LAW
AND
ORDER

MORE MYSTERIES FROM THE
BERKLEY PUBLISHING GROUP . . .

LAW
AND
ORDER

EDITED BY
Cynthia Manson

STORIES FROM
Ellery Queen's Mystery Magazine
AND
Alfred Hitchcock Mystery Magazine

BERKLEY PRIME CRIME, NEW YORK

LAW AND ORDER

A Berkley Prime Crime Book / published by arrangement with
Dell Magazines

PRINTING HISTORY
Berkley Prime Crime edition / April 1997

All rights reserved.
Copyright © 1997 by Dell Magazines.
This book may not be reproduced in whole or in part,
by mimeograph or any other means, without permission.
For information address: The Berkley Publishing Group,
200 Madison Avenue, New York, NY 10016

The Putnam Berkley World Wide Web site address is
http://www.berkley.com/berkley

ISBN: 0-425-15781-4

Berkley Prime Crime Books are published
by The Berkley Publishing Group,
200 Madison Avenue, New York, NY 10016.
The name BERKLEY PRIME CRIME and the BERKLEY PRIME CRIME
design are trademarks belonging to Berkley Publishing Corporation.

PRINTED IN THE UNITED STATES OF AMERICA

10 9 8 7 6 5 4 3 2 1

CONTENTS

COPS
···

LAWYERS/COURTROOM
···

PRISON

INTRODUCTION

LAW AND ORDER features a variety of characters in pursuit of crime and punishment. We have cops and detectives in search of those who break the law; we have lawyers defending their clients or prosecuting the innocent and the guilty; we have judges presiding over the courts, and, finally, we have prisoners behind bars, some on death row.

The storytellers include a strong line-up of well-known authors such as Jonathan Kellerman, John D. MacDonald, Lawrence Block, and Michael Gilbert. The short stories in this collection range from Donald Westlake's "After I'm Gone" featuring Detective Abraham Levine, shot in the line of duty, to Agatha Christie's "The Witness for the Prosecution" in which a lawyer is determined to prove his client innocent against all odds. Also included are Erle Stanley Gardner's "The Case of the Irate Witness," which is the first published short story featuring Perry Mason, and Jeffery Deaver's "Interrogation," a brilliant study of a detective's obsession to get inside the mind of a killer.

Within these pages you will meet heroic and dedicated men in blue, street savvy detectives, sleazy attorneys, arrogant judges, innocent victims and cold-blooded killers. There is something for every fan of crime fiction in this diverse collection of stories.

—*Cynthia Manson*

I ALWAYS GET
THE CUTIES

❦

John D. MacDonald

KEEGAN CAME INTO MY APARTMENT, FROSTED WITH WIN-
ter, topcoat open, hat jammed on the back of his hard skull,
bringing a noisy smell of the dark city night. He stood in
front of my birch fire, his great legs planted, clapping and
rubbing hard palms in the heat.

He grinned at me and winked one narrow gray eye. "I'm
off duty, Doc. I wrapped up a package. A pretty package."

"Will bourbon do, Keegan?"

"If you haven't got any of that brandy left. This is a
brandy night."

When I came back with the bottle and the glasses, he
had stripped off his topcoat and tossed it on the couch. The
crumpled hat was on the floor, near the discarded coat.
Keegan had yanked a chair closer to the fire. He sprawled
on the end of his spine, thick ankles crossed, the soles of
his shoes steaming.

I poured his brandy and mine, and moved my chair and
the long coffee table so we could share either end of it. It
was bursting in him. I knew that. I've only had the vaguest
hints about his home life. A house crowded with teen-age
daughters, cluttered with their swains. Obviously no place
to talk of his dark victories. And Keegan is not the sort of

1

man to regale his co-workers with talk of his prowess. So I am, among other things, his sounding board. He bounces successes off the politeness of my listening, growing big in the echo of them.

"Ever try to haggle with a car dealer, Doc?" he asked.

"In a mild way."

"You are a mild guy. I tried once. Know what he told me? He said, 'Lieutenant, you try to make a car deal maybe once every two years. Me, I make ten a day. So what chance have you got?' "

This was a more oblique approach than Keegan generally used. I became attentive.

"It's the same with the cuties, Doc—the amateurs who think they can bring off one nice clean safe murder. Give me a cutie every time. I eat 'em alive. The pros are trouble. The cuties leave holes you can drive diesels through. This one was that woman back in October. At that cabin at Bear Paw Lake. What do you remember about it, Doc?"

I am always forced to summarize. It has got me into the habit of reading the crime news. I never used to.

"As I remember, Keegan, they thought she had been killed by a prowler. Her husband returned from a business trip and found the body. She had been dead approximately two weeks. Because it was the off season, the neighboring camps weren't occupied, and the people in the village thought she had gone back to the city. She had been strangled, I believe."

"Okay. So I'll fill you in on it. Then you'll see the problem I had. The name is Grosswalk. Cynthia and Harold. He met her ten years ago when he was in med. school. He was twenty-four and she was thirty. She was loaded. He married her and he never went back to med. school. He didn't do anything for maybe five, six years. Then he gets a job selling medical supplies, surgical instruments, that kind of stuff. Whenever a wife is dead, Doc, the first thing I do is check on how they were getting along. I guess you know that."

"Your standard procedure," I said.

"Sure. So I check. They got a nice house here in the city. Not many friends. But they got neighbors with ears. There are lots of brawls. I get the idea it is about money. The money is hers—was hers, I should say. I put it up to this Grosswalk. He says okay, so they weren't getting along so good, so what? I'm supposed to be finding out who killed her, sort of coordinating with the State Police, not digging into his home life, I tell him he is a nice suspect. He already knows that. He says he didn't kill her. Then he adds one thing too many. He says he couldn't have killed her. That's all he will say. Playing it cute. You understand. I eat those cuties alive."

He waved his empty glass. I went over and refilled it.

"You see what he's doing to me, Doc. He's leaving it up to me to prove how it was he couldn't have killed her. A reverse twist. That isn't too tough. I get in touch with the sales manager of the company. Like I thought, the salesmen have to make reports. He was making a western swing. It would be no big trick to fly back and sneak into the camp and kill her, take some money and junk to make it look good, and then fly back out there and pick up where he left off. She was killed on maybe the tenth of October, the medical examiner says. Then he finds her on the twenty-fourth. But the sales manager tells me something that needs a lot of checking. He says that this Grosswalk took sick out west on the eighth and went into a hospital, and he was in that hospital from the eighth to the fifteenth, a full seven days. He gave me the name of the hospital. Now you see how the cutie made his mistake. He could have told me that easy enough. No, he has to be cute. I figure that if he's innocent he would have told me. But he's so proud of whatever gimmick he rigged for me that he's got to let me find out the hard way."

"I suppose you went out there," I said.

"It took a lot of talk. They don't like spending money for things like that. They kept telling me I should ask the L.A. cops to check because that's a good force out there. Finally I have to go by bus, or pay the difference. So I go by bus. I found the doctor. Plural—doctors. It is a clinic deal, sort of, that this Grosswalk went to. He gives them his symptoms. They say it looks to them like the edge of a nervous breakdown just beginning to show. With maybe some organic complications. So they run him through the course. Seven days of tests and checks and observations. They tell me he was there, that he didn't leave, that he *couldn't* have left. But naturally I check the hospital. They reserve part of one floor for patients from the clinic. I talked to the head nurse on that floor, and to the nurse that had the most to do with Grosswalk. She showed me the schedule and charts. Every day, every night, they were fooling around with the guy, giving him injections of this and that. He couldn't have got out. The people at the clinic told me the results. He was okay. The rest had helped him a lot. They told him to slow down. They gave him a prescription for a mild sedative. Nothing organically wrong, even though the symptoms seemed to point that way."

"So the trip was wasted?"

"Not entirely. Because on a hunch I ask if he had visitors. They keep a register. A girl came to see him as often as the rules permitted. They said she was pretty. Her name was Mary MacCarney. The address is there. So I go and see her. She lives with her folks. A real tasty kid. Nineteen. Her folks think this Grosswalk is too old for her. She is tall Irish, all black and white and blue. It was warm and we sat on the porch. I soon find out this Grosswalk has been feeding her a line, telling her that his wife is an incurable invalid not long for this world, that he can't stand hurting her by asking for a divorce, that it is better to wait, and anyway, she says, her parents might approve of a widower, but never a guy who has been divorced. She has heard from Grosswalk that his wife has been murdered by a prowler and he will be out to see her as soon as he can. He has known her for a year. But of course I have told him not to leave town. I tell her not to get her hopes too high because it begins to look to me like this Grosswalk has knocked off his wife. Things get pretty hysterical, and her old lady gets in on it, and even driving away in the cab I can hear her old lady yelling at her.

"The first thing I do on getting back is check with the doctor who took care of Mrs. Grosswalk, and he says, as I thought he would, that she was as healthy as a horse. So I go back up to that camp and unlock it again. It is a snug place, Doc. Built so you could spend the winter there if you wanted to. Insulated and sealed, with a big fuel-oil furnace, and modern kitchen equipment, and so on. It was aired out a lot better than the first time I was in it. Grosswalk stated that he hadn't touched a thing. He said it was unlocked. He saw her and backed right out and went to report it. And the only thing touched had been the body.

"I poked around. This time I took my time. She was a tidy woman. There are twin beds. One is turned down. There is a very fancy nightgown laid out. That is a thing which bothered me. I looked at her other stuff. She has pajamas which are the right thing for October at the lake. They are made from that flannel stuff. There is only one other fancy nightgown, way in the back of a drawer. I have found out here in the city that she is not the type to fool around. So how come a woman who is alone wants to sleep so pretty? Because the husband is coming back from a trip. But he couldn't have come back from the trip. I find another thing. I find deep ruts off in the brush beside the camp. The first time I went there, her car was parked in back. Now it is gone. If the car was run off where those ruts were, anybody coming to the door wouldn't see it. If the door was locked they wouldn't even knock maybe, knowing she wouldn't be home. That puzzles me. She might do it if she didn't want company. I prowl some more. I look in the deep freeze. It is well stocked. No need to buy stuff for a hell of a while. The refrigerator is the same way. And the electric is still on."

He leaned back and looked at me.

"Is that all you had to go on?" I asked.

"A murder happens here and the murderer is in Los Angeles at the time. I got him because he tried to be a cutie. Want to take a try, Doc?''

I knew I had to make an attempt. ''Some sort of device?''

''To strangle a woman? Mechanical hands? You're getting too fancy, Doc.''

''Then he hired somebody to do it?''

''There are guys you can hire, but they like guns. Or a piece of pipe in an alley. I don't know where you'd go to hire a strangler. He did it himself, Doc.''

''Frankly, Keegan, I don't see how he could have.''

''Well, I'll tell you how I went after it. I went to the medical examiner and we had a little talk. Cop logic, Doc. If the geography is wrong, then maybe you got the wrong idea on timing. But the medico checks it out. He says definitely the woman has been dead twelve days to two weeks when he makes the examination. I ask him how he knows. He says because of the extent of decomposition of the body. I ask him if that is a constant. He says no—you use a formula. A sort of rule-of-thumb formula. I ask him the factors. He says cause of death, temperature, humidity, physical characteristics of the body, how it was clothed, whether or not insects could have got to it, and so on.

''By then I had it, Doc. It was cute. I went back to the camp and looked around. It took me some time to find them. You never find a camp without them. Candles. They were in a drawer in the kitchen. Funny looking candles, Doc. Melted down, sort of. A flat side against the bottom of the drawer, and all hardened again. Then I had another idea. I checked the stove burners. I found some pieces of burned flaked metal down under the heating elements.

''Then it was easy. I had this Grosswalk brought in again. I let him sit in a cell for four hours and get nervous before I took the rookie cop in. I'd coached that rookie for an hour, so he did it right. I had him dressed in a leather jacket and work pants. I make him repeat his story in front of Grosswalk. 'I bought a chain saw last year,' he says, acting sort of confused, 'and I was going around to the

camps where there are any people and I was trying to get
some work cutting up fireplace wood. So I called on Mrs.
Grosswalk. She didn't want any wood, but she was nice
about it.' I ask the rookie when that was. He scratches his
head and says, 'Sometime around the seventeenth I think
it was.' That's where I had to be careful. I couldn't let him
be positive about the date. I say she was supposed to be
dead a week by then and was he sure it was her. 'She
wasn't dead then. I know her. I'd seen her in the village.
A kind of heavy-set woman with blonde hair. It was her
all right, Lieutenant.' I asked him was he sure of the date
and he said yes, around the seventeenth like he said, but
he could check his records and find the exact day.

"I told him to take off. I just watched that cutie and saw
him come apart. Then he gave it to me. He killed her on
the sixteenth, the day he got out of the hospital. He flew
into Omaha. By then I've got the stenographer taking it
down. Grosswalk talks, staring at the floor, like he was
talking to himself. It was going to be a dry run. He wasn't
going to do it if she'd been here in the city or into the
village in the previous seven days. But once she got in the
camp she seldom went out, and the odds were all against
any callers. On his previous trip to Omaha he had bought
a jalopy that would run. It would make the fifty miles to
the lake all right. He took the car off the lot where he'd
left it and drove to the lake. She was surprised to see him
back ahead of schedule. He explained the company car was
being fixed. He questioned her. Finally she said she hadn't
seen or talked to a living soul in ten days. Then he knew
he was set to take the risk.

"He grabbed her neck and hung on until she was dead.
He had his shoulders hunched right up around his ears
when he said that. It was evening when he killed her, nearly
bedtime. First he closed every window. Then he turned on
the furnace as high as it would go. There was plenty of oil
in the tank. He left the oven door open and the oven turned
as high as it would go. He even built a fire in the fireplace,
knowing it would be burned out by morning and there

wouldn't be any smoke. He filled the biggest pans of water he could find and left them on the top of the stove. He took money and some of her jewelry, turned out the lights and locked the doors. He ran her car off in the brush where nobody would be likely to see it. He said by the time he left the house it was like an oven in there.

"He drove the jalopy back to Omaha, parked it back in the lot, and caught an 11:15 flight to Los Angeles. The next morning he was making calls. And keeping his fingers crossed. He worked his way east. He got to the camp on the twenty-fourth—about 10 in the morning. He said he went in and turned things off and opened up every window, and then went out and was sick. He waited nearly an hour before going back in. It was nearly down to normal temperature. He checked the house. He noticed she had turned down both beds before he killed her. He remade his. The water had boiled out of the pans and the bottoms had burned through. He scaled the pans out into the lake. He said he tried not to look at her, but he couldn't help it. He had enough medical background to know that it had worked, and also to fake his own illness in L. A. He went out and was sick again, and then he got her car back where it belonged. He closed most of the windows. He made another inspection trip and then drove into the village. He's a cutie, Doc, and I ate him alive."

There was a long silence. I knew what was expected of me. But I had my usual curious reluctance to please him. He held the glass cradled in his hand, gazing with a half smile into the dying fire. His face looked like stone.

"That was very intelligent, Keegan," I said.

"The pros give you real trouble, Doc. The cuties always leave holes. I couldn't bust geography, so I had to bust time." He yawned massively and stood up. "Read all about it in the morning paper, Doc."

"I'll certainly do that."

I held his coat for him. He's a big man. I had to reach up to get it properly onto his shoulders. He mashed the hat onto his head as I walked to the door with him. He put his big hand on the knob, turned, and smiled down at me.

"I always get the cuties, Doc. Always."

"You certainly seem to," I said.

"They are my favorite meat."

"So I understand."

He balled one big fist and bumped it lightly against my chin, still grinning at me. "And I'm going to get you too, Doc. You know that. You were cute. You're just taking longer than most. But you know how it's going to come out, don't you?"

I don't answer that any more. There's nothing to say. There hasn't been anything to say for a long time now.

He left, walking hard into the wild night. I sat and looked into my fire. I could hear the wind. I reached for the bottle. The wind raged over the city, as monstrous and inevitable as Keegan. It seemed as though it was looking for food—the way Keegan is always doing. But I no longer permit myself the luxury of imagination.

AFTER I'M GONE

~~~

Donald E. Westlake

AFTERNOON VISITING HOURS AT THE HOSPITAL WERE FROM two till five, so when Detective Abraham Levine of Brooklyn's Forty-third Precinct got off his tour at four P.M. he took a Rockaway Parkway bus to the hospital and spent thirty-five minutes with Detective Andy Stettin. Levine and Andy had been together when Andy was hit, a bullet high on the left side of the chest, fired through a closed door. Andy, a promising youngster, a hotshot, one of the new breed of college-graduate cops, had been close to death for a while, but was now on the mend, and very bored and impatient with hospital routine.

It wasn't really necessary for Levine to go through this ritual every day, nor did he have that much to say to the youngster. In fact, he knew full well he was only doing it because he so much didn't want to. There was a certain amount of guilt involved, since Levine was secretly happy that the bullet had ended his brief partnership with Andy Stettin, but in truth Andy wasn't the main point here at all. The main point was the hospital.

To Andy Stettin, healthy and self-assured, the hospital was merely a nuisance and a bore. To Abraham Levine, fifty-five years of age, short and stocky, overweight and short of wind, with a tired heart that skipped the occasional beat, the hospital was a horrible presentiment, an all-too-possible future. Those sad withered men, shrunken within their maroon or brown robes, shuffling down the wide featureless corridors in their Christmas-present slippers, were a potential tomorrow that could be very close indeed. Going to the hospital every afternoon was for Levine a painful repeated confrontation with his worst fears.

Today, a Thursday, Levine told Andy that there continued to be no break in the case of Maurice Gold, during the investigation of whose murder Andy had been shot by a drug dealer who, unfortunately, was not Gold's killer. Andy shrugged, not really interested: "Gold is gonna stay Open," he said.

Levine had to agree. With some sort of reverse logic, when a case became inactive the Police Department phrase was that it was Opened. "Open that," meant in reality to close it, to cease to work on it. The reason behind the Newspeak phraseology was that only an arrest could Close a case; an inactive case could always be reactivated by fresh evidence, and therefore it would remain—unto eternity, most likely—Open.

Levine and Andy also talked a while about Levine's regular partner, Jack Crawley, a big, shambling, mean-looking harness bull with whom Levine had a very easy and reassuring relationship. Crawley had just come back on duty this week after his convalescent leave—he had been, several months ago, shot in the leg—and the long spell of inactivity had made him more bristly and bad-tempered than ever. "I think he'll arrest *me* pretty soon," Levine said.

Andy laughed at that, but what he mostly wanted to talk about was a nurse he had his eye on, a pretty young thing, very short and compact, squeezed into a too-tight uniform. Both times the girl passed by while Levine was there, Andy did some elephantine flirting, very heavy-handed arch remarks that Levine found embarrassing but which the girl appeared to enjoy. The second time, after both men had watched the provocative departure of the nurse, Andy grinned and said, "The sap still rises, eh, Abe?"

"The sap also sets," Levine told him, getting to his feet. "See you tomorrow, Andy."

"Thanks for coming by."

Levine was walking down the wide corridor, not meeting the eyes of the ambulatory patients, when a hand touched his elbow and a gravelly voice said, quietly, "Let's just walk around here a while."

Surprised, Levine looked to his right and saw a short, blocky, pugnacious-looking man of about his own age, wearing an expensive topcoat over a rather wrinkled suit, and an old-fashioned snap brim hat pulled low enough to make it difficult to see his eyes. Levine noticed the awkward bunchiness of the man's tie-knot, as though he had got himself up in costume like a trick-or-treater, as though his real persona existed in some other mode.

The man gave Levine a quick sidelong glance from under his hatbrim. His hand held firmly to Levine's elbow. "You're a cop, right? Abraham Levine, detective. Visiting the cop in there."

"Yes?"

"So let's talk a little bit."

They had reached an intersection of corridors. The elevators were straight ahead, but the man was pulling Levine to the right. "Talk about what?" Levine asked, trying to shake loose.

"Cops and robbers," the man said. "I got a proposition."

Levine planted his feet, refusing to move. Peeling the man's fingers from his elbow, he said, "What sort of proposition?"

With darting movements of his head, the man shot wary glances along the corridors. "I don't like it here," he said. "Exposed here."

"Exposed to what?"

"Listen," the man said, moving closer, his breath warm on Levine's chin, his hatbrim nearly touching Levine's face. "You know Giacomo Polito," he said.

"I know who he is. Mafia chieftain. He controls one of the five families."

"I'm a soldier for him," the man said, his voice low but harsh, pushing with intensity. "I know Giacomo's whole life story."

Levine frowned, trying to see this too-close face, read meaning into the tone of the husky tense voice. Was this an offer of information? The setting was unusual, the manner odd, but what else could it be? Levine said, "You want to sell that life story?"

"Don't rush me." Another darting glance. "Giacomo disappeared my son," the man said, still in the same breathy way. "He knows I know."

"Ah."

"You take your bus, like you do," the man said. "Look out the back window. When you see a green Buick following, you get off the bus. There's a kind of a flower on the aerial."

"And who are you?" Levine asked him. "What's your name?"

"What's the dif? Call me Bobby."

"Bobby?" The incongruity of that name with this man made Levine smile despite himself.

The man looked up, facing Levine more directly than before. He too smiled, but with an edge to it. "That was my son's name," he said.

THE GREEN BUICK WITH THE RED PLASTIC CHRYSANTHE-mum taped to its antenna followed the bus for a dozen blocks before Levine decided to follow through. Then he got off at the next stop, stood at the curb while the bus drove off, and waited for the Buick to stop in front of him.

The delay had been because Levine wasn't entirely sure what he thought of "Bobby" and his story. A Mafia soldier who decided to defect usually did so when under indictment himself for some major crime, when he could trade his knowledge for softer treatment from the courts. Simple revenge between criminals rarely included squealing to the police. If Bobby's son had been killed by Giacomo Polito, in the normal course of events Bobby would simply kill Polito, or be himself killed in the attempt. The Mafia tended to run very much along the lines of a Shakespearean tragedy, with few roles for outsiders.

In addition, if Bobby had decided that *his* vengeance required selling Polito to the police, why not do it the normal way? Why not simply drive to Manhattan and go to the Organized Crime Unit in Police Headquarters and make his deal there? Why talk to some obscure precinct detective in the depths of Brooklyn—and in particular why do it in a hospital corridor? Why all this counterspy hugger-mugger?

What finally decided Levine to take the next step was that he couldn't think of any rational alternative explanation for Bobby's actions. If someone had decided to murder Levine, of course, this would be an excellent ploy to put him in a position where it could be done. But Levine could think of no one at the moment who would have a motive. He wasn't due to be a witness in any upcoming trials, he hadn't made any potentially dangerous arrests recently, nor had he received notification within the last year or so of any felons, arrested by himself, who had been released from prison. Also, if Bobby's story were merely a charade for some sort of con game, how could it hurt Levine? He wouldn't pay anything or sign anything or even necessarily believe anything. And finally, there had been the real brimstone aura of truth in that last direct stare from Bobby when he'd said, "That was my son's name."

So for all those reasons Levine had ultimately stepped off the bus and stood waiting until the Buick pulled to a stop in front of him. But before getting into the car, he did nevertheless check the floor behind the front seat just to be absolutely certain there was no one crouched back there with a pistol or a knife or a length of wire.

There was nothing—just some empty beer cans. So Levine opened the front passenger door and bent to enter the car, but Bobby was leaning over toward him from the steering wheel, saying, "Uh, would you take down the, get rid of the flower?"

"Of course."

Masking tape had been wrapped around both antenna and flower stalk. Levine tugged on the plastic stalk and the tape ripped, releasing it. He then got into the car and shut the door, feeling vaguely foolish to be sitting here with a red flower in his lap. He tossed it atop the dashboard as Bobby accelerated away from the curb, checking both the inside and outside mirrors, saying, "I did shake 'em, but you never know."

"You're being followed?"

"Oh, sure," he said, shrugging as though it was an everyday event. "They wanna know I'm not going anywhere before the big day."

"What big day?"

"Wipeout," Bobby said, and ran a finger along his neck. "Giacomo's got a contract out on me."

"You're sure of that?"

Bobby gave him a quick glance, almost of contempt, then went back to his fitful concentration on the road ahead and both mirrors. "I'm sure of everything," he said. "When I'm not sure, I shut up."

"So you want police protection, is that it?"

"Why don't *I* tell *you* what I want, okay?"

Levine smiled at the rebuff. "Okay," he said.

Bobby turned a corner. He seemed to be driving at random, though trending northwest, away from the hospital and in the general direction of Manhattan, several miles away. "Giacomo's got a young wife," he said. "The old Mama died, all over cancer, right? So Giacomo went to Vegas to work out his grief, he come back with a bride. A dancer at the Aladdin, calls herself Terri. With an I."

"Uh huh."

"My son—"

"Bobby."

"My *son*. Got hooked on this Terri. He was like a dog,

there's a bitch in the neighborhood in heat, you cannot keep that dog in the house.''

''Dangerous.''

''She says he raped her,'' Bobby said. ''He didn't rape her, she was asking for it.''

Levine kept silent. He watched Bobby's fingers twitch and fidget on the steering wheel.

''A bodyguard found them at it,'' Bobby said: ''Naturally she had to cry rape. My son told his story, the bodyguard said forget it, my son went home. Terri with the I, she went to Giacomo. She talked to Giacomo, but Giacomo didn't talk to nobody, not to me, not to my son, not to nobody. The bodyguard got disappeared. My son got disappeared. I said, 'Giacomo, we know one another a long time, why don't you talk to me first, ask me a question?' He still don't talk. I go away, and he puts a contract on me, he puts shadows on me to be sure I'm still here for the hit.''

''There's a special time for the—hit?''

''Saturday night. Day after tomorrow. I still got friends to whisper me things. At Barolli's Seafood House in Far Rockaway upstairs in the private dining room there's gonna be a banquet. It's Giacomo's first wedding anniversary.'' Bobby spoke the words with no apparent irony. ''That's where they're gonna take me out. By the time they're at the coffee and cigars, I'm at the bottom of Jamaica Bay.''

''Pretty.''

''Businesslike,'' Bobby said.

''If it's police protection you want—''

Levine was stopped by Bobby's cold eyes looking directly at him. ''You gonna explain life to me, Mr. Levine?''

''Sorry.''

''I know about police protection,'' Bobby said. He lifted his right hand from the steering wheel and rubbed his thumb back and forth over the pads of his other fingers. ''With this hand,'' he said, ''I have paid protective police to be blind and deaf while the subject of their concern was falling out a window. You are an honest cop, Mr. Levine, and that's very nice, that's why you and me are talking, but let me break you the sad news. There are one or two rotten apples in your crowd.''

"I know that.''

"I also know about the Feds and their witness protection plan,'' Bobby said. "They will give me a new name, a new house in a new city, a new job, a new driver's license, a whole entire new life.''

"That's right.''

"All they take away is my old life,'' Bobby said. "That's what Giacomo has in mind, too. I *like* my old life.''

"So far,'' Levine said, "I'm not sure why you're telling me all this.''

"Because I have a scheme,'' Bobby said, "but my scheme is taking too long. I won't be able to leave town until the middle of next week. I'm okay until Saturday, but when I don't show at the celebration they'll start looking for me. It'll be tougher for me to move around town.''

"I can see that.''

"I need a courier,'' Bobby said. "I need protection and assistance. I need an honest cop to run my errands and see that nobody offs me.''

"Tell me your scheme,'' Levine said.

"I am assembling information,'' Bobby told him. "I am talking into a tape recorder, I am giving facts and names and dates, I am nailing Giacomo to the cross. And I am getting the physical evidence, too, the contracts and the photos and the letters and the wiretaps and everything else.''

"Giacomo shouldn't have killed your son,'' Levine said.

"Not without talking to me.''

"You'll turn over all this information next week?''

"To the law?'' Bobby grinned, a kind of distorted grimace that created deep crevices in his cheeks. "You got the wrong idea,'' he said.

"Then who do you give it all to, all this proof and information?''

"Giacomo's partners,'' Bobby said. "His friends. His

fellow *capi*. His business associates. What I'm putting together is what he's done to *them* over the years. I have stuff Giacomo himself can't remember. I have enough to get him offed ten times from ten different people.''

"I see," Levine said. "You ruin Giacomo with the mob, and his contract on you ceases to matter."

"*And* he's dead. And the Terri with him."

"Why do you think I would help you?" Levine asked.

Again the wrenching grin. "Because I'm gonna give you some scraps from my table," Bobby said. "Just a few things you'd like to know."

"About Giacomo."

"Who else?" Under the wide-brimmed hat, under the darting, dashing, anxious eyes, Bobby smiled like a death's head. "Just enough to put Giacomo in prison," he said. "Where it'll be easier for his friends to kill him."

FOR FORTY MINUTES LEVINE SAT AT LIEUTENANT BARker's desk and looked at pictures, front and side views of Caucasian males, page after page of tough guys in living color, behind clear plastic. The infinite variety of human appearance became confined here to variations on one theme: the Beast, without Beauty.

"Him," Levine said.

Inspector Santangelo leaned over Levine's shoulder and whistled. "You sure?"

"That's him, all right."

It was Bobby, no question. Without the hat, he was shown to have a low broad forehead, thick pepper-and-salt hair that grew spikily across his head, and cold eyes that seemed to slink and lurk behind half lowered lids. Without the hat he looked more like a snake. The name under the photos was Ralph Banadando.

Inspector Santangelo was visibly impressed. Crossing the lieutenant's office to resume his seat on the sofa, he said, "No wonder he knows where the bodies are buried. And no wonder he called Polito by his first name."

Lieutenant Barker, chief of the precinct's detective

squad, whose office this was, said, "Who is he?"

"Benny Banadando," the inspector said. "He's Giacomo Polito's right-hand man—they came up through the ranks together. He's the number-two man in that mob." Grinning at Levine, he said, "That's no soldier. He told you he was a soldier? That's a General." Nodding at Barker, seated in what was usually the visitor's chair, he said, "You did right to call me, Fred."

"Thanks."

It was Friday morning, nearly noon. Yesterday, saying he would get in touch with Levine sometime today to hear his answer, whether or not he would accept the proposition, Bobby—Ralph "Benny" Banadando now—had let Levine off six blocks from his home, giving Levine ten minutes to walk and think. At home, he had at once phoned the precinct to give Lieutenant Barker a brief recap of the conversation. Given the truth of Bobby's remark about the "one or two rotten apples" in the Police Department, they'd agreed not to spread the story very widely, and Barker had phoned his old friend Inspector Santangelo, now assigned to the Organized Crime Unit. This morning Santangelo had come down to the Forty-third Precinct with his book of mug shots, and now Levine had a name for Bobby. He said, "Does Banadando have a son?"

"He did," Santangelo said in a dry tone. "Fellow named Robert, not very sweet. What do you want to do, Abe? Can I call you Abe?"

"Sure."

"And I'm Mike," Santangelo said. "You want to turn this thing over to me, or do you want to follow through yourself?"

"You mean, do I want to tell Banadando yes or no."

"That's what I mean." Grinning at some private thought, Santangelo sat back on the sofa, stretching his long legs in the small office. "Before you answer," he said, "let me say this. I don't want to bring this news back to my shop, because if I do it'll get to Polito and he won't wait for the symbolic moment of his anniversary dinner."

Levine nodded. "That's what we thought, too."

"In addition," Santangelo said, "you'll be marked yourself, Abe, because Polito won't be sure how much Banadando told you."

Lieutenant Barker said, "He won't try to kill a cop."

"Probably not," Santangelo said. "But if he's nervous enough, it's a possibility. From our point of view, it's better if Banadando can work his scheme in peace and quiet. But what that means, Abe, we can't provide backup."

"I can," Lieutenant Barker said. "Abe's partner, Jack Crawley, can back him up."

"That's not quite the same as three busloads of TPF," Santangelo said. "You see what I'm getting at, Abe? This could be dangerous for you."

Levine said, "What happens if I tell Banadando no?"

"I pull him in," Santangelo said. "I try to convince him his scheme is busted anyway and he might as well cooperate with us."

"He'll say no."

Santangelo shrugged. "It's worth a try."

Levine said, "You won't have to. I'll tell him yes."

"GOOD," SAID BANADANDO'S HUSKY, LOW, INSINUATING voice on the phone. It was twenty to five on Friday afternoon and Levine was in the hospital again, visiting with Andy Stettin. Andy's phone had rung and it was Banadando, for Levine.

Conscious of Andy's curious eyes on him, Levine said into the phone, "What happens now?"

"Nothing. I can still play my own hand till tomorrow night. You know Long Island well?"

"Pretty well."

"About fifty miles out there's a town called Bay Shore. On the Great South Bay."

"I know it."

"Go there Sunday morning, around nine. Go down to the end of Maple, park there."

"What will I—?" But Banadando had hung up.

Levine replaced the receiver and Andy said, "What was that? Sounded like a real sweetheart."

"Mobster," Levine said. "He's gonna give some evidence. For some reason he made me the intermediary."

"Why's he giving evidence?"

Levine was reluctant to hold back—it wasn't as though he mistrusted *Andy*—but he had to maintain a habit of reticence in this situation. "Some of his pals have a contract on him," he said.

Andy's lip curled. "Let 'em kill each other off. Best thing that can happen."

"I suppose so," said Levine slowly, but the words were ashes in his mouth. He understood why what Andy had just said was the common, almost the universal belief among the police; whenever one mobster killed another, great smiles of happiness lit up the faces in the precinct houses. But Levine just couldn't take pleasure from the death of a human being, no matter who, no matter what he had done in his life. He supposed it was really selfishness, really only a matter of projecting their deaths onto himself, visualizing his own end in theirs, that made him troubled and sad at the cutting short of lives so stained and spoiled, but nevertheless he just couldn't bring himself to share in the general glee at the thought of a murdered mobster.

A little later, as he was leaving Andy's room, he paused in the doorway to let a wizened ancient man pass by, moving slowly and awkwardly and painfully with the help of a walker. *That's me*, Levine thought, and behind him Andy said, "If they start bumping one another off, Abe, just step to one side."

Levine looked back at him, bewildered, his mind for an instant filling with visions of doddering oldsters bumping one another off: "What do you mean?"

"Your mobster pals. They love to kill so much, let 'em kill each other. It isn't up to us to stop it, or to get in the way."

"I'll stay out of the way," Levine promised. Then he

smiled and waved and left, walking around the ancient man, who had barely progressed beyond the doorway.

MAPLE AVENUE IN BAY SHORE ENDED ON A LONG WIDE dock, covered with asphalt and its center lined with parking meters. Levine found a free meter, got out of the car, and strolled a bit, smelling the salt tang. Once or twice he glanced back the way he had come, without seeing Jack Crawley; which was as it should be.

Out near the end of the dock, several small boats were offloading bushel baskets and burlap bags, all filled with clams. Two trucks were receiving the harvest, and the men working there called cheerfully at one another, talking more loudly than necessary, but apparently filled with high spirits because of the clarity and beauty of the day.

Nine A.M. on the third Sunday in October. The air was clear, the sun bright in a sky dotted with clouds, the water frisky and glinting and cold-looking. Levine inhaled deeply, glad to be alive, barely even conscious of the straps around his shoulders and chest, under his shirt, holding the recording apparatus.

He strolled aimlessly on the dock for about fifteen minutes and then turned at the sound of a *beep-beep* to see a small inboard motorboat bobbing next to the dock, with Banadando at the wheel. Banadando gestured, and Levine crossed over to stand looking down at him. "Come aboard," Banadando said. "We'll go for a run on the bay."

CLAMMERS AND FISHERMEN WERE IN OTHER SMALL BOATS dotting the bay. Long Island was five miles or so to the north, the barrier beach called Fire Island was just to the south, and Banadando's boat—*Bobby's Dream* was the name painted on the stern in flowing golden letters—was simply another anonymous speck on the dancing water.

Bobby's Dream was compact but comfortable, its cabin where Levine now sat containing a tiny galley-style kitchen, cunning storage spaces, a foldaway table, and a pair of long upholstered benches that converted to twin beds. "Nice, huh?" Banadando said, coming down into the cabin after cutting the engine and dropping anchor.

"Very clever," Levine said.

"That, too," Banadando agreed. Today he wore a long-billed white yachting cap edged in gold, the bill shielding his eyes as yesterday's hat had done. In blue blazer, white scarf, and white pants, he was almost a parody of the weekend yachtsman. Sitting on the bench across from Levine, he said, "After dark I take the inlet, I go out to the ocean, I sleep in comfort and safety. Nobody knows where I am or where I'll be next. I land where I want, when I want. Until I leave town, this is the safest place in the world for me."

"I can see that," Levine said.

"You wired?"

"Of course," Levine said.

Banadando shook his head, smirking a bit. "We all go through the motions, right? You know I know you're gonna be wired, so I know you know I won't say anything you can use. But still you got to go through the whole thing, strap it on, walk around like a telephone-company employee. You broadcasting or taping?"

"Taping," Levine said, wondering if Banadando would insist on being given the tape.

But Banadando merely smiled, saying, "Good. If you were broadcasting, we'd be too far out for your backup to read."

"That's right. Mr. Banadando, we—"

Banadando made a face. "I figured you'd find that out, who I am, but I don't like it. How many cops know about our little conversation?"

"Four, including me. We're already aware of the existence of rotten apples. Don't worry, we won't alert Polito through the department."

"Don't tell me not to worry, Mr. Levine."

"Sorry."

"You're a long time dead."

"I agree," Levine said.

Banadando took from an outside pocket of his blazer a
sheet of white typewriter paper folded into quarters. Opening this, smoothing it on the tabletop, he turned it so the
handwriting faced Levine. It was large block-printed letters
in black ink. He said, "You see all this?"

"Yes?"

"I'm not giving you this paper, you're remembering it.
Or you'll listen to your tape, later. You see what I mean?"

Levine looked at him. "Why do you think I'm going to
be in that much trouble, Mr. Banadando?"

"Because I don't know how smart you are," Banadando
said. "Maybe you're very dumb. Maybe one of the three
cops you talked to is right now on the phone to Giacomo.
Maybe you get nervous in the clutch. Maybe all kinds of
things. I can't see the future, Mr. Levine, so I protect myself from it just as hard as I can. Okay?"

"Okay," Levine said.

Banadando's fingertip touched the first word on the sheet
of paper. His hands were thick and stubby-fingered, but
very clean, with meticulously groomed nails. The effect,
however, was not of cleanliness but of a kind of doughy
unhealthfulness. "This," Banadando said, his sausage finger tapping the word, "is a telephone number."

Levine frowned. The word, all alone near the top of the
sheet, was VANDYKE. "It is?"

"The phone dial doesn't just have numbers," Banadando
reminded him. "It has letters. Dial those letters. You'll call
just after noon today—this is back in the city, it's a city
number."

"All right."

"You got to call no later than ten past twelve or he won't
be there."

"All right."

"When the guy answers, you tell him you're Abe. That's
all he knows about you, that's all he needs to know. He'll
tell you does he have the stuff yet or not. If it's no, he'll
tell you when to call again."

"What is this stuff?"

"Let it be a surprise," Banadando said.

Levine took a breath. "Mr. Banadando," he said, "I have to tell you something you should already know. If any evidence of crime is put in my possession, I'm going to turn it over to my superiors."

"Sure you are," Banadando said. "You'll take the package, you'll sniff all over it like a bird-dog, you'll get nothing out of it. The next thing that happens, you'll bring it to me."

"But you realize we'll study it first."

"I am not here to be stupid," Banadando said. His finger moved down to the next item, below VANDYKE. There was the word KOPYKAT, and under it an address: 1411 BROADWAY. "This is a copying service," he said. "It's a chain, there's Kopykats all over the city. This is the Broadway one. You got it?"

"Yes."

"They're open on Sunday. This afternoon, any time this afternoon, you go there and pick up the package for Mr. Robert. If there's no package, don't worry about it."

"All right."

The stubby finger moved down to the last item on the sheet of paper: BELLPORT on one line, and under it HOWELL'S POINT. "Tomorrow morning," he said. "It's farther out from the city, so let's say ten o'clock. You bring me the Kopykat package and the other package, and I tell you what next."

"And the scraps from your table?"

With a thin smile, Banadando shook his head. "We pay at the end," he said.

"No," Levine said. "We have to have something now, to prove it's worthwhile."

Banadando sat back, brooding. The small movements of the boat were comforting at first, but then insistent.

A large white ferry went by, on its way to Fire Island, and its wake made the *Bobby's Dream* heave on the water like something alive and in pain.

"Upstate in Attica," Banadando said at last, "in the state

pen there, you got a guy named Johnson, serving five consecutive life terms. He's never coming out. He'll be the only Johnson there with that sentence.''

Levine smiled faintly. ''I guess you're right.''

''In Vermont,'' Banadando said, speaking slowly, picking his words with obvious care, ''there used to be a ski lodge called TransAlpine, had a big Olympic indoor skating rink. Burned down. No link between that and Johnson at all, right?''

''You tell me,'' Levine said.

''Johnson did things for Giacomo sometimes,'' Banadando said. ''Giacomo had a piece of TransAlpine. Not right out in front, but you could find it.''

''And?''

''Johnson hired the torch.''

''It was arson?''

''Nobody ever said it was,'' Banadando said. ''Not up there in Vermont. All I say to you is, Johnson hired the torch. Johnson and TransAlpine, there's no link there, so nobody ever talked to Johnson about that. Now all of a sudden I'm giving you a link. And what has Johnson got to lose?''

''The same as the rest of us,'' Levine said.

The man who answered the Vandyke phone number had a thin raspy voice. He said, ''I got everything but the gun. You want?''

''Yes,'' Levine said.

''In Manhattan,'' the raspy voice said, ''Seventy-ninth Street and Broadway, there's benches at the median, middle of the street, where people sit in the sun. Around two o'clock there'll be an old guy there with the package, gift-wrapped. Tell him you're Abe.''

Levine followed directions and found half a dozen elderly men on the stone bench there, faces turned to the thin clear autumn sun. The faces were absorbing the gold, hoarding it, stocking it up for the long cold time in the dark to come.

One of the old men held in his lap a parcel that looked

like a box of candy gaily wrapped in Happy Birthday paper. Levine went to him, identified himself as Abe, and took delivery. When Levine asked him how he'd come by the package, the old man said, "Fella give it to me half an hour ago with a five-dollar bill. Said you'd be along, said he couldn't wait, said I had an honest face."

The next old man over laughed, showing a mouth without teeth. "I said to the fella," he announced, "what kinda face you think *I* got? Paid me no never mind."

Carrying the Happy Birthday parcel, Levine went down Broadway to Kopykat, where he picked up the package for Mr. Robert. Then he continued on downtown to hand the material over to Inspector Santangelo at the Organized Crime Unit. "People upstate are talking to Johnson," Santangelo said.

"But is he talking to them?"

Santangelo grinned. "He will."

THE NEXT MORNING, SANTANGELO BROUGHT THE TWO packages to the Forty-third Precinct and handed them back to Levine in Lieutenant Barker's office. The Kopykat package had turned out to be copies of about forty ledger pages, but only numbers and abbreviations were filled in, making it useless by itself; you'd have to know what business those pages were connected to, and presumably Banadando's intended customer would know.

As for the birthday present, that box had contained a jumble of sales slips, for items ranging from automobiles and furs to coffee tables and refrigerators, plus a bunch of photos and negatives. There were a dozen pictures of what appeared to be the same orgy, pictures of a man getting into a car on a city street, pictures of a man at a construction site, of a truck being loaded or unloaded at the same site, of two men exchanging an envelope in the doorway of an appliance store.

Everything had been fingerprinted and photographed and brooded over, but there wasn't so far much value in the material. "It's puzzle parts," Santangelo said. "Just a couple of stray puzzle parts. Banadando has the rest."

MONDAY WAS A LESS PRETTY DAY THAN SUNDAY HAD been, the broad sky piling up with tumbled dirty clouds and a damp breeze blowing from the northeast. With Banadando's packages on the front seat beside him, Levine drove out the Long Island Expressway and took the turnoff south for Bellport. He found Howell's Point, left the car, and saw Banadando approaching on a bicycle, dressed in his yachting outfit, with a supermarket bag in the basket. Banadando looked unexpectedly human and vulnerable, not at all like the tough guy he really was. Levine was pleased with the man, almost proud of him, for how matter-of-factly he carried it off.

Dismounting, Banadando said, "Take the groceries, okay? The boat's just over here."

Banadando walked the bike and Levine followed with the bag and the two packages. The bag contained milk, tomatoes, lettuce, English muffins, a steak. Levine found himself wondering: Does Banadando have a wife? Is she part of his escape plan, or is he abandoning her, or does she not exist? Maybe she's already gone on ahead to prepare their next home. Banadando's style was that of the complete loner, but on the other hand he was only involved in this problem because of his emotional attachment to his son.

That was why Levine had never been able to go along with the idea that a murdered mobster was something to be happy about. Even the worst of human beings was still in some way a human being, was more than and other than a simple cartoon criminal. No death should be gloated over.

Aboard the boat, Banadando lashed the bike to the foredeck, then cast them off and headed out onto the bay, while Levine went below and put away the groceries. Coming up again on deck, where Banadando sat in a tall canvas chair at the wheel, steering them on a long gradual curve eastward into Bellport Bay, Levine said, "I'm not wired today. Thought you'd like to know."

Banadando grinned at him. "Waste of good tape, huh?"

"You won't say anything useful while I'm recording you."

"I won't say anything useful at all. Not the way you mean."

They ran southeast for fifteen minutes, then Banadando dropped anchor near Ridge Island and they went below together to talk. Levine explained that the Vandyke man had said he had everything but the gun, and Banadando waved that away: "I don't need the gun. I got enough without the gun."

"Well, here it all is," Levine said, gesturing to the two packages on the table.

Banadando nodded at the packages and grinned. "Made no sense to you, huh?"

"That's right."

"It'll make sense to some people," Banadando said. "And that's all it has to do. What about Johnson?"

"He's being talked to."

"He'll be very interesting, Johnson. Okay, time to memorize."

It was another sheet of paper, instructions on another two pickups. Levine listened and nodded, and when Banadando was done he said, "How long am I your messenger?"

"Two more days," Banadando said. "Tomorrow morning you bring me this stuff, I give you the last shopping list. Wednesday morning you bring me the last of it, I give you a nice package for yourself. The Johnson stuff is just a teaser—Wednesday morning I give you a banquet."

"And you leave."

"That's right," Banadando said. "And if you keep your ear to the ground the next few months, Detective Levine, you will hear some faraway explosions."

Their business done, they both went up on deck, and Levine sat in the second canvas chair while Banadando steered back toward Bellport. Even though the sky was lowering with clouds and there was a chill dampness in the air, there was something extraordinarily pleasant about being out here in this boat, skimming the choppy little wavelets, far from the cares of the world.

Not far enough. They were almost to Howell's Point. Levine could actually see his own car and a few other cars and some people walking along the pier when Banadando suddenly swore and spun the wheel and the *Bobby's Dream* veered around in a tight half circle, lying way over on its side into the turn, spewing foam in a great white welt on the gray water.

It wasn't till they were far from shore, out in the empty middle of the bay, that Banadando slowed the boat again and Levine could talk to him, saying, "Friends of yours back there?"

"Friends of *his*," Banadando said, his voice vibrating like a guitar string.

Tension had bunched the muscles in his cheeks and around his mouth, and his lips were thin and bloodless.

Levine said, "I wasn't followed, I can tell you that. My back-up would have known."

"The supermarket," Banadando said. "I can't even go to the supermarket. This is *rotten* luck, *rotten* luck."

"Now he knows about the boat."

"He can put people all around this bay, Giacomo can," Banadando said. "If he knows there's a reason. And now he knows there's a reason."

"I'll just mention police protection once," Levine said.

Banadando nodded. "Good," he said. "That was the mention. Look here."

From an enclosed cabinet under the wheel, Banadando pulled out a Defense Mapping Agency book of Sailing Directions, found the pages he wanted, and showed Levine what he intended to do.

"Long Island's a hundred twenty miles long," he said. "From where we are here, there's like another seventy miles out to the end. But I can't stay on the South Shore any more, so here's what I'm gonna do. I don't have to go all the way out to Montauk Point at the end of the island. Here by Hampton Bays I can take the Shinnecock Canal through to Peconic Bay, then I only have to go out around Orient Point and there I am on the North Shore. Then I head west again, across Long Island Sound. Look here on this map, west of Mattituck Inlet, you see this little dip in the coastline?"

"Yes."

"There's a dirt road there, comes down from Bergen Avenue. I know that place from years ago. There's a little wooden dock there, that's all. Nobody around. That's where we meet tomorrow, let Giacomo and his boys search the South Shore all they want."

Looking at the maps, Levine said, "That's a long way to go in a small boat like this."

"A hundred miles," Banadando said, dismissing it. "Maybe less. Don't worry, Levine, I'll be there. Between now and Wednesday, let's face it, the only way I stay alive is to do things Giacomo thinks I won't do or can't do."

"You're right," Levine said.

"I'm always right," Banadando said. "I can't take you back to your car. I'll drop you at Center Moriches, you can take a cab back . . ."

Levine made that day's pickups with no trouble, and that evening, as rain tapped hesitantly at the windows, the four policemen who knew about Banadando—being Levine and Jack Crawley and Lieutenant Barker and Inspector Santangelo—met in the lieutenant's office at the precinct to decide what to do next.

Jack Crawley, a big beefy man with heavy shoulders and hands and a generally dissatisfied look, had no doubt what *he* wanted to do next: "Bring in everybody," he said. "Inspector, you bring in your whole Organized Crime Unit, we bring in plainclothes *and* uniformed people from the precinct, and we surround that mother. I don't want Abe to spend any more time in the middle of some other clown's argument."

"I'm already in, Jack," Levine said. "We're on the

verge of getting some very useful information. I think Banadando actually is as smart as he thinks he is, and that he'll manage to elude Polito for the next two days. It's only until Wednesday, after all. The minute I step off that boat on Wednesday you can phone Inspector Santangelo at Organized Crime, tell him I'm out of the way, and send in the entire police department if you want."

"He'll be long gone by then," Crawley said, and Lieutenant Barker said, "I tend to agree with Jack."

"I'm sorry," said Levine, "but I don't. In the first place, he *won't* be long gone. I believe he actually will make it around the island tonight, but it won't be an easy trip. Those little boats always *feel* like they're going fast, but they're not. What's the top speed of a boat like that on choppy open water? Twenty miles an hour, maybe a little more? And they gobble up gasoline, he'll have to stop once or twice at marinas. This rain will slow him down. Traveling as fast as he can, on a small boat pounding up and down over every wave, he'll be lucky if it only takes him seven or eight hours to get around to where he's supposed to meet me tomorrow."

Lieutenant Barker said, "Meaning what, Abe? How does that connect?"

"Meaning," Levine said, "he can't disappear from us all that easily."

Santangelo said, "That's not such good news, Abe. If *we* could find Banadando just like that, why can't Polito?"

Levine shrugged. "Maybe he can, I hope not. But we have the entire law enforcement apparatus behind us to help, and Polito doesn't. We can bring in the Coast Guard, Army helicopters, anything we need."

Smiling, Santangelo said, "Not necessarily at the snap of our fingers."

"No, but it can be done. Polito can't begin to match our manpower or our authority."

Crawley said, "Never mind all of that after-the-event stuff, Abe. What it comes down to is, Polito's people got to that pier today within an hour of *you* getting there. What if they'd been an hour earlier?''

''A lot of different things could have happened,'' Levine said.

''Some of them nasty,'' Crawley told him.

Santangelo said, ''The decision has been Abe's from the beginning, and it still is. Abe, I'll go along with whatever you decide. But I have to say, there's a lot in what your partner says.''

''I'll stay the course,'' Levine told him.

Santangelo said, ''There's something else to consider. If something goes wrong, if Banadando gets killed or slips through our fingers, we could all be in trouble for not reporting the situation right away.''

Levine spread his hands. ''If you're worried about that, you rank me, you could take the decision out of my hands.''

''No, I don't want to,'' Santangelo said. ''I think we're handling it right, but I want you and Fred and Officer Crawley to know there could be trouble for all of us down the line. Within the Department.''

Lieutenant Barker said, ''Let's count that out of the decision-making.''

''Fine with me,'' Santangelo said.

THE LONG ISLAND EXPRESSWAY ENDED JUST SHORT OF Riverhead, seventy-five miles from Manhattan but still another forty-five miles from the end of the island at Montauk Point. The last dozen miles the traffic had thinned out so much that on the long straightaways Levine could see in the rearview mirror Jack Crawley's car, lagging way back. The rain had stopped sometime during the night but the sky was still cloud-covered and the air was cooler and still damp. In midmorning, the sparse traffic here at the eastern end of the Expressway was mostly delivery vans and a few private cars containing shoppers, the latter mainly headed west toward the population centers.

The land out here seemed to imitate the wave-formations of the surrounding sea—long gradual rolls of scrub over which the highway moved in easy gradients, long sweeps steadily upward followed by long gradual declines. It was on the upslopes that Levine would catch glimpses of Jack Crawley's dark-green Pontiac far behind and on the down-slopes that he was increasingly alone.

At the Nugent Drive exit, two miles before the end of the highway, a car was entering the road, a black Chevrolet. Levine pulled accommodatingly into the left lane, passed the car, saw it recede in his mirror, and a moment later was over the next rise. Signs announced the end of the road.

The Chevy reappeared over the crest behind him so abruptly, moving so fast, that Levine hardly had time to register its presence in his mirror before it was shooting past him on the right and there were flat cracking sounds like someone breaking tree branches and the wheel wrenched itself out of Levine's hands.

He'd been doing just over sixty. The Chevy was already far away in front and Levine's car was slewing around to-ward the right shoulder, the wheel still spinning rightward. Levine grabbed it, fighting to pull it back to the left, his right foot tapping and tapping the brakes. Blowout, he thought, but at the same time his mind was overriding that normal thought, was telling him, no, they shot it out, they shot the tire!

Banadando! They found him, they're going after him—they cut me out of the play!

He was recapturing control of his emotions and his thoughts and the car when its right tires hit the gravel and dirt beside the road and tried to yank the steering wheel out of his hands again. He hung on, his foot tapping and tapping, pressing down harder as they slowed, daring to assert more and more control until at last, in a swirl of tan dust of its own creation, the car jolted to a stop and skewed slightly at an angle toward the highway, seeming to sag in exhaustion on its springs.

Levine opened his mouth wide to breathe, but the con-striction was farther back, deep in his throat. He leaned forward, resting his forehead on the top of the steering wheel, feeling its bottom press hard into his stomach. His trembling hand went up to cup his left ear, the position in which, he had learned, he could best hear his heart.

Beat, beat, beat—

Skip.

Beat, beat, beat—

Skip.

Beat, beat, beat, beat—

Skip.

Beat, beat . . .

All right. Straightening, Levine took a deep breath, finding his throat more open, the act of breathing less painful. That had been a scary one.

Generally, the skips came every eighth beat, but excitement or exercise or terror could shorten the spaces. Three was about the closest it had ever come, and this near-accident had matched that record.

Accident? This was no accident. His entire body still slightly trembling, Levine struggled out of the car, walked around it, and saw that both right-side tires were flat. They showed garish big ragged entry holes in their sides. A sharpshooter, worth the money Polito would be paying him.

Polito. Banadando. Feeling sudden urgency, Levine looked up the empty roadway toward the top of the slope he'd just come down. Crawley should have appeared by now, he wasn't that far back.

They've taken him out, too.

Jesus, what's happened to Crawley? Levine had actually trotted a few paces toward that distant crest when over it came a rattly white delivery van and he remembered his other urgency instead: Banadando. In going for Levine's tires, Polito's men had made it clear they weren't interested in killing police today, so they'd undoubtedly taken out Jack Crawley the same way. The man in real trouble was Banadando.

Pulling his shield out of his jacket pocket, waving it in the air, Levine flagged the approaching van to a halt. A big boxy contraption advertising a brand of potato chips on its side, it was driven by a skinny bearded man who stood up to drive. He was frowning at Levine with a kind of hopeful curiosity, as though here might be that which would rescue him from terminal boredom.

It was. The tall door on the right side of the van was hooked open. Climbing up into the tall vehicle, still showing the shield, Levine said, "Police. I'm commandeering this truck."

"*This* truck?" The young man grinned, shaking his head. "You got to be kidding."

"Drive," Levine told him. "As fast as this thing will go." To encourage the young man, he added, "We're trying to stop a murder."

"You're on, pal!"

But no matter how enthusiastic the young man might be, the van's top speed turned out to be just about fifty-two. Levine kept leaning his head out the open doorway, looking back, hoping to see Jack Crawley after all, but it never happened.

The interior of the van was piled high with outsize cardboard cartons, presumably containing potato chips. Levine leaned against the flat top of the dashboard under the high windshield and wrote a note on a sheet of paper torn from his memo pad:

"NYPD Detective Abraham Levine, 43rd Precinct. Partner Jack Crawley in apparent accident on LIE. Underworld informant under attack. Follow caller to site."

After the highway ended, the young man followed Levine's instructions along Old Country Road and Main Road and Church Lane and Second Avenue. "It'll be a dirt road," Levine said. "On your left."

When they finally found it, the young man was going to swing to the left and drive down the road but Levine stopped him. Handing over the note, he said, "Go to the nearest phone, call the Suffolk County police, read this to them, tell them where I am."

"You might want me along," the young man said. "Maybe you could use some help."

"*Bring* me help," Levine told him. Stepping down to the shoulder of the road, he slapped the tinny side of the van as though it were a horse, calling to the driver, "Go on, now. Hurry!"

"Right!"

The van lumbered away, motor roaring as the young man tried to accelerate too rapidly up through the gears, and Levine trotted across the road and started down the dirt road, seeing the fresh scars and streaks of a car having recently passed this way.

First he saw the water through the thin-leaved birch trees—Long Island Sound, separating this long tongue of land from Connecticut. Then he saw the automobile, a small fast low-to-the-ground Mercedes-Benz sports car painted dark-blue. The black Chevy was nowhere in sight. Polito apparently employed specialists.

There was only the one car, and it contained seating for only two. Levine unlimbered his .38 S&W Police Special from its holster on his right hip and moved forward, stepping cautiously on the weedy leaf-covered ground. Yellow and orange leaves fluttered down, sometimes singly or, when the breeze lifted, they dropped in platoons, infiltrating their way to the ground.

Beyond the Mercedes, muddy ground sloped down to an old wooden dock. Tied beside it, very close to shore, was the *Bobby's Dream*. Revolver in hand, his eyes on the boat, Levine approached and, as he passed the Mercedes, a big-shouldered man in dark topcoat and hat came up out of the boat onto the dock, his arms full of boxes and packages, a couple of which Levine recognized—things he had brought to Banadando himself. He stopped, arm out, revolver aimed, and quietly said, "Just keep coming this way."

The man stopped, staring at Levine, his expression one of total amazement. Then, in a blindingly swift move, he flung the boxes away and his right hand stabbed within his topcoat.

Levine didn't want to kill, but he did want to stop the man. He fired, aiming high on the man's torso on the right

side, wanting to knock him down, knock him out of play,
but still leave the breath of life in him. But the man was
ducking, bobbing, just as Levine fired. When he jolted
back, his pistol flying out of his clothes and arcing away
to fall into the water, Levine had no idea where he'd been
hit. He went down hard, the sound a solid thud on the
wooden boards of the dock, and he didn't move.

A sudden burst of pistol fire flared from the boat and
Levine flung himself backward, putting the low bulk of the
Mercedes between himself and the gunman. The firing
stopped, and Levine sat on the leafy ground, revolver in
his right hand, left hand pressed to his chest, mouth
stretched wide. The constriction . . .

Hand cupped to ear, he counted beats, and after the
fourth came the skip. Not too bad, not so bad as a little
while ago in the car.

To his right, where he was sitting, were the hood and
bumper and left front tire of the Mercedes, and out at an
angle beyond them were the dock and the boat and the
unmoving man Levine had shot. To his left, pressing
against his arm, was the narrow graceful trunk of a birch
tree. Levine sagged briefly against the tree, then pulled himself up onto his knees and looked cautiously over the hood.

Immediately the pistol cracked over there, and a fluttering of branches took place somewhere behind Levine, who
ducked back down. When nothing else happened, he called,
"Banadando!"

"He don't feel like talking!" yelled a voice.

"Send him out here!"

"He don't feel like walking either!"

So he was dead already, which would give the man on
the boat nothing to lose by holding out. Still, Levine called,
"Come out of there with your hands up!"

"I'll tell him when he comes in!"

"You won't get away!"

"Yeah? Where's your army?"

"On its way!" Levine called, but the constriction closed

his throat again, chopping off the last word. Get here soon, he prayed.

The man on the boat swore loudly and fired twice in Levine's direction. Headlight glass shattered and Levine couldn't help flinching away, his entire body clenching at each shot. "I'm comin' right through you!" yelled the voice.

"Come right ahead!" Levine yelled back. But he didn't yell it, he hoarsely coughed it. The tightness in his throat was making his head ache, was putting metal bands around his head just above his eyes. He *couldn't* pass out, he *had* to hold this fellow here. Bracing himself between the Mercedes and the tree trunk, he extended his arm forward onto the hood, where the revolver would be visible to the man in the boat. Hold him there. Hold him, no matter what.

Another shot pinged off the car's body—merely frustration and rage, but it made Levine wince. His free hand went to his ear. He sat looking at a leaf that had fallen into his lap.

Beat, beat, beat—
Skip.
Beat, beat—
Skip.
Beat, beat—
Skip.
Beat—

THE SUFFOLK COUNTY COPS WERE ALL OVER THE DOCK, the boat, the foreshore. Boxes of Banadando's evidence were being carried to the cars. The gunman from the boat had already been taken away in handcuffs, and now they were waiting for the ambulance and the hearse.

Crawley stood with the Medical Examiner, who straightened and said, "He was dead at least a quarter hour when you got here."

"Yeah, I thought. And this one?"

They left Abe Levine's body and walked over to the wounded man on the dock, still unconscious but wrapped now in blankets from the police cars. "He'll live," the M.E. said.

"The wrong ones die," Crawley said.

"Everybody dies," The M.E. said.

Crawley turned and looked back at his partner. Abe was braced between the car and the tree, arm out straight, revolver just visible to the boat. He had died that way, his heart stopping forever but his body not moving. Sirens sounded, approaching.

"How do you like that," Crawley said. "He was dead, and he finished the job anyway. His corpse held that punk covered until we could get here."

"Maybe they'll give him a medal," the M.E. said, and grinned, showing uneven teeth. "A posthumous medal. The first legit posthumous medal ever, for performance above and beyond the call of death."

The hearse and ambulance were arriving. Crawley looked at the M.E. and pointed at Abe. "No plastic body bag," he said. "He gets a blanket."

THE QUESTIONER

Jonathan Kellerman

SANTIAGO HAD WAITED FOR THE PHONE TO RING SIX TIMES, unanswered, before the intercom button flashed and the buzzer sounded.

It was de Mauro, calling from the room.

"He's ready, Jorge. It shouldn't be a difficult one."

"I'll be there in three minutes."

Santiago stood up, straightened his tie, took a deep breath, and walked to the door. It had been a vaguely troubling day. It was good that this wasn't going to be a difficult one. He needed time to clear his brain, to stop and think. Already his skull was bursting.

He left his office and began the familiar walk down the long white-tiled corridor. Each step was choreographed by the past, every movement of his tall ascetic body was well planned. That was the key to his success, good planning. It had always separated him from the others. The ability to set the stage, to prepare and rehearse precisely the correct stimuli so that the probability of eliciting the desired responses was maximized. One did not always succeed, Santiago knew, but one maximized the probabilities. There was nothing that could be done about the rare psychopath who, totally cut off from the anxieties of interpersonal relationships, did not budge. But that was not his fault. He was not God.

He had first noticed that he was different when he was a child. It was, he reasoned, a gift, a talent, just like being able to paint, or play the cello. In his mind there was some confusion as to whether his own talent had begun immediately after a particularly virulent attack of fever had swept through his village, leaving him delirious and sweating in the rear of his parents' house. He had been little more than eight or nine and everyone said it was a miracle he had survived and even more of a wonder that his brain had not been affected. Of the latter, Santiago was sometimes not totally sure, though he knew his mind was intact—no doubt more intact than most others.

In school, the teachers had noted, first with amusement and relief and then with increasing concern, how they could leave the classroom, entrusting the behavior of the other children to young Santiago, and upon returning find the children more composed, disciplined, and quiet than before. One teacher had peeked through the doorjamb in an attempt to find out exactly what the boy did, for his ability to maintain order surpassed that of the adults. To the teacher's surprise, he noted nothing. The boy made a few statements about rules and regulations and the other children just seemed to listen. There was a curious air of tension in the room, but nothing tangible. The teacher relayed this observation to his colleagues and they shrugged, laughed nervously, and said how they were lucky to have a boy like Santiago, an unpaid deputy, and how he would go far, a boy like that.

Santiago himself wasted little time exploring the origins of his talent. It was a visceral thing. Literally. The squirm in his stomach. He could sense a lie coming from another person before the false words left loose lips. It cued him, so that by the time the lie had been spoken he was ready to counter it, to challenge, attack, parry delicately—whatever maneuver was appropriate. The split-second delay between the squirm and the other person's voice gave

Santiago just the extra edge he needed to win: to ferret out
the lie, to scoop it loose like a surgeon shelling a tumor,
to expose it to his mind and watch the liar recede into
helplessness. At first he was upset by the squirm—it was
startling, vibratory, like a low grade electric shock. As time
passed, however, he began to recognize the utility of it and
adapted to the pain.

He was the best thing they had, the colonels said. With
Santiago there was no need to torture. He was cleaner, more
efficient, and no bleeding hearts from the Red Cross would
ever complain. He had played a large role during the wave
of political convulsions that had washed across the country
several years before, questioning prisoners to the point of
physical exhaustion, pinpointing the lies, saving those who
told the truth. That period of unrest was over now and he
had achieved his rank; he was a man who commanded respect. Not a colonel, to be sure, but a captain of the highest
rank. A man to be reckoned with. He had a whitewashed
villa in the suburbs, an official chrome-colored Mercedes,
and the young daughter of a rich man—a truth teller—as
his wife. It was a good life for Santiago at this point in
time. And all he had to deal with now were the murderers,
arsonists, rapists, thugs, and thieves who insisted upon in-
flicting themselves upon an otherwise orderly new republic.
Small challenge for him.

THE PRISONER HAD BEEN PREPARED. HE HAD BEEN TOLD
that he was going to be questioned by Captain Jorge Santiago. He had been informed by a smiling de Mauro that
Captain Santiago was the best questioner in the republic,
that he had a knack for knowing when the truth was being
told and when it was not. That Captain Santiago never
failed (miniscule hyperbole offered in the service of truth).
Having been so informed, the prisoner was then left alone
to wait in an empty room decorated only by two chairs and
the static hum of air-conditioning. The prisoner waited for
eighteen minutes. Then Santiago entered. If the prisoner
smoked, Santiago brought cigarettes that had been denied

for days. If he was a coffee drinker, Santiago offered a steaming mug of a good brew. If he was an addict, Santiago brought coca leaves to chew. Santiago smiled, sat down, crossed his legs, pulled out a sheaf of official-looking papers, and examined them for a few minutes. Then he faced the prisoner.

He was a young man, barely into his twenties. Thin, fine-boned, with pale skin and a thick unruly tangle of black hair. He had not shaved for several days and Santiago noted that his beard was incomplete. Stubble showed over his upper lip and on his chin, and there were sprinkles of hair in the region of his sideburns, but his cheeks and jaw were baby-smooth. A boyish-looking man, thought Santiago.

The prisoner tried to avoid Santiago's eyes, but he had been seated in such a way that this could not be accomplished without closing his eyes or looking down at his feet. It was the latter that he chose, as they usually did. Closed eyes implied pain. And guilt. Such was their logic. The repetitiousness of human behavior!

The questioner looked full face at the prisoner.

"How did you feel," he asked gently but clearly, "when you first found out about the girl's death?"

The young man was shaken. The unexpected question. The conversational tone of the questioner's voice. He had expected a barrage of interrogation about his whereabouts, details, alibis. And here he was presented with a question that even went so far as to assume his innocence—when he had *first found out.*

"I don't remember. It was—"

"When you first found out, when you heard the news about her death," Santiago repeated, probing but still gentle, "were you angry? Scared? Sad? Stunned?"

"Sad! I was sad!"

"You were sad." Santiago nodded, expecting more.

"She was beautiful—it was sad that so beautiful a creature was gone."

"Like a beautiful bird? Like a creature with magnificent

plumage who has been plucked from the air and thrown to the ground?"

The prisoner looked at Santiago with stunned eyes.

"A compassionate response, Luis—that is your name, isn't it? A very compassionate response, and an aesthetic one too. Sadness at beauty lost."

"She was a beautiful person too," whispered the young man. He spoke with remembrance in his voice.

"I'm sure she was beautiful." Santiago crossed his legs again and waited a moment before speaking. "Still, Luis, I must say it is an unusual response. I would have thought that your response would have been anger—a desire to avenge the death of a beautiful creature—a beautiful *woman*, whose beauty you have known. You were intimate, were you not?"

"We were lovers." The young man trembled visibly.

"Beauty that you have tasted, a woman who was yours. I would have thought there would be a desire on your part to avenge her death, to strike out at the coward who pulled her from flight."

"Of course." The prisoner was trying to compose himself. "There was anger too. But first, sadness."

"Strange." Santiago shook his head. "But then again, I am only an officer of the police. I am not a psychologist."

The young man was a smoker, so Santiago offered him a cigarette. An expensive foreign brand that the prisoner was known to have favored. The young man hesitated, then took the cigarette. Santiago lit it for him, moving his chair closer in the process so that when the smoke cleared the questioner's face loomed unexpectedly larger before the prisoner's eyes.

"I saw the pictures of her, you know," said Santiago softly. "She was not beautiful. There were bruises around the face. Her throat had been cut—cleanly, I might add. And the ants—" he sighed "—those miserable jungle ants. They had begun their dirty work."

The young man was struggling with his emotions, not knowing whether to emphasize his grief or to remain calm and impassive. The struggle left him agitated, and it was at this point that Santiago felt the first tiny squirm in his stomach.

"I'm sorry," he said, "if the details are so gruesome. I felt you had a right to know."

"It's—all right."

"After all, you were her lover."

"Yes, yes." The prisoner got up from his chair and paced the room.

"You were her only lover?"

Squirm.

"Yes."

"Of this you are sure?"

Squirm.

"Yes."

"It is good to be so secure in love, to know that one is unchallenged by another man."

Squirm.

"Yes. It is—it was good." The prisoner's voice cracked. He turned away from Santiago, standing in a corner of the room, facing the wall, one hand touching the smooth white tile.

"That is why you were sad, of course. I can understand now. You were a king, unchallenged, and you had lost a creature of beauty and so you were sad."

"I don't understand. I'm confused."

"I'm confused too, Luis." Santiago's voice rose. "I don't understand how a virile, feeling man who loses his true love can reduce a human being to the level of a *creature*, can only feel a sophisticated, understated emotion like sadness! I don't understand, Luis. I am only a captain of police, but it baffles me how such a man can remain so calm."

"I am a calm person." The prisoner spoke between clenched jaws.

"This I understand. You are a student of law at the university. A student of law *must* be calm. But even the calm of reason recedes before the image of a smooth white throat with a barely separating wound stretching from ear to ear."

The young man began to retch.

"That is fine, Luis. You may vomit. Don't search for a bucket, we will clean your vomit from the floor."

The young man clutched at his stomach and heaved, but nothing came from his mouth except a dry choking sound.

"Go ahead, Luis. You may throw up your pain. Let the burning out of your intestines."

A bubble of spittle formed at the prisoner's mouth and he blew it to the floor. He coughed, heaved, and convulsed unproductively.

"It is a shame how the sourness and the burning stays inside, You would feel much better if you were able to vomit it up. Come back, Luis, sit down, relax."

The prisoner obeyed.

"I am sorry to put you through this," continued Santiago. "It is somewhat of an absurdity, a pretty horror, that in this life—the one life given to both of us—that we have to occupy our time in bringing up pain."

The prisoner was terrified. He looked at the questioner as if he were a madman.

"There is too much pain in life, is there not?"

The prisoner nodded.

"Do you think she felt pain?"

Squirm.

"I don't know."

"The medical officers could not determine if she had been knocked unconscious by the blows to the head before her throat was cut or if she felt the blade."

"I hope she felt no pain."

As the young man spoke Santiago's stomach was assaulted by a rain of squirming pain.

"You hope? You don't know?" Squirm.

"No! Of course not!"

"You don't remember?"

"No!"

"Oh, you do remember?" Squirm.

"I do—I don't—there is nothing to remember. I was not there."

"You are lying." Squirm.

"No."

"Not no, yes. Quite simply yes. You are lying. I have sat in this room and questioned thousands of men and I know who lies and who does not. But no matter, you will come to the truth yourself when you find that you will not be able to vomit out your pain—and your guilt." Santiago spoke in a matter-of-fact voice, not accusing, merely predicting.

The young man buried his face in his hands.

Santiago allowed silence to settle between them. Then he spoke:

"I have my own theory—it is not a sophisticated theory, Luis, but one that you might be interested in. My theory is that your feeling of sadness is delicately linked with your guilt. You killed your lover and when you did so you were another person—not literally, but psychologically another person. Perhaps you were consumed with anger at her infidelity—these are emotions one man can understand in another.

"As this other person, transported by, shall we say, another state of being, you killed her, plucked her from the sky. Later, when you first found out what you had done—I don't know when that precise moment was, maybe it was as you looked at her bleeding into the soft jungle soil where you dragged her body, maybe it was not until after you had returned home, or perhaps you did not return to yourself until you heard the news on the radio—but at that moment of revelation you did indeed feel a sweeping sense of sadness. Sadness at having left your own self and having stepped into the persona of another, at having taken away a beautiful creature.

"For it was only if you were able to see her as a creature—a thing, a prize game hen, a *creature*—that you would be able to cut her throat, to beat her around the head. You could do those things to a creature, but not to the woman who whispered to you between the sheets.''

Santiago let his words sink in.

"I don't know your precise motive, Luis, though I imagine it is one that I and any other man could sympathize with. Perhaps our medical officers upon conducting the post mortem examination—'' he consulted his watch ''—at this very moment, only a few feet away will discover inside of her the sperm of more than one man, the seed of many men.''

The young man looked up. There was fury in his eyes.

"The motive will emerge. It always does." Santiago shrugged. "The important thing is you, Luis. How will you be judged? I am no psychologist, as I told you before, but I will be able to recommend to the score of psychologists who will examine you that your emotions at the time were congruent with those of a man who did not know what he was doing, who was operating within the shell of another's persona. I will tell them that your initial emotion was sadness and that such an emotion is characteristic of the murderer who has acted without reason and who later discovers the consequence of his act. I will base my opinion upon thousands of hours of experience as a questioner and I will be believed. You will be treated with compassion if I do these things, but this is dependent upon you.''

"What can I do?''

"You must be truthful. You must write the truth down on paper. Simple white paper.''

"I must confess.''

"Tsk. I am not a priest. Your repentance does not concern me. You will never do such an act again.''

"What if I am not guilty?''

"My dear Luis, we could concern ourselves with theoretics all day and you would still not be able to vomit up your pain. The truth is, you are guilty—but only in an abstract sense, of course.''

"And if I insist that I am not?''

"Then you are lying." Santiago patted his midriff. "I can feel it here. In me. It is a talent I have had for some time. When you lie I can feel it. We could hook you up to a complicated set of machinery, but the result would be the same.''

''You cannot prove anything.''

''There will be no need to. We will find the passerby, the neighbors who heard your occasional fight, perhaps someone who saw you slap her or saw her slap you. We will find witnesses at the clubs and restaurants in which she was seen with other men. We will set the stage. I will testify that you lied frequently and that you gave calculated, premeditated testimony here today. That you resemble a cold-blooded murderer whose existence poses a threat to society. It will not be a pretty orchestration, but short of your giving us the truth it will be our only way.''

''The only alternative is—'' The young man was broken. Santiago knew a brief fluttering sensation of triumph.

''The truth. On simple clean white paper.''

''You have this paper?'' Tears were streaming down the prisoner's face.

Santiago reached inside the pocket of his jacket and drew forth the familiar sheet. He handed the young man his own gold-plated pen, a gift from the colonels.

The prisoner took them and the sound of hurried scratching writing filled the room.

ONCE THE PRISONER HAD BEEN REMANDED IN THE CUS-tody of two uniformed officers and Santiago was able to shrug off the effusive admiring comments of de Mauro, he slipped quietly out of the Ministry of Police building and into his Mercedes. It was a warm, pleasant night and the fragrance of the jungles, though miles away, came to him in a perfumed rush.

At home, Salvador served him a tall cool mixture of rum and fruit juice and told him that Madame would be down for dinner shortly. He relaxed in a chair on the veranda and listened to the wind.

She came down the stairs quietly and was at his side before he could rise to greet her.

"Good evening, Jorge."

"Good evening, darling."

They walked together to the dinner table and as he held out her chair he noticed that her face looked unusually flushed. Her hair was tied back in gleaming ebony plaits and her shoulders were warm and brown. A beautiful woman, his wife. He kissed her cheek softly and returned to sit opposite her at the well set table.

"You know, darling," he said, spreading a stiff linen napkin across his lap, "I called you earlier this afternoon. The phone rang several times and nobody answered."

She was answering him in a hesitant, tinkling tone of voice, telling him she had given Maria and Salvador the day off and had gone shopping with a friend, but Santiago was not listening. For while she spoke, in fact a split second before she opened her mouth, he found his stomach writhing in hot, acid, squirming pain.

DON'T FEAR THE
REAPER

〰

David Dean

JULIAN SAT SLUMPED IN THOUGHT IN THE PASSENGER SEAT of the patrol car, looking south down Island Drive. His partner, a summer officer, sat ramrod straight behind the wheel of the idling cruiser, his hands clenched in a death grip on the steering wheel.

Every summer, the Camelot Police Department augmented its small force with a dozen or so Class II officers drawn from criminal justice programs at various colleges. All the communities on the Jersey shore followed this pattern during the tourist season, when the populations of the islands would suddenly explode with do-or-die fun-seekers. The hordes would occupy their newly acquired kingdoms from Memorial Day until Labor Day, when the call of unseen forces would compel them to fold their tents and move on, leaving behind their stunned, but richer, subjects.

Julian's musings came to a halt as the event they had been waiting for began. He sat up a little straighter in order to witness the nightly ritual of bar closing and glanced over at his partner, who remained on alert, reminding him of a retriever waiting for a signal from his master. His gelled flattop nearly quivered in anticipation.

"Think there'll be a fight?" he asked, with a little more enthusiasm than Julian liked to hear.

"Um . . . could be. Possibly," Julian responded noncommittally.

Naturally, that was why they and several other cars were there. To forestall, as much as possible, the usual fights, vandalism, and the like, that tended to occur when several thousand drunk youths gathered together in one place. That place happened to be the Camelot Bar and Grill. A mammoth, rambling old hotel that occupied a city block and boasted three separate bars, a liquor store, and pool tables. The actual hotel, which had occupied the upper two stories, had been closed for many years now.

As they watched, the crowd began to pour out of the building, rushing through the now-open double doors that dotted the side of the structure and spilling onto the sidewalk and overflowing into the street. Many of them were drenched in sweat, their shirts plastered to their bones. Some seemed to be gasping for air, lifting their arms to the skies as if thankful for deliverance from the crush inside. Julian felt a drop of perspiration slowly working its way down his chest and tugged his protective vest away from his body to let some of the heat escape. It was quite warm for two in the morning.

He pointed out one young woman to his partner. She was on her hands and knees at the curb, puking up her paycheck. "Well, at least someone had a good time," Julian remarked.

The mob spread out to block half the traffic circle in front of the Camelot. Southbound cars were going in the wrong direction around the circle to avoid them. Northbound cars were taking evasive action to escape collision with the southbound rebels. One of the other patrol units began to ease its way into the milling crowd, slowly cutting a swath through them, forcing them to cross the street or to get back up on the sidewalk. Julian remained in place, ready as backup. He carefully scanned the crowd for signs of trouble, alert for the arching beer bottle that could turn this exodus into a melee.

"Where are they, do ya think?" he asked his younger partner.

"Who's that?" Franklin replied, a puzzled look on his seamless face.

"The piggyback couple." There was a pause while the young officer mulled this tidbit over.

"The piggyback couple?" he finally stammered. "Who's that?"

Julian was amused to see a furrow of concentration actually form a crease on his shiny young forehead.

"Franklin, I'm shocked at you. You're not aware of the piggyback couple?" Franklin looked worried now, knowing he was being set up. "Soon they will come out of that bar, as they come out of that bar every night. As they come out of every bar in this town every night. Nay, as they come out of every bar in every town in this state every night, sooner or later. And yet, you, a police officer, if only a Class II, know nothing of them. I'm disappointed in you, Franklin."

Franklin responded cautiously, "Oh yeah, right."

"Ah, here they are," Julian murmured.

As if on cue, the piggyback couple came jogging out into the night. A very drunk young man carrying an equally drunk young woman, squealing with delight, on his back. Julian chuckled. It never failed, no matter the bar. It was a phenomenon, peculiar to the summer perhaps, that cops witnessed with unfailing regularity. The couple made it to the corner before falling victim to gravity and the effects of alcohol. They disappeared, flailing, into some shrubbery.

"How'd you know that?" Franklin gasped.

Julian didn't answer, but spoke into the microphone of the car radio, "Eleven-oh-seven will take that call. We're eight blocks south of it." He turned to Franklin and said, "Turn us around and take us to Thirteenth. A caller heard screams in the vicinity."

Franklin executed a hard U-turn, cutting off an oncoming car and slamming Julian against the door.

"Jesus, Frank, take it easy. I'd like to get there alive."

"I didn't hear that call," Franklin said, almost under his breath.

Julian could hear the self-recrimination in his tone and offered some consolation. "Yeah, I know. You were too busy worrying about the piggyback couple. It'll all be in my report."

Franklin floored the gas pedal and they careened northward.

As they approached the area of Thirteenth Street, Julian had his young partner slow the squad car down to a crawl and kill the headlamps. "Keep your eyes open for anybody wandering around down here," he instructed. "And roll down your window and listen." He reached over and switched off the FM radio and at the same time informed dispatch that they were in the area and that nothing was showing. He heard Eleven-hundred tell dispatch that they were in the area also, cruising south on Island Drive. Julian could just make out their darkened car, creeping ghostlike along the curb several blocks away.

Julian looked around, noting the desolation of the neighborhood after the press of the bar crowd a mere quarter-mile away. No one seemed to be out, and there were few houses showing lights at this hour. They were crawling past the public-works yard, with its chain-link fence running the length of the block, when Julian switched on the alley light, throwing the various trucks, tractors, earthmovers, and surfrakes into sudden relief. There was no movement. No quarry was flushed from hiding. He switched off the light and told his partner to stop the car. They came to a halt underneath the water tower.

"I'm gonna take a walk around. You go ahead, but stay close. If you stop anybody, call Eleven-hundred for backup. They'll be able to get to you quicker than I will on foot." Julian eased himself from the car and quietly clicked the door shut. He leaned back in the window and said, "Don't forget about me, okay?'' and walked quickly into the shadows.

He waited for the patrol car to leave the area and listened. Still nothing. Just an increase in traffic due to bar break. He checked to make sure his portable was on low and began to ease along the perimeter of the fence, keeping in the shadows.

He followed the fence around the corner where the water tower stood and stopped. A ragged piece of black fabric fluttered weakly from the strands of barbed wire that topped the fence. He could just make out some lettering on the cloth. It appeared to be ''ALLICA.'' He noted that the strands were pressed down onto the chain-link, and that section of the fence leaned out over the sidewalk as if crushed down by a great weight. Julian looked up and was struck square in the forehead by a drop of liquid. He gasped and stepped back, his hand going involuntarily to the spot. It came away glistening with water. The water tower was sweating in the warm night air. He peered up two hundred feet to where the vast squat tank rested on its enormous legs and became aware now of an occasional plop of water on the nearby sidewalk. He risked a look with his flashlight but saw nothing on the catwalk that girded the belly of the tower. He flicked off the light and the tower seemed to retreat, making him feel as if he were falling backwards or that the tower was in its final moments of balance prior to crashing to the earth in an asphalt-splitting explosion of water. He stepped back, stumbling, and forced himself to look down to counteract the effects of vertigo. His portable crackled into life, causing him to start.

''Eleven-oh-seven to Eleven-hundred, I'll be out with two subjects at Twelfth and First.''

That was Franklin, and Julian began to walk quickly east on Thirteenth to back him up. As he reached the next corner, he heard Eleven-hundred sign out with his Class II and slowed. He could see the little gathering just a block north of him now on First. Three officers and a young couple.

Julian approached quietly from behind as the two Class

II's let the full-timer, Shane McPherson, do the talking. Julian just listened as Shane did his thing. There was no one better in the department at this kind of encounter, in Julian's opinion. Even though he was overweight and nobody's idea of a recruiting poster cop, Julian had great respect for him. What he lacked in appearance, he more than made up for in quickness of wit.

Julian sidled around to have a quiet look at the subjects. They were younger than he thought, not more than nineteen from the looks of them. The female noticed him immediately, casting a sullen, guarded look in his direction. The male's attention was completely on Shane's massive presence, a stupified expression on his face. He was tall and thin, with a bad complexion and bangs that hung into his eyes that he kept nervously brushing away. Julian noted that his Blue Oyster Cult T-shirt was sticking to his starved-looking frame in several places. The girl seemed out of breath.

She caught him looking and Julian thought he saw a moment's alarm flash across her white, fleshy face. It was gone in an instant, replaced by an angry determination that glinted in her small green eyes. She swung back to Shane and launched into a low, forceful monologue, forcing Shane to focus his attention on her. The boyfriend was shunted aside, literally taking a step back.

Julian drew closer to catch what she was saying and observed her right hand disappear beneath her great thatch of orangy-red hair and grip her neck, massage it lightly, and drop again, nonchalantly, to her side. Ignoring Julian completely now, she stood with her short, plump body planted firmly in front of Shane and explained, in exasperated terms, that, yes, she and her boyfriend had been in the neighborhood a few minutes ago taking a walk, as if that were a crime, and may have had a little difference of opinion on a few things. No big deal! The hand crept up to her neck again. It happened, or didn't the cops know that? Now, could they get on with their lives without any more police interference?

Shane looked amused. The boyfriend looked smug, staring admiringly at the girl. Shane took the lead. "So, what are you sayin'? That you two had a fight and maybe you did a little screamin'? That's what the neighbors heard?"

She answered Shane, her voice dripping with contempt. "Yes, Officer, that's what I'm saying. Now, may we go?"

Shane plowed on, impervious. "So, why?"

"Why what, Officer?"

"Why the screamin'? He hurt ya, or what?"

She glanced over at her boyfriend and a tight little smile crept onto her face. "No, he didn't hurt me. No one hurts me. We're on a different plane than that."

"I kinda figured that," Shane replied without missing a beat. "So, you had a fight, you did some screamin', you didn't get hurt, and here we are."

She visibly relaxed, the hand went back to the neck. "Yes, exactly."

Julian stepped forward. "So, what's wrong with your neck?"

She swung to face him, the hand quickly retracted. Fury contorted her already plain face into ugliness. "What?" she hissed.

Julian directed the beam of his flashlight to her neck, revealing a livid red line beginning at her jugular and vanishing beneath her mass of hair. It looked like a rope burn, but much narrower, and recent. The throat area was unmarred.

"How'd that happen, miss?"

There was a pause as she mastered herself. Julian could almost hear her thinking. "In a volleyball game," she began, her voice low and her eyes focused on the ground. "We were having a volleyball game at the house when someone's hand got caught in my necklace." Her eyes met his now. "It was an accident. Nothing to do with this. No concern of yours."

Julian glanced over at Shane. They understood each other. There was nothing for them here. They'd found their screamer and that would have to be that. If there had been

violence between these two, there was nothing they could
do with what they were getting. "You got some ID from
them and a local address?" Julian asked, as he began to
walk to the patrol car.

"Yeah, just waitin' on dispatch to verify their DL's,"
Shane called to his retreating back.

As they drove away, Julian looked back at the newly
released couple. They were making their way down the
sidewalk, their arms wrapped around each other as if for
support. Their disparate gaits caused them to wobble as
they walked, and they never looked back.

IT WASN'T UNTIL AFTER FOUR A.M. THAT JULIAN REMEM-
bered the patch of black cloth at the water tower. The Class
II's had all been released at four and he was now teamed
up with Shane. The sun was just starting to lighten the
eastern sky with a rosy hue.

He pulled up to the base of the tower and pointed it out
to Shane. "This is what I thought was going on last night
with the screamin'. I figured someone had tried to scale the
fence to the tower and got cut." Julian opened the car door.
"Let's take a look."

They ambled over to the damaged fencing and Shane
pulled the fabric loose and studied it. "It's a torn shirt,"
he announced. Julian peered through the linkage into the
tall, yellow grass beneath the tower. He spotted a brand-
name sneaker lying on its side. Farther in, he could make
out two large depressions in the grass, maybe some clothing. "Yo, Jules, I think there's some blood on this shirt."

A slight morning breeze swayed the foliage surrounding
the depressions and Julian felt himself falling again, like
last night. Sweat instantly coated his palms. He gripped the
chain-links and turned to Shane. "There's two bodies in
there," he said tightly. "I think one of them belongs to the
shirt."

WITHIN FORTY MINUTES OF THEIR SUMMONS, THE SCENE
was transformed from the breathless quiet of dawn to a

place of controlled confusion and subdued chatter. Following standard operating procedure, Julian had had the dispatcher notify the detective on call, the chief, the prosecuter's office, and the M.E., and all had duly arrived in various stages of stupor. Even though the sun had risen well above the horizon, it was not yet five-thirty. The scene had been taped off, and another patrol car had taken over shooing away the morbidly curious, though at this time of the morning they consisted only of the occasional jogger or elderly dog-walker. Even coffee had been sent out for. The various officers and technicians stood in idle groups, having completed the photography, and waited for the medical examiner to finish her preliminary examination before they began to process the scene for physical evidence. Julian stood over the body of a young white male as the M.E. crouched beside it, making some notes. She clucked and hmmed.

She turned her head and looked up at him. "So, you and Shane found the bodies?"

"Yeah," Julian quietly replied. "There was a report of screams in the area around two A.M. We didn't find anything here, but I noticed the shirt. We came back for another look when it got light. We also found how they got in. The lock is missing off the maintenance gate. They fell?"

She had started writing again. "Looks that way, or jumped. Do you know either of them?"

Julian gazed down at the broken body of the boy. He lay on his back, one leg almost completely folded under his body. The remaining flap of shirt showed the letters MET and a garish print of a guitar-playing skeleton. The chest, exposed where the T-shirt had been torn away, revealed numerous serrations made by the barbed wire and subsequent punctures from the top edge of the chain-link fence. He could see the purple-black line of lividity running lengthwise along the boy's back, where the blood had settled after his heart stopped beating. It left the rest of him dead-white. The face appeared too large and asymmetrical as a result of the shattered skull shifting under its fleshy cover. Julian thought of the boy's parents and suddenly, yearningly, of his own children, safe at home, dreaming in their tousled beds.

"Yeah, I know him. He lives, or did, a few blocks from here on First. He was seventeen. His name's Ryan Louper. The kids called him Loopy. I had him on a drug charge about two months ago and he'd agreed to supply me with some info on who's dealing LSD to the juvies around here. Acid's made a big comeback lately. I'd yet to hear from him."

The M.E. looked at Julian thoughtfully. "Think that has anything to do with this?"

"I thought you said they had fallen or jumped?" he shot back.

After a short pause, she replied, "Yeah, I did." She turned and walked a straight and careful line to the next body. Julian followed, placing his footsteps in hers. When he reached the girl, he almost retreated a step. In spite of the fact that she had missed the fence and had less obvious damage, the result of the unbroken impact had been devastating. She looked as if a giant had stepped on her and carefully ground her into the earth. Her eyes had almost distended from their sockets.

Julian looked away and said, dry-mouthed, "I don't know this one. I don't think I've ever seen her before."

The M.E. clucked and hmmed again. She began jotting on her notepad.

Julian cleared his throat and began again. "I don't think Ryan was the kind of kid that would kill himself. He knew the score. He knew that juvenile charges don't carry much weight. The worst he would have been facing was counseling or drug rehab, probably. If he didn't want to snitch on the dealers, he would have just said so. It was no big deal. In fact, he hadn't snitched on anybody and probably wasn't going to. He was just stringing us along, more than likely." He stopped, realizing how defensive he sounded.

And felt. He had been warned about using juvenile inform-
ers, how volatile they could be.

Julian looked up to the tower catwalk and back to the
sagging fencing that Ryan's body had struck. It wasn't far
from the base of the tower, but would a simple slip and
fall have taken him even that distance? And how did he
explain the girl? How did she happen to fall also? He
looked down at her broken body again and sighed. A silly,
adolescent notion came to him. Maybe they were holding
hands at the moment of the fall . . . or jump. It was then
that he noticed her clenched fist, two slender pieces of
leather, or rawhide, dangling from it.

"Doc, what's she holding there?"

The M.E. unhurriedly turned her attention to the corpse's
right hand and carefully pried it open. Lying there was a
cheap-looking silver cross. Julian squatted down to get a
better look, resisting the impulse to pick it up. On closer
inspection, he could see that it was a type of cross, but with
a difference. The head of the cross ended in a loop. The
leather thong was threaded through a small opening at the
top of the loop and broken, ending in two pieces. It was
obviously meant to be worn around the neck.

"That's what I think is called an ankh," the doctor murmured. "Egyptian, if I remember my history of religious
classes correctly. I believe it symbolizes eternal life." Neither chose to comment on the irony.

It suddenly occurred to him how they could have both
"fallen" at the same time. "Doc, do you think Ryan could
have been wearing this? It would make sense that if she
started to fall, that she would reach out to grab something.
Maybe she grabbed this necklace and pulled Ryan over
with her."

The doctor looked thoughtful. "That's a pretty theory,
but I saw no abrasions on the neck of the male during
prelim. Still, an autopsy will tell us more. You can let the
others know that I'm done here." She stood and stretched
as Julian made his way to the cluster of officers.

As Shane pulled away from the curb, Julian looked back

at the technicians fanning out beneath the tower, the bodies once again hidden from view. Even in the light of day, the water tower now looked evil to him, like a great heathen idol, gloating over its sacrifices and its secrets. An involuntary shudder coursed through his tired body, and a flash of memory surfaced like a striking fish. A picture of a girl on a darkened street rubbing the back of her neck and wincing in pain.

THE LOUPERS WERE HOME, AS JULIAN FEARED THEY would be. He imagined they had had another sleepless night, thanks to Ryan.

He had not wanted to pull this duty, but since it was technically his investigation and there was the identity of the girl to clear up, it fell to him. He had Shane stop just around the corner from the Louper's rented house. The father's pickup was still in the drive, and the mother was clearly visible at the kitchen table. She was still in her housecoat, staring angrily out the window. Julian looked at Shane. They had already discussed what they would do.

As soon as they stepped into view, Mrs. Louper rose from her chair and took several steps toward the door. Her face was set and grey, vestiges of fear showing in her darkened eyes. She stopped herself from rushing to the door. As they climbed the steps, they heard her call out her husband's name. He appeared abruptly behind her as she opened the door to their knock.

"Do you have him down at the station again?" she asked immediately.

Her husband's face was loose with exhaustion, frightened. He was seeing more clearly than she. He saw that this was different. If they had had Ryan at the station, they would have just called, wouldn't they? That's what they'd always done in the past. Just called.

Julian began, "Could we just come in for a moment? I think we all need to sit down."

A spark of fear and suspicion animated the woman's face and was quickly subdued. She folded her arms across her chest and remained blocking the door. "You've got him, don't you? Well, I hope you've put him in a cell this time! If he's going to keep fooling around with drugs that's what he deserves!"

Julian pictured Ryan's shattered body lying naked on a mortuary slab and wanted nothing more than to stop her from saying these things that she would have all of her life to regret. He continued on up the steps, forcing the woman to step aside, and entered the kitchen. "Ryan was with a young lady last night. Do you know who she was?"

The question threw them both off guard. He could see them visibly relax. Problems with a girl, this was something normal. Something they could understand. Julian felt cruel, delaying the blow he knew he must deliver, but if he waited they might not be in any condition to identify the dead girl. After all, she too probably had parents frantic with worry that she had not returned.

Mr. Louper spoke. "He went out with his girlfriend last night. She's from Bayshore Township." Bayshore was a down-at-the-heels town in the south of the county. Julian recalled that Ryan had run into some trouble down that way not too long ago. "He said they were going over to a friend's house to listen to some music. He promised me that it wasn't a party."

"Her name?" Julian asked.

"Becca . . . Rebecca Tournquist. Are they in some kind of trouble, Officer Hall?"

Julian ignored his question. "Could you describe her for me?"

Mrs. Louper answered. "She's seventeen, the same age as Ryan, has black, wavy hair just past her shoulders, and is kinda tiny . . . you know, petite. Is that what you needed to know?"

Julian faltered. That was the girl he had found. Now for the hard part. "Yes, Mrs. Louper, that's very helpful." He took a breath. "Now, I have some very hard news for you. Maybe we should sit?" No one moved. The Loupers, all color drained from their faces, remained immobile, waiting for the blow. "Ryan and Rebecca were killed last night in an accident." He stopped; he could feel his hands shaking and he placed them in his pockets. The woman began to sway, a low moan breaking from her ashen lips. Shane was quickly at her side, easing her into a chair. Suddenly Louper slammed his hand down on the tabletop, causing the dishes to jump and startling the officers.

"They didn't have a car, damn you!" he shouted. "It's still out front! They walked to where they were going!" he finished triumphantly, desperately.

"It was a fall, you see," Julian resumed quietly. "They apparently were on the water tower and fell." He refrained from mentioning any other possibility. "Mr. Louper, is there anyone you would like us to call? A priest or minister? If you like, we could get someone here to stay with you and your wife."

Louper, his hands still on the tabletop, supporting his full weight now, looked up. The hot tears were streaming from his eyes. "You're sure? You're sure it's Ryan?"

Julian just nodded. Mrs. Louper began to wail, a soft, keening sound. Her husband made no effort to go to her. Each was engulfed in their own grief and guilt. Julian heard someone clattering down the stairs from the second floor.

"Mom, Dad? What's wrong, what's happened?"

The little sister, Julian thought. I forgot about the little sister. Oh God.

SEVERAL HOURS LATER, SHANE AND JULIAN WERE BACK at the station, drained and exhausted. They had summoned a doctor, who had medicated the survivors, leaving them zombielike in their quiet house. No TV, no radio. Just silence.

Before they left, Julian had secured permission from Louper to search Ryan's room. He had explained that it was normal procedure in a case such as this. Louper had simply nodded yes. It was Shane who had discovered the sheets. There were three of them. Each had fifty hits of blotter acid on a sheet of notebook-sized paper that was expertly perforated into fifty tabs for easy detachment. Each tab contained the LSD in the likeness of a dancing bear surrounded by roses. Childlike images. No suicide notes.

A quick field test confirmed their suspicions, and Julian packaged a sheet for examination by the prosecutor's lab for a definitive analysis. The other two he set aside for latent fingerprints. He was anxious to know who else had handled these sheets besides Ryan. Tomorrow, he intended to rattle some cages.

JACOB SCOTLAND WAS SHOOTING HOOPS AT THE REC CENter when Julian found him the following evening—a small, thin boy of sixteen, with a clear, milky complexion and a guileless, baby face. Julian noted that despite his size he held his own against the larger boys on the court. Since the age of fourteen, Jacob had successfully broken into a dozen or more homes, using a second-floor technique that required a good deal of dexterity and wiry strength. He had been caught twice already and showed little inclination to reform. In fact, his M.O. had recently resurfaced in a string of B&E's in the lagoons.

This was the person that Ryan and Becca had told the Loupers they were going to visit on the night of their deaths. Julian waited for halftime and signaled Jacob over. He approached in his usual carefree manner, wiping himself down with a dirty-looking towel, as if being summoned by a cop during a basketball game was commonplace. His angelic face beamed.

"Officer Hall, how ya doin'?" he began.

Julian didn't smile back. He was in no mood for the usual adolescent banter. He had already decided to cut right to the chase.

"You know about Ryan and his girlfriend?"

Jacob's cherubic features clouded briefly. "Yeah, it's all over town. Bummer, huh?" The smile broke through the clouds again. Irrepressible.

Julian resisted the impulse to strangle this kid. "Yeah,

Jacob, it's a bummer. I can see that you're real tore up about your buddy.''

"Yo, man, Ry and Becca followed their own path. That's nothin' to do with me. They had free will.''

Julian was caught off guard by Jacob's record-jacket philosophy. "So, what are you saying, Jacob? That they walked out of your place, climbed the tower, held hands, and jumped? Did you watch all of this, Jacob?''

Alarm rippled across Jacob's face. "No, man! I wasn't there! They didn't even come to my house that night!''

Julian already knew that, having checked with Jacob's parents. He bluffed. "There's no law against suicide, Jacob, but there is one for assisting. If I find out you were there and did nothing, or helped them, by God, I'll have you tried as an adult!''

The smile had completely vanished and looked like it might never return. That was what Julian wanted. "If they weren't with you before they went to the tower, who were they with? And this had better be the truth, Jacob, 'cause I'm gonna check.''

Julian watched him weigh his options, and as usual he chose self-preservation. "They were probably hangin' with some dudes over at Eleventh and Camelot. An old house on the corner. They went there sometimes when they told their folks that they were at my house. Ry had been hangin' out there a lot since you guys busted him.''

"Who are these people, Jacob? What's up with them?''

Jacob considered this for a moment. "It's a girl and a dude. They're a little older than us, eighteen or nineteen, but they're cool. A little different, maybe, but cool.''

Julian felt his scalp tingle. "A red-haired girl and a tall, skinny guy?''

Jacob brightened a little. "Yeah, Gabriel and Morgan, you know 'em?''

There they were again. "Yeah, I've met them. Jacob, do a lot of people know about Ryan being busted?''

"It's been around town. You know Ry could never keep his mouth shut.''

Julian digested the double meaning in Jacob's statement. If Ry had blabbed about his acid bust, had he also told everyone about how the cops wanted him to be an informant? The buzzer sounded for the game to resume.

"One last thing, Jacob. What makes you think they killed themselves? Why would they do that?"

Jacob had already started to walk away and he stopped in mid-stride, the towel slung over his shoulder. "You should talk to those dudes on Eleventh about that, man. All I know is that since Ry started hangin' there he's been different . . . or was different," he corrected himself. "They got a different way of lookin' at life over there. I'm not into it, but it's cool. Ry said they were teaching him not to be afraid."

"Afraid of what?" Julian asked.

"Anything, dude. Parents, cops, life, death, you know, everything."

"He said that? Even death?"

"That was the main thing he said they believed. If you didn't fear death, nothing could touch you. That there was freedom on the other side." Jacob walked away. Over his shoulder, the smile fully in place again, he called out, "Don't fear the reaper!"

Julian recognized the line from a popular rock song in which the singer urges his lover to commit suicide with him. "Bullshit," he muttered under his breath and walked away.

TWO DAYS LATER, JULIAN RECEIVED A COPY OF THE MEDical examiner's findings. It contained no surprises. Both deaths were ruled accidental as a result of their plummet from the water tower. Suicide was not mentioned, both as a courtesy to the families and due to the absence of suicide notes or other corroborating evidence. The serology examination revealed traces of lysergic acid diethylamide, which was listed as a possible contributing factor in the deaths.

Julian pondered that for a moment. LSD kept popping

up in this case. First, he had nabbed Ryan with a sheet of
acid several months ago. Second, Ryan agrees to put him
on to the source of the local network. Third, Ryan, according to the possumlike Jacob, starts to hang out with the
Eleventh Street couple. Fourth, Ryan and his girlfriend take
a two-hundred-foot header off the local water tower and
their autopsies reveal the presence of LSD in their blood-
streams. Finally, he and Shane find three sheets of blotter
acid in Ryan's room.

A hundred and fifty hits was way too much for personal
use. Had Ryan moved into dealing shortly before his death?
Had he cut into some other dealer's territory and suffered
the consequences? It seemed unlikely. Money just wasn't
a motive in street-level acid dealing. It was only three to
five dollars a hit, for God's sake! Acid dealers weren't like
crack or heroin pushers. They weren't in it for the money.
They tended to see themselves as purveyors of an alternate
lifestyle. Modern-day shamans offering their followers a
glimpse of paradise . . . or hell. It was a power trip, really,
with the dealer as both holder of the key and guide once
you had entered the gate. Among the very young, it could
be a powerful, and dangerous, position.

Ryan just didn't fit the bill. He wouldn't have had the
organizational skills for such a role. He was Loopy, remember? Essentially a good-time Charlie.

There was another possibility, however. Maybe Ryan had
hidden those sheets as evidence, intending to turn them
over to Julian. It would be just like Ryan to go half the
distance and get distracted or change his mind. But had he
shot his mouth off about that as well? Whereas money
might not be a motive to an acid dealer, prison certainly
could be.

Julian opened the bag containing Becca's clothing and
belongings, which had been sent over with the M.E.'s report, and carefully withdrew the silver ankh with its broken
leather thong. He had specifically requested a DNA test be
run on any flesh found adhering to the leather at the point
where it had been broken. The M.E.'s office had been just

as specific. In the absence of evidence of homicide and the lack of any suspects, no tests would be run. There was no way they could justify the expense and, besides, the use of DNA in forensic science simply had not yet reached a level where it was accepted as definitive by the judiciary system. At this point, the myth was a more powerful tool than the reality. There had been no mention in the report of whether the necklace had been identified by the girl's parents or not. He pulled the phone over to him and dialed their number.

Rebecca's mother did not recall ever having seen her daughter wear a necklace of that description, and it was unique enough that she would have remembered. Julian thought he knew its owner.

THE HOUSE WASN'T HARD TO FIND, SITTING EXACTLY where Jacob had said it would be at the corner of Eleventh Street and Camelot Avenue. It was a ramshackle Victorian monstrosity sprouting turrets and cupolas from unlikely places, a hangover from the days when the rich brought their servants with them to the shore. With three floors and an attic, there was plenty of room for everyone. Usually, the attic was where the servants ended up. They were like rabbit warrens, cut up into a half-dozen rooms or so. They must have been insufferably hot in the summer, Julian thought.

As Julian approached, he noticed that the paint had worn away in a number of places and that shingles were missing from both the roof and the siding. The broad wooden steps leading to the wrap-around veranda sagged under his weight and the wood looked spongy. The veranda itself sloped towards the heavy, ornate front door, reminding him of a carnival fun house where once you enter, you cannot go back. Julian glanced at the forbidding entrance, expecting to see a sign above the door that read, "Abandon Hope, All Ye Who Enter Here!"

He could see no one through the tall windows that fronted the house. The inside looked to have been better kept up than the exterior, but still had a forlorn, unkempt appearance, cluttered, dark, and dusty. Julian returned to the door and peered through the tulip-patterned etched glass framed in the woodwork. At the end of the dimly lit hall he glimpsed a shawled figure gliding silently from one room to the next. He felt his hackles rise in spite of himself. He slammed the blackened brass door-knocker several times to dispel the goose bumps. After all, this phantom had red hair.

After what seemed like a very long wait, Julian heard someone shuffling down the hallway towards the door. Gabriel's face appeared briefly in the glass and vanished. Another pause ensued and Julian wondered if he was going to open the door or not. Just as he raised the knocker again, the door swung inward a few inches. Gabriel thrust his acne-scarred face out, his long, stringy forelocks covering one eye.

"Yeah?" he ventured.

"Is it Lurch's day off?" Julian asked, straight-faced.

Gabriel seemed to consider this. "Say what?" he finally responded.

Julian didn't want to waste any more time with repartee on an unarmed opponent. "Could I come in?"

Once again, the boy seemed befuddled, unsure. Julian could see a bead of sweat run down his long, dirty-looking neck as he turned to look back into the house. His face came around again. "Um, just a minute." With that he closed the door.

Was the girl standing behind him? Did he have to consult her before allowing the police in? He's either very stupid or very nervous, Julian thought.

After another long pause, the door opened again. This time it was Morgan. She was no longer wearing the shawl and her great thatch of orangy hair hung unbound to her waist, a mass of snarls and split ends that made her look like a flaming Medusa. Her paper-white face looked serene and confident. She began to speak, but had to stop to clear her throat. She tried again.

"How may I help you, Officer?" she asked, with just the slightest trace of peevishness.

"I'd like to talk with you inside, if I may. With you both," he added.

She seemed to consider this. The door opened all the way and she invited him in with, "Come in, if that is what you choose." Gabriel was nowhere to be seen.

"Isn't that what Dracula said to Jonathan Harker?" Julian joked. Nonetheless, this house and these people gave him the creeps.

She turned back from the parlor entrance and eyed him without a trace of humor. "I don't know what you're talking about," she replied flatly.

"You're right," said Julian. "I think it was 'Enter of your own free will.' " He had given it his best Hungarian accent.

Spots of color appeared at the girl's cheeks. Julian could see that she wasn't used to being toyed with. "You may come into this room," she said. "But no farther. The rest of the house is off-limits to you." Now it was Julian's turn to get steamed. Gabriel sat cross-legged on an antique sofa with the stuffing spilling out, watching this exchange. Julian walked on in, intentionally not replying, not acknowledging her implied control of him.

Julian smiled warmly at Gabriel. "Long time, no see, pardner!" Once again, the humor went right over the boy's head and he just looked startled. His eyes sought Morgan's. Julian decided that he would focus on the boy. The girl, who had settled herself in an upholstered, wing-backed chair, regarded them both imperiously. Julian chose not to sit and leaned back against the mildewed wallpaper. He plowed on. "Gabriel," he said overloudly, "when's the last time Ryan Louper and his girlfriend were in this house?" The eyes looked fearful now.

The girl interrupted. "Officer, this is my house. I think I have a right to know why we are being questioned and what it's about."

"This is your house? When did you buy it?" Julian asked pleasantly.

She was caught off guard at his change of direction. "Well, it's my grandfather's actually, but he's let me live here for as long as I choose." The spots of color returned.

That word again. "Choose." She seemed intentionally to avoid words like will and must. "I see. So it's not 'your' house." He let that hit home and continued. "I'm investigating the deaths of Ryan Louper and Rebecca Tournquist, a young couple you're both familiar with, I've been told. You've read about it in the paper, I assume?"

"We don't read the papers," she responded coolly. "They're full of lies, half-truths, and distortions. The real truth lies within."

Julian digested this for a moment. "Well, miss, the real truth is that two friends of yours are dead. I found them myself. You can take it from me, they're as dead as you can get." Julian could hear Gabriel breathing through his mouth now, hoarse, ragged.

Morgan glanced sternly in his direction. "What makes you think they were friends of ours? Who told you that? I'd like to know who that could be."

I just bet you would, thought Julian. "Miss, I'm just trying to determine their movements prior to the 'accident.' It's pretty routine, actually. And seeing as how you two were in the vicinity of the water tower at the time of their fall, I thought you might have seen or heard something. In fact, I thought you all might have been together that evening." He finished up looking at Gabriel, who sounded as if he might have an asthma attack at any moment.

She was standing now, rigid. "We've already told you, Officer. We didn't know them and they were never with us!" She wasn't going to give Gabriel a chance. She spoke for them both now. "We've told you all we know, which is nothing!"

"Actually," Julian cut her off, "old Gabriel here hasn't told me anything. Have you, Gabe?" He reached down and patted his knee in a friendly, confidential manner. "Maybe we'll talk later.'' Gabriel looked ashen and terrified. Julian noted that it wasn't he Gabriel was looking at though, it was the girl. ''Mind if I use the bathroom?'' he asked, seemingly oblivious to the girl's blatant hostility and the tension-laden atmosphere. ''Is it down the hall here?'' He walked rapidly out of the room and turned left toward the back of the house.

The girl was instantly behind him. ''I want you to leave now!'' she hissed.

Julian kept walking and opened the door he had seen her come out of earlier. ''This it?'' he called over his shoulder.

The room he was looking into was radically different from the rest of the house. It was brilliant with a kaleidoscope of light supplied by a bank of large, stained-glass windows lining the rear wall. The furnishings consisted of mounds of cushions forming divans for reclining.

His attention, however, was captured by the inner wall, which was a pulsing mural of colors depicting a landscape of people meeting their deaths in a variety of graphic ways. Head-on collisions seemed to predominate. In each case, the person's soul was shown flying heavenwards, white-robed and rapturous, from the crushed or bleeding body. It was the end of the world and the beginning of the hereafter. Julian recognized it as a crude reproduction, with numerous liberties taken, of a frightening painting known as ''The Rapture.'' It's like looking into her squirming little brain, Julian thought.

Morgan pushed by him and slammed the door shut in his face. ''Get out!'' she screamed.

''Oops, thought that might be the loo,'' Julian responded. He turned and started for the front door, leaving Morgan guarding her inner sanctum. Gabriel stood peering nervously into the hallway from the parlor entrance. ''I'm really sorry for all the upset, Gabriel. I was just hoping to clear up this accident business and I thought you guys might be able to help. Hey, cops are people. We all screw up.''

Julian stopped abreast of the boy and leaned into him

conspiratorially. He removed something from his pocket and held it in his closed fingers. "Listen, Gabe, I feel awful about upsetting your girlfriend like this. Maybe this will make her feel better. I found it right after we stopped you guys on First Avenue the other night." He opened his hand and there lay the ankh.

Almost smiling with relief, Gabriel reached out for it. "Morgan's ankh!" he breathed. "She was afraid she'd never get it back. It was so dark . . ." With a gasp, he stopped in mid-sentence and snatched his hand back as if Julian were holding a scorpion. The realization of what he had said was written all over his face. Over the boy's shoulder, Julian could see the girl, who had crept silently down the hall and witnessed the exchange. Her normally pasty face was even paler and the flesh hung loose with shock. Only the tiny, muddy green eyes looked alive, glittering with malice.

Julian held the necklace up so that she could clearly see it. "Gotcha!" he said and went out the door.

Back in the car, he placed his head down on the steering wheel, trying to master his excitement and fury. On the one hand, he now knew with certainty that Morgan and Gabriel had been on that tower with Ryan and his girlfriend on the night of their deaths. The motive, now that he had caught a glimpse of Morgan's character, was just as clear. She had known, just as Jacob and everyone else in their little circle had known, that Ryan was an informant for the police. That was why he had taken up with this odd couple in the last few months of his life. He was setting them up. But Morgan set him up first. There was no way that she could spend a day "inside." Not her. The queen of her domain, the mistress of her own fate. May, not shall.

On the other hand, Julian knew that he didn't have a shred of usable evidence. In the absence of witnesses or a confession, they would continue as if they had never stood at the top of that bloated tower looking down at those shattered young bodies. Julian thought of the mural and briefly pictured the souls of Ryan and Rebecca flying heavenwards, in terror, from the earth. He started the car and drove away.

Back at the station, a large manila envelope was waiting for him. It was the report on the latents from the state police. Almost holding his breath, Julian tore it open and read the report.

THEY HIT THE HOUSE AT TWO IN THE MORNING WITH THE search warrant. Julian was a great believer in visiting suspects in the wee hours, when they were at their physical and psychological low ebb. Defenses were down and truth tended to be less elusive.

The Automated Fingerprint Identification System, or AFIS, as it was more commonly called, had done the trick. Not only had it proven that the Acid Queen and her joker had handled the sheets of LSD that had been found in Ryan's room, thereby giving Julian a shot at a distribution charge, it also revealed that both had faced similar charges in the past. More importantly, they could no longer deny that they had known the dead couple.

Morgan had been smart enough to destroy any sheets they had lying around the castle after Julian's visit, but she had underestimated the cops. Something Julian had privately counted on. The chemicals for making her brew were found in various locations throughout the house. In the servants' quarters, they had found a paper perforator and a hand-operated silkscreen press. The stencil had been a dancing bear.

Morgan had been carried out screaming that she was a chemistry major. Gabriel had remained silent. Julian saw to it that they were transported separately to the station and kept that way.

JULIAN WAS SITTING FACING THE DOOR OF THE INTER-view room when they brought Gabriel to him. He took a long moment just to look at the boy, who was shivering like someone with St. Vitus's Dance. He looked down at the floor to avoid Julian's eyes and wrapped his arms around himself. Julian, with careful enunciation, read him his Miranda warning. He nodded his head to indicate that he understood his rights. He doesn't trust himself to speak, thought Julian. So he began.

"Gabriel," Julian said softly, "there's very little I need from you in reference to the drug charges you're facing here. I think the evidence will stand alone on that pretty well. Do you understand me?"

Gabriel's teeth began to chatter, making a slight clacking sound in the concrete room. He nodded again.

"There's another reason I have you in here. I think you know what that is, don't you?"

Gabriel looked up at Julian now. His eyes wet, beseeching. Julian couldn't tell if he wanted him to stop or go on and get it over with. His hope buoyed. If ever a suspect was on the verge of breaking, this was him. . . .

"The water tower, Gabe, that's what we need to talk about." The young man began to rock back and forth now, his eyes tightly shut. "I think you can tell me what happened up there that night, can't you? I know you were there, and I think you need to tell someone. If you help me with this, I'll go to bat for you with the prosecutor. I can't make any promises, but I'll try." The tempo of the rocking increased and Julian saw that he was biting hard on his lower lip. Still nothing.

"It's the girl, Morgan, isn't it? Are you trying to protect her, Gabriel? Is that it?"

Gabriel stood suddenly, still rocking like a crazy person. Julian stood too.

"I know what happened up there wasn't your fault, Gabriel. It was her idea, but she needed you, didn't she? Because there were two of them, she needed you up there."

Without warning, Gabriel slammed his forehead into the cinder block of the wall, hard. Before Julian could get around the desk that separated them, he did it again. Julian grabbed him and spun him around. Gabriel's forehead was red and abraded, spots of blood showing.

"You don't understand her!" he wailed. "You don't understand her!"

"Then tell me!" Julian demanded.

They looked at each other and Julian could see the struggle in the other's face. After a moment, Gabriel simply murmured, "I can't."

Julian felt the elation of the day's events draining from his system and being replaced by a loathing for this bizarre couple that he could barely contain. He could see his chance of convicting the girl for the murders of Ryan and Rebecca falling away from him. The boy was a coward, more afraid of Morgan than the police.

"You're terrified of her, aren't you?" Julian hissed.

Something like dignity tried to make its way into Gabriel's face and failed. "We made a pact," he whispered. "We made a pact for as long as we live on this plane of existence."

Julian backed up a step, disgusted. "Get out of here, Gabriel. A medic'll take a look at your head before you go back to your cell."

Alone, with his face in his hands, Julian weighed his remaining options.

IT WAS DAWN WHEN HE HAD MORGAN BROUGHT IN. SHE looked exhausted but defiant. Julian knew that bail money for both of them was en route from her generous grandfather. He ignored the preliminaries, having made his decision in the quiet predawn hours. Anything that was said in this room would never end up in a court of law.

They sat staring at each other like battle-weary vets. Tired, but not vanquished. Julian knew better than to bluff that her partner had squealed on her. She would find out the truth as soon as their bail arrived. No doubt she knew her man pretty well in any case. Julian broke the silence.

"Morgan, I'm not going to detain you for long. As you know, our case against you for the manufacture and distribution of LSD is rock-solid."

"That's bullshit!" she spat out. "I'm a chemistry major and I've got the transcripts to prove it!"

Julian cut her off. "I'm sure you do. Not just any idiot can whip up a batch of acid. However, some of the chemicals you had in your possession are illegal in themselves, and taken together with your little setup upstairs, I don't think we'll have any problem proving our case."

He let her glare at him while it sank in.

"Your problems go just a little deeper than that though. You've got priors. Probation won't even be an issue in your case. You will do time. Five to ten years . . . for starters."

"What the hell is that supposed to mean, starters?"

Julian noticed that her choice of words and phrasing was cruder now than in their previous meetings. She was tired, ragged. He began the lie.

"It means this." He threw the ankh onto the desktop and let it lie there between them. For the first time, he saw actual fear in her face. She looked as if she wanted to run from the room. The look was gone in a second, replaced by the roiling clouds of fury that seemed her natural state.

"Your boyfriend has already identified this as belonging to you, but I took it a step further. See where the thong is broken?" He held up the ends for her to see. "I had the prosecutor's lab take some scrapings from it for DNA analysis. It'll take a few days for the report. Then I'll be coming after you with a court order for some blood. I think you know what the results will be. How is your neck, by the way? All better?"

Like Gabriel, she stood up suddenly. Julian remained in his seat.

"You can stand, if you like, Morgan, but you 'may' not leave." She looked wildly at him. "So, you see, Morgan, that sample is going to place you at the scene—opportunity, it's called. Your fingerprints on the sheets of acid that Ryan got from you provide a motive. Motive, opportunity, and means. And the means were simple enough. You got them stoned and suggested a trip to the water tower. I imagine you guys had been up there before. It must be a great place to watch the world from when you're stoned. After they got settled, leaning over the railing and watching the world go by, you launched them. You took the girl, obviously, since we found your necklace in her hand. Gave you a bit of trouble, did she?''

"You're making all this up, you lying bastard!'' she screamed.

Julian reached out and placed his hand over the ankh. "Morgan, you're going to spend the rest of your life in prison . . . following other people's orders. That'll be the hateful part for you, I imagine, no longer being in control and controlling others, but on the receiving end. That's what this has all been about, hasn't it? You lost control of Ryan, or thought you had, and he presented a threat to your little world, so you removed him . . . and the girl. Just to make sure. It wasn't murder, though. You were just sending them to the 'other side' . . . a little early, maybe. But rest assured that if anyone should dare to suggest the death penalty, I'll be the first to protest it, because that would be the easy way for you, wouldn't it? After all, you don't fear the reaper, do you, Morgan? Do you?''

She launched herself at him, scratching three grooves down his cheek before Shane rushed in and dragged her back to her cell. They were both released that same morning. Julian didn't have to wait long.

THIS TIME THE JUMPERS WERE SPOTTED RIGHT AWAY, thanks to the spotlights the borough had newly placed at the bottom of the tower to illuminate the catwalk. Quite a crowd had gathered even before the police had arrived. The girl wasted little time, according to witnesses, but dove with arms spread wide, flashing briefly in the glare of the lights before vanishing into the darkness at the base of the tower.

The young man remained motionless, with his back pressed against the wall of the tank, and the giant letters CAMELOT emblazoned above his head.

He was still there when Julian arrived and found Shane trying to talk him down with a loudspeaker. Julian left his car and walked up to his perspiring partner. "Shane, when you get him down from there, bring him to me. He has something he can tell me now." With that he turned and started back for his patrol car, thinking of two young people who would never grow old and their grieving parents and wondering if his own children were asleep yet.

THE VERDICT

~∞~

Lawrence Treat

THE CASE WAS MURDER, FIRST DEGREE. PLENTY OF MAL-
ice, plenty of forethought. Sergeant Wenzel, Criminal Investigation Department, handled it.

He was a small man with delicate features and quick
movements. His energy was inexhaustible and he walked
with short scurrying steps that left bigger men panting to
keep up with him. He liked to remind his colleagues that
he was the only State Trooper with a perfect record. To a
man they disliked him, as did his wife.

When he saw the corpse slumped over in the front seat
of the ten-year-old car he remarked on how pretty she must
have been.

Then he laughed, that low, cold, superior neigh of his.

The car was parked about a hundred feet back from the
road, in a grassy, rutty lane that sliced into the forest and
went nowhere. An assortment of beer cans, candy wrappers,
and miscellaneous litter indicated what the road was mostly
used for.

The sergeant's keen eyes spotted a piece of material that
had somehow got wedged in the buckle of a damaged seat
belt. The material was wool, a gray herringbone pattern
such as might have come from a man's sports jacket. A

plaid cap, folded and crumpled up, was caught between the side edge of the back seat and the wall of the car.

The sergeant picked up the cap and studied it thoughtfully. "I'll bet it wasn't left here last night," he said. "Still, I'm damn well going to find out whose cap it is."

He looked at the inside. It bore the label of a fashionable Chicago haberdasher. There were no initials on the sweatband or on the lining. The sergeant filled out an identification tag and wired it through the crown of the cap.

Following orthodox procedure he ordered his men to search the surrounding area. One of them found the murder weapon. It was an S & W "38" that was later identified from its numbers as part of a batch sent to an Oregon police department eight years before. The entire shipment had been stolen and some of the weapons had turned up in a gangster's arsenal seized not long ago. The gun in question, however, was not listed as among those recovered, and its history was not known.

Sergeant Wenzel had no trouble identifying the girl. Her name was Judith Gorman and she worked for a real estate firm in the city. She commuted to work and she lived a half mile down the road, which dead-ended just past her house. The sergeant punned on the words "dead end," and one of the troopers laughed. The others merely glared.

"I'd guess," the sergeant said, grandstanding, "that our dear little Judith was probably pregnant, and that she had a tryst with a lover who had better plans for himself than marrying her. He saw no way out except this. Dreiser's *An American Tragedy* all over again."

Wenzel was sharp. He not only made sound deductions, but he was quick to find the holes in even his own logic. His thinking was flexible, and when he was wrong he was the first to spot the error. Except that, with his flair for detective work, he rarely made mistakes.

He sent his men up and down the road to gather information, while he himself went to the Gorman house and interrogated Judith's mother.

"Was your little girl pregnant?" he asked in a low voice.

Mrs. Gorman, dazed and shocked by the question, shook her head. "No—no—not Judith. She would have told me. She came to me with everything."

"Yes? Did she tell you where she was going last night?"

"No, but I'm sure it's not what you think."

"Who was she with?"

"I don't know."

"Ah!" the sergeant said. His tone was accusing. In the course of his interview with Mrs. Gorman he wrung her dry and may well have shortened her life by several years; but he got the information he wanted.

Judith had had several boy friends that Mrs. Gorman knew of, and Sergeant Wenzel overwhelmed her with questions about them. Whom had Judith gone out with the night before last? The night before that? The previous week? What names had she mentioned? What phone calls had she made, received? Mrs. Gorman had listened in on them, Wenzel could tell she was nosey, so what had Judith said? He pestered, cajoled, insulted, coaxed. He managed to compile a list of names and establish a clear picture of Judith Gorman's life and character. Then he got permission to go through her personal possessions.

He fingered her underwear lovingly, and while no one else was in the room he pocketed a bra to keep as a souvenir. Nevertheless he was efficient in his search. He located her address book, a pad with some phone numbers, and then some miscellaneous notes and jottings on scraps of paper and old envelopes, all of which he eventually discarded as clues. He found a souvenir cigarette lighter that had been given out at a trade-book convention in Miami three years ago.

Later, of course, with painstaking thoroughness, the sergeant checked out every name and every phone number, but Judith's known boy friends had ironclad alibis for the time of her death.

But before leaving the Gorman house the sergeant had another interview with Mrs. Gorman who, thanks to the ministrations of a couple of neighbors, had begun to calm down. Wenzel knocked on her bedroom door and after explaining that he merely wanted to make sure she was all right, he was permitted to enter. She looked up at him and said, pathetically, that if she'd only insisted on finding out who Judith's unknown boy friend was, Judith might be alive today.

The sergeant agreed and told Mrs. Gorman that he was glad she was now facing facts—a statement which provoked her to tears and further self-recriminations. He stared down at her and then, politely, he asked her whether she'd like some pictures of her daughter's corpse. Mrs. Gorman went into hysterics. The sergeant, satisfied with what he'd accomplished thus far, left the house.

Back at the scene of the murder he found that the Medical Examiner had arrived. The M.E. announced that Judith Gorman had died of a bullet wound at about midnight the previous evening. The sergeant observed that that was hardly news, and he bruskly ordered the M.E. to make a thorough autopsy.

"What the hell kind of autopsies do you think I make?" the doctor demanded.

"Doctor, Doctor," Wenzel said, "I'm just reminding you. That's my job, to see that everybody does the best work he's capable of."

The doctor growled, and the sergeant chuckled contentedly. Then his men started coming in to report.

Several of the Gorman neighbors, like so many people living on small, country roads, were car watchers. They counted and identified all the cars that went by. They knew who had visited the Gormans, when the plumber came and when the electrician passed, and how long they stayed. They knew the local cars by sight and sound and knew who owned which, and they stated that on three evenings within the last couple of weeks Judith had driven out shortly after dinner, and had returned (the time was a guess, based on the sound of a car heard heading toward the Gormans') around midnight. In other words, Judith had gone to meet her date secretly, rather than have him call for her.

Audibly, Wenzel made a slight change in his original analysis of the case. "Her love," he said, "might have been a married man."

The sergeant was also told that there had been a party at the Wallensacks' last night. The Wallensacks owned the big house at the head of the road, a fifteen or twenty minute walk to the Gorman house and maybe a five minute walk to the lane where the body had been found. The sergeant drove to the Wallensack house.

He and Mrs. Wallensack got along famously. She told about her party, and they joked over the antics of the Wallensacks' dog. It was a thoroughbred puli and they called it Tosca. It had long soft hair which a few years ago Mrs. Wallensack had clipped and then spun and woven into a scarf. She showed the sergeant the scarf and she preened herself in front of him. He'd never heard of a puli, but he shifted the conversation to other breeds and told stories about a retriever he pretended he'd once had. She laughed uproariously and invited him to come back when he was off duty.

After a while they discussed the Gorman case. Mrs. Wallensack called Judith "that little Gorman girl." Wenzel asked why she hadn't been invited to the party. Mrs. Wallensack was taken aback at the mere idea. A little thing like that, who worked in a real estate office? Of course not. And her mother, Mrs. Gorman—simpleminded. That was the best you could say for her. And they certainly didn't rate social acceptance.

The sergeant left with a list of Mrs. Gorman's guests. He was surprised to find Harlan Bancroft's name there. Bancroft, an ex-cop who was now head of his own investigation agency—had he been there as a guest or on business? The sergeant wondered. Then, back in his office, he sat down and compared the Wallensack names with those in Judith's address book. One name appeared on both lists. Cyrus Larrabie.

The sergeant knew him. A few weeks ago Larrabie had been involved in an auto accident that the sergeant had investigated. Larrabie had suffered some minor cuts, and the sergeant had taken him home. No charges had been brought.

So—Cyrus Larrabie. The sergeant had his man.

He proceeded slowly nevertheless, for the sergeant was careful, cautious, and conscientious. He called the state's technical research laboratory.

"I want a thorough job on the Gorman car," he said. "I want hair samples, fingerprints, smudges, samples of dirt and dust. I want everything you can find and I want a complete analysis. I want you to go over the whole car with a vacuum cleaner. In particular I want to know if there's any blood that isn't typed as the Gorman girl's. I want you to examine the seats, the door latches and door handles for any threads or fragments of clothing. I want—"

"Look," the research man said, "we know our job. Just tell us what you don't want."

"I don't want any mistakes," Wenzel said, and hung up.

The lab men did a painstaking job, because they knew that Wenzel would spot any oversights. They found a trace of blood, AB type, subgroup m, RH negative. It was a type so rare as to be almost identifying. By contrast Judith's was the very common O type. As for the patch of wool which had been caught on the edge of the door, the lab men indulged in the gobbledy-gook of technical findings, and then called it wool of the highest quality and asked for a sample to compare it with. Further, they found an assortment of hair ends which they neatly classified as to sex, color, race, and probable age of subject. As usual several of the hairs, and the only usable fingerprints, belonged to police officers who had examined the car.

Wenzel was pleased with the lab report. Meanwhile he had called Larrabie's number and been told that Larrabie had left this morning on a business trip and would be back in three days. He worked as a textbook salesman and specialized in paperbacks.

The sergeant, posing as a friend of Larrabie's who was in town for a few days, called Larrabie's publishing firm.

Larrabie, the sergeant claimed, had promised to show him
around town and he, Wenzel, was real disappointed. One
of Larrabie's colleagues suggested that Wenzel meet him
for a drink, around 5:30 that evening.

Sitting at the bar, Wenzel steered the conversation
around to Larrabie. It seemed that Larrabie, a bachelor, was
something of a swinger. None of the secretaries in the office
was safe from him, but Larrabie was going to be married
shortly and he was expected to calm down. He knew how
to pick 'em, too, because this Libby Millman he was engaged to, she not only was a looker, she was loaded. In the
daytime she drove around in a yellow Lincoln convertible.
Her other Lincoln was a black sedan. She used it nights
only.

The rest of Larrabie's chicks? The friend smiled. There'd
be some broken hearts, but Larrabie had given his friend a
list of names. Would Mr. Wenzel like to try one of them
tonight?

Wenzel hedged, but he continued to show interest in the
list. Someone by the name of Gorman. Judith Gorman. Did
the friend know anything about her? No, he didn't. Never
even heard of her.

The following morning the M.E.'s report came in and
stated that Judith Gorman had been four months pregnant.
The sergeant, reading the findings, smiled, and he kept on
backtracking on Larrabie and consolidating the case against
him. He found out that Larrabie had often been in Chicago
on business. Since plaid caps are not sold in large quantities
and since the label in the cap was that of an exclusive men's
shop, Wenzel sent a detective to Chicago to identify the
cap and bring back samples of gray herringbone suiting.

Wenzel was lucky. The store kept a list of customers and
of their purchases, so that they could duplicate any order
at any time. One Cyrus Larrabie had bought a plaid cap
from them three years ago. He had also bought a gray herringbone sports jacket. A swatch of the material was available, and it checked exactly with the piece found in the car.

Meanwhile the sergeant interviewed most of the guests

who had been at the Wallensack party the other night. The upshot was precisely what he'd hoped for. At a party of thirty people nobody could possibly prove he'd been in the house every single minute. To slip out for a half hour or so without being seen—it would have been easy.

The composite account that the sergeant built up showed that Larrabie had had a few drinks, but was far from drunk. He'd flirted with a couple of girls and he'd got one of them as far as the porch, when the puli had appeared. Larrabie was frightened of dogs, and he made some remark about bitches butting in, and went back into the house.

"I was pretty mad," the girl said. "Such a gentle dog, such fine lovely hair."

The sergeant felt pleased with himself. He swore out a search warrant and waited for Larrabie to come home. Shortly after he did he was brought to the sergeant's office.

Wenzel's first question was a model of sophisticated interrogation. The question did not divulge any information, gave the suspect no indication of why he was being questioned, but nevertheless pinned him down to a position from which there was no retreat.

"Do you or did you," the sergeant said, "at any time know one Judith Gorman?"

The answer was prompt and unequivocal. "No."

"You claim you never saw her?"

"Never even heard of her until I read about her in the paper."

"Good." The sergeant positively beamed. His difficulty lay in placing Larrabie at the scene of the crime at or about the time it had been committed. By asking the lesser question the sergeant had set a clever trap. Larrabie's denial that he knew Judith could be proved a lie, on the basis of the victim's address book, and from that moment on Larrabie was doomed.

To give him his due, however, Larrabie was consistent and he made no damaging admissions. He denied everything right down the line, except to owning a gray herringbone sports jacket.

"Yes, I have such a jacket," he said, "but I haven't worn it in months."

"I think that you wore it on a certain night, and that there is now a tear in it."

"If there is I know nothing about it.

"You killed Judith Gorman," the sergeant said coldly, "and I can prove it."

"You're crazy," Larrabie said, but there was more than a hint of fear in his voice.

"I ask your consent for a sample of your blood and for some hairs that the laboratory needs for comparison purposes."

Larrabie ran his hand through his hair, pulled, and came out with a few strands. "Here," he said shakily. "Take my blood next, and then let's end this nightmare."

A gray herringbone jacket with a small tear was found in Larrabie's closet. The fibers found in the car matched the fibers in the jacket. Larrabie's hair ends matched some of the hairs found in the car, his blood was type AB, subgroup m, RH negative, and he admitted having attended the Miami convention when the souvenir lighters were given out.

The D.A. congratulated Wenzel on the thoroughness with which he'd gathered the evidence.

"I wish there were more police officers like you," the D.A. said. "With evidence like this I can't help but get a conviction."

"Thanks," the sergeant said, "but my investigation was nothing out of the ordinary. It was logical and thorough, but that's what I'm paid for."

At the trial the D.A. presented the overload of evidence that Wenzel had gathered, and Wenzel took the stand and made his usual good impression. Cross-questioning merely substantiated his statements. Nevertheless the jury brought in a verdict of Not Guilty.

The judge was shocked. He polled the jury, and each of them stood up and said firmly, "I find the defendant Not Guilty."

The judge gave them a tongue lashing, said it was the worst verdict he'd ever heard in his courtroom, and dismissed them without thanks. But privately he tried to find out what had gone wrong.

The jurors refused to talk either to him or to reporters. The D.A. was as mystified as the judge. The defense attorney suggested, the merest innuendo, that he knew the reason, but everyone said he was simply trying to take credit for winning the case.

Sergeant Wenzel was more dissatisfied than anyone else. He not only had an innate need for correct answers, but this was his case and an acquittal was almost a personal insult. He therefore determined to force someone to tell him what had gone on in the jury room.

After due study of the names of the jurors and their backgrounds he fastened on one George Miles. Miles owned a restaurant, and since no restaurant can conform completely to all the laws and ordinances covering its operation, the sergeant dined there and made a few discreet inquiries. He found what he wanted, then armed with a list of violations he visited Miles. The proprietor saw the point and answered the sergeant's questions freely.

"The reason we refused to talk," Miles said, "was that the judge instructed us not to use any special knowledge of our own, that it would be unethical, but to decide the case only on evidence presented in court. And—well, you see, I know pulis. They're my hobby."

"What do you mean by that?"

"I breed them. I tell you, I know pulis."

"What about them?"

"The puli is a Hungarian sheepdog, bred as a herder, to keep sheep together in the flock, but the instinct is so deep that he'll herd anything including people. If I go walking with some of my friends and one of them becomes separated or even lags behind, my pulis go after him. Those dogs of mine will nudge and push and nip and snarl, and bring that person right back to the group. And a puli is a pretty big dog."

"I still don't get it," the sergeant said.

"Larrabie took a girl out to the porch, and the Wallensack puli forced him back inside—remember that bit of evidence? And Larrabie was afraid of dogs, so he couldn't have left the party. Impossible. The puli wouldn't let him.

"The first vote we took was eleven to one for conviction. I dissented. Believe me, it took a lot of arguing, but in the end nobody wanted to convict Larrabie of murder if that puli would have kept him from leaving the house. The other jurors finally agreed." Miles licked his lips. "Sergeant, you got the wrong man."

Wenzel was furious. He not only had his record to think of, but if any of the jurors spoke up publicly, if it was ever discovered that Sergeant Wenzel had pulled the most colossal boner of his career—accusing an innocent man—he'd be through. He wouldn't be demoted, not after his commanding officer had okayed the case and backed him, but the sergeant's pride and self-confidence and reputation for infallibility would be gone. All the people on whose toes he'd stepped, and he'd stepped on plenty, would laugh at him. And he'd have to take it.

The sergeant wrestled with the problem of what to do, and he came to a decision. As a result of it he called on Larrabie and questioned him at some length. Afterward the sergeant had a session with Colonel Ide, his commanding officer. The sergeant told of his interview with Miles.

"I would like," Wenzel said, "permission to reopen the case."

"Any new leads?" Colonel Ide asked.

"I think so. I saw Larrabie and he said that about fifteen years ago he and a man named Eddie Cannon were roommates and close friends. Cannon was engaged to a girl named Harriet Mann, and the threesome saw a lot of each other. Harriet kissed the pair of them good night after every date, and Larrabie was scheduled to be best man at the wedding. But the wedding never took place, because Larrabie ran off with the bride-to-be."

"What did Cannon do?"

"Nothing. Larrabie and Harriet moved out to the coast, where they lived together, but without getting married. Eventually, Larrabie says, he saw that they weren't made for each other and he left her. Three months later, in despair at being pregnant and friendless and deserted, she committed suicide, although Larrabie claims he had no news of it until much later.

"He and Cannon met at a party about ten years ago, which was five years after the suicide. Larrabie says he explained that he and Harriet had parted by mutual consent and that he'd had no idea at the time that she was pregnant. He says that, after his account, he and Cannon made up, but I have my doubts as to how sincere this Eddie Cannon could have been. I'd like to investigate him." The sergeant's eyes gleamed. "I want to nail him for this."

"You think he framed Larrabie for the Judith Gorman murder?"

"Somebody did," Wenzel said.

"You think Cannon killed a perfectly innocent girl, with no motive except to frame Larrabie?"

"It's possible, although maybe Cannon got her pregnant and wanted to get rid of her for that reason. I don't know, and I'd like to clear up the case."

"Somebody framed Larrabie," Colonel Ide said. "If Cannon did it you'll have to show how he planted Larrabie's lighter in Judith's room. You'll have to prove Cannon stole, or could have stolen, that cap, ripped a piece of cloth from the gray jacket, gotten hold of an untraceable gun, obtained hair samples and a blood sample, and, finally, left no trace of himself among Judith's possessions. That's a tall order, Sergeant."

"A friend could do most of it," Wenzel remarked.

Colonel Ide leaned back in his chair. "Go ahead," he said. "Somebody killed her, and we've got to find out who."

The sergeant was lucky. The first thing he discovered was that Eddie Cannon worked as a private detective for the Harlan Bancroft Investigative Agency. And a private detective has connections—the kind, for instance, that can procure him an untraceable gun. And a private detective could have the know-how to transfer a blood sample. And he could break into an apartment and take a cap and a scrap of jacket and a cigarette lighter and a few hair ends. Or even better, with a little resourcefulness, he could obtain those particular items while visiting a friend.

So—the cap, the jacket, the lighter. By itself, Eddie Cannon's occupation went a long way toward showing that he had the expertise to frame Larrabie. And then the sergeant found out that Larrabie had paid his friend Cannon $500 to investigate Judith Gorman's death, for the purpose of proving Larrabie's innocence.

The sergeant sensed that he had something important, but he did not go to Cannon directly. Not yet. Instead he called the Bancroft agency. He had no trouble getting the information that Cannon had asked for and had received a leave of absence in order to work for a friend. The day after getting the leave, Cannon had flown to Hawaii, where he'd stayed for six weeks.

The sergeant went to Hawaii. Investigation revealed that Cannon had registered at a good hotel, made love to two girls, learned how to surf, and gained ten pounds. Then Cannon returned. He arrived home shortly before the trial and had not spoken to Larrabie since.

The sergeant's next step was to locate witnesses who had seen Eddie Cannon and Judith Gorman together. For that he covered selected drive-ins, bars, restaurants, and motels, where he showed Judith's picture along with Cannon's. He explained who they were and asked, "You saw them together here, didn't you?"

Witnesses like that are easy to get. They say yes because they want the notoriety of having seen the defendant. They know that a little publicity will bring in business to a bar or a restaurant. The sergeant had no illusions about their motives, and he did not vouch for their accuracy. He merely knew that juries are impressed by people who get up on the stand and say unhesitatingly, "Yes, I saw them together.'' If the D.A. wanted to use this type of witness, that was up to him.

Still, Wenzel was making progress and he felt he was getting close to building up a solid case. He had motive and opportunity, and the Cannon-Gorman connection was established. All that remained was to place Cannon on the scene of the crime.

He now saw Cannon for the first time. The sergeant approached him in a friendly manner and made no accusations. He managed, however, to slip in the question as to where Cannon had been on the night of the murder.

"Working," Cannon said, "on a confidential case."

Wenzel didn't push it, but the next day he went to see Bancroft with the same question. "What was Eddie Cannon doing on the night that Judith Gorman was killed?" he asked.

Bancroft, resenting the question, insisting that Cannon's work was privileged and private, told the sergeant to get out and stay out. Back at headquarters, the sergeant took up the matter with Colonel Ide.

"Nobody," the sergeant said, "can kick a State Trooper out of his office and get away with it. I'll get the information all right, but I want an apology, too."

"I'll have Bancroft here," Colonel Ide promised, "at ten o'clock tomorrow morning."

"With his file on Eddie Cannon," the sergeant said.

Colonel Ide nodded. "He'll bring it. I want a showdown on this case."

The interview was not pleasant for anyone, and they all knew it. Bancroft led off.

"Sergeant," he said, "you're making a serious accusation. I know my men, I make exhaustive inquiries before I hire them, and they're not criminals. If you have any evidence let's hear it."

"Good," the sergeant said, and he gave it. It was detailed, lengthy, and impressive, and Bancroft listened attentively.

"You've made a fairly convincing case," he said, after

the sergeant had finished, "to show that Larrabie was framed and that a professional probably did it, but you haven't proved that Eddie Cannon was the one."

"Who else?" Wenzel said.

Bancroft spoke sharply. "You," he said. "Ever since you started investigating Eddie Cannon, *he's* been investigating *you*. And he found out some interesting things.

"First of all he traced the gun, which we know was part of that stolen Oregon shipment. You were on the five-man detail that eventually recovered those guns, but you didn't hand all of them in. Each one of you appropriated one for himself, and Eddie has written statements by the other four to that effect.

"Next, you brought Larrabie home from that car accident of his, where he was cut up a little. He told Cannon that he'd mentioned the Wallensack party to you, and that was probably when you got the idea of framing him. Simple to carry out, wasn't it? Larrabie was shaken up and bleeding, nothing easier than getting hold of a blood sample of his and then walking out of his place with his cigarette lighter, his cap, and bit of material torn from his jacket. And, like any hat or cap, a few hair ends were caught in the lining.

"On the night of the murder you parked among the other cars at the Wallensacks' and then you walked down to your meeting with Judith and shot her. After she was dead you planted your clues. If there was any evidence of your affair with her, you had ample opportunity to destroy it when you went to her house the next morning, supposedly to investigate. And that was when you wrote Larrabie's name in her address book, and that can be proved, too. You know enough about handwriting and inks to realize that."

"A bunch of theories," the sergeant said coldly. "And the first thing Cannon had better explain is why he accepted five hundred dollars to clear Larrabie, and then went to Hawaii and did nothing. Nothing at all."

"On the contrary," Bancroft said. "Eddie Cannon earned his fee. Among other things he told Larrabie's lawyer all about pulis, and when Larrabie was lucky enough to find a juror who was a breeder of pulis and therefore knew all about them, that was a lot better than putting an expert on the stand where he'd be cross-questioned at length. Maybe it wasn't too ethical on the lawyer's part, but—''

Bancroft shrugged, and Colonel Ide, grim and scowling, finished the remark. "Effective," he said. "Damned effective."

FRUIT OF THE POISONOUS TREE

≈≈≈

John Dobbyn

TREVOR TOWNSEND, JUDGE OF THE SUPERIOR COURT IN and for the County of Suffolk, Commonwealth of Massachusetts, is, by any measure, a piece of work. We were no more than twenty minutes into the argument on my motion for an injunction against Boston Bank & Trust, one of His Honor's favorite charities, when I could actually count six male gophers tunneling through the walls of my stomach. Understandable, since the judge had that finely honed bent of the incurably self-satisfied for meeting every legal argument with a barb dipped in the vitriolic oil of sarcasm.

The afternoon break came mercifully at three o'clock. I rose to the bailiff's cry of "All rise" with the thought of purging my mind with a chocolate blitz at the Bailey's downstairs. The whim died aborning, however, with a crook of Judge Townsend's finger as he departed the bench for chambers. I looked at counsel for the defense for any light she could shed on the summons. She shrugged, smiled, and passed quickly to the free world outside.

Reluctance doesn't begin to characterize my entrance into the judge's chambers. He had shed the robe and sat like Torquemada, ready to welcome the next guest of the Inquisition.

I took his nod as a gracious invitation to make myself comfortable. Tea and macaroons would be served momentarily. Perhaps not.

"Mr. Knight, I assume I have your confidentiality. I wish to retain your services to represent my son in a criminal matter."

There are jump-shifts in conversation that affect the hinge of your jaw, such that you wonder if you will ever get your mouth fully closed again. This qualified. I think it was seeing the unexpectedly human motion of concern on the judge's Mount Rushmore features that brought me back.

"On what charge, Judge?"

"The allegation is murder in the first degree. My son is a junior at Harvard. He attended a party of college students—not Harvard—at an apartment on Beacon Street last evening. The incident occurred there."

"Where is he now?"

"He is being detained at the Charles Street prison. They're reluctant to depart from the usual bail disallowance in a capital case because of the delicate position of his relationship to a judge. I'm loath to ask special favors for the same reason."

"Certainly not, Judge. Can't soil the old robes just for the sake of getting the kid out of the reach of every rapist at Charles Street, that wants to get back at the old man."

Actually, I didn't say that. I just nodded.

"May I assume that you will take the case, Mr. Knight?"

There are two things you don't do as an attorney. One is appear at a medical convention unarmed. The other is turn down a sitting judge.

As LONG AS I WAS AT THE SUFFOLK COURTHOUSE ANY-way, my first stop was the District Attorney's office. No need sparring with the assistant D.A.s. The top lady herself, Ms. Lamb by name, if not by temperament, would sooner surrender her flesh to the torturers than give up one juicy headline from this case to an assistant.

She was surprised to see me, since nearly all of the criminal practice I took on was in federal court. I had clerked for a federal judge after law school, and a steady stream of indigent appointments came from that source. During my seven years with the firm of Bilson & Dawes (the last two as junior partner), my seniors had harrumphed and scowled over my accepting even federal criminal appointments. It tarnished the pristine image of the three-piece suits who practiced not trial work but civil li-ti-ga-tion. The bearded, whiskey-breathing slouches who frequently populated the firm's waiting room when I took a criminal appointment did nothing to loosen firm policy.

"You've got to be joking. You represent young Townsend?"

I smiled pleasantly in spite of the inference. "Strange bedfellows, what? Shall we talk business?"

"There's no business to discuss, unless you're offering the full plea of guilty. Have you talked to your client?"

"My next stop. Why are we being inflexible here?"

"Because I'm going to personally walk your boy to the electric chair."

"Might we go through the inconvenience of a trial first?"

She grinned that half grin that they get when they're holding the real cards.

"I'll give him the formality, if he insists, but when the jury reads his confession..." Her hands and eyebrows went up in unison. I hate that gesture.

"He confessed?"

"To every detail. He dictated a statement, read it, signed it, and then went through the whole thing again for the video camera. I'll send copies of both of your office."

She leaned in for the killer. "Count on it. He'll burn, at least for this one."

Youth led me to take the bait. "You imply there's more?"

"Four unsolved strangulation-rapes in the last two years. I don't suppose you get beyond the financial pages up at Bilson."

If there was anything soft and cuddly about Ms. Lamb as an infant, she had managed to ossify it in her eighteen years at the bar. At five foot eight, one hundred and twenty-five pounds, dark hair in a bun so tight her nostrils flared, she was one lean, mean, prosecuting machine. Not uncharacteristically in the trade, word had it that she was waiting for the case that could transport her to the state house. This one sent up flares.

"I assume the Miranda warnings reared their ugly heads in the process."

"Right up there at the front."

"I'd have bet on it. And the autopsy report, you'll be pleased to share it?"

"You'll be the second one to see it."

Ms. Lamb's grinding arrogance made me long for the warmth of Judge Townsend's courtroom.

CHARLES STREET PRISON AFFORDS A CLUSTER OF INTIMATE dwellings measuring six by eight, where the accent is less on privacy than on togetherness. It seemed to have been constructed around the era of the Tower of London, and probably shared the architect.

I sat waiting in the attorney's room until I found myself looking up a six foot four inch frame to the palest features I have ever seen on an eighteen-year-old. I've seen feeder goldfish thrown into a tank of piranhas looking more in their element than young master Townsend.

I had been fully prepared to resent him, with his Brooks Brothers tweed over chinos over oxblood loafers (no socks)—the uniform of those who were born to attend Harvard. Oddly, there was a humility in his eyes that did not seem born of his present circumstances. I found, out of reflex, that I liked the boy. I fought against it.

"I'm Michael Knight. Your father asked me to come around."

I would have said "represent you," but I still hadn't gotten used to the idea. He held out a well-muscled hand that clamped mine with authority. I raised an eyebrow. He caught my meaning and forced a shy smile.

"Crew."

"And pretty good too." I caught part of the inscription on his T-shirt where the top shirt folded open. Filling in the rest of the letters, my guess was that he had won a regatta singles championship. "I bet a ring went with that."

He flushed a little and then seemed to go into himself when he said, "They took it when I came in. I think they said I could have it when I go to court."

From his expression, my guess was that remembering past victories made the embarrassment more painful.

I nodded him into the wooden straight-back across the table. He hung over the table like a puppy about to be scolded.

"You want to tell me about it, Trevor?"

"Chip."

His eyes came up from the table. I didn't blame him for going for a nickname. I only hoped it was not "off the old block."

"What happened, Chip?"

He was leaning on elbows wide enough apart to accommodate a Mazda. I noticed that his eyes did not retreat to the table. Good sign.

"I got an invitation from a girl I knew to a party at an apartment on Beacon Street around Berkeley. I guess four or five girls live there. It was mostly a group from different colleges around town. I got there about seven-thirty. Had a couple of drinks. I started to feel dizzy, sick. Someone brought me up to one of the bedrooms. I fell on the bed and went out cold."

He took a breath before the tough part.

"I woke up about nine . . ."

"How did you know it was nine?"

"There was a clock beside the bed."

I nodded.

"There was a girl in the room. In the bed. I think we'd been arguing."

"After you woke up?"

His eyes drifted. He stood up and walked over to the window that was an eighth-inch glass and a quarter-inch grime that had been collecting since John Adams last washed it. His voice was calm and deliberate.

"I took the belt from a terrycloth robe that was lying on the bed. I put it around her neck and tied a slipknot. I pulled it taut until the breathing stopped. I could see her eyes close. She fell backwards on the bed."

I waited, but there was no more. The wet beads on his forehead belied the quiet tone of voice.

"Why?"

He turned back, almost surprised to see me.

I said, "Why?"

He thought about it. "I think we'd been arguing."

"About what?"

"I can't remember."

"Was she the one who invited you?"

"No. I didn't know her before last night."

"What happened then?"

"I must have passed out. I don't remember anything until somebody dropped me onto the bed in my apartment in Cambridge."

"Any idea of the time?"

"Yes. Ten o'clock. I heard someone say it. It seemed so early, I checked the clock. That was all I remember until the police woke me up. They came sometime early in the morning."

I jotted down some notes and let it sink in.

"What were you drinking?"

He came back to the chair. "Some kind of punch. I don't know. I think it was gin."

"Did you take it, or did someone bring it to you?"

He thought. "One of the fellas there brought the first one. I took the second."

"Any drugs?"

He shook his head.

"What was the girl's name, the one that invited you?"

"Sue . . . ah, Sue Banner . . . Bannister. I just met her the week before at a football game. I didn't know her well. She called me the night before to tell me there was going to be a party."

"Did you know anyone else there?"

"Couple of the fellas went with me."

He caught me with his eyes before I got the next question out.

"I appreciate what you're trying to do, Mr. Knight, but I did it. There's no point in trying to make a defense. Can we just get it over with?"

WHAT HAD SO FAR BEEN A PERFECT LOSER OF A DAY headed downhill when I got back to the firm. I could read the vicarious pain in my secretary's eyes when she handed me the message slip.

"SEE ME NOW! A.D."

Ask any associate and most of the junior partners what "A.D." stands for, and they'll whisper, "Angel of Death." Alex Devlin— "Lex" to those who are permitted the liberty, which includes the Dalai Lama and a few others—is one who suffers not the foibles of juniors gladly. He has a body like Spencer Tracy, a jaw that could plow snow, and a nose that was designed by the man who laid out the Boston streets.

Word had it that he had been the best of the best in the criminal bar. Ten years ago he hung up his spurs and pulled out of criminal defense work entirely. Nobody at my level knows why, and nobody at his level is talking. They say he had a taste for the grape, but then so does half the trial bar.

Actually he didn't hang up his spurs. He traded them for polo boots. After a year in never-never land, the firm recruited him for the courtroom magic that he still performs in the clean arena of civil litigation.

Word of my summons had apparently circulated, because every associate I passed on my way to the gates of hell took one last look at me in life. I smiled the smile of the brave as I entered the inner sanctum.

He was standing at the window, back to me, and even from that angle the aura was formidable. When he turned around, I was moved by the power of the man's presence. It wasn't fear as much as awe.

"You've taken the Townsend defense. Why?"

"I didn't have much choice, Mr. Devlin. It was put to me as a command performance. I still have no idea why he wanted me."

I could feel the heat of his eyes and pitied any witness on cross-examination.

"He didn't want you. He wanted me. Now he's got me."

The blank look on my face asked the question. He answered it.

"You carry the firm's name. This case will fill the first three pages of the *Record-American* every night. He knew I couldn't afford to stay out of it."

"If he wanted you, which I don't doubt, why didn't he ask you?"

"He knows I'm out of criminal work." His shoulders sloped a bit, and I couldn't read the look in his eyes as he sat down at the desk.

"Apparently I'm back in it. What have you got?"

I sat opposite him and took out my notebook. I told him everything I knew about the case. My secretary had handed me a manilla envelope from the D.A.'s office when she gave me the note from Mr. Devlin. I opened it and found the signed confession of Chip Townsend and a videotape. I handed over the confession. Mr. Devlin read it and threw it back.

"Read it. Tell me if it squares with what he said."

I ran through it. ". . . belt from a terrycloth robe . . . lying on the bed . . . around her neck . . . slip knot . . . pulled it taut . . . breathing stopped . . . see her eyes close . . . fell backwards on the bed.

"That's it. They also got it on videotape."

I held it up. He gestured to the VCR and television in

the corner of the office—standard equipment for trial counsel. I slipped in the tape and turned on the TV. It was a full-body shot of Chip in the D.A.'s interrogation room. After the Miranda warnings, he said his piece.

"I took the belt from a robe that was lying on the bed. I put it around her neck and tied a slipknot. I pulled it taut until the breathing stopped. I could see her eyes close. She fell backwards on the bed."

The lines over Mr. Devlin's eyes told me he caught the same thing I did, but I thought I'd let him say it.

"Let me see that confession again."

I took it over. He reread it and looked up at me. Something came alive in his eyes. I nodded.

"Check your notes."

"I just did. Verbatim. He told the story in exactly the same words three times. What are the chances of that?"

He leaned back. His eyes focused vaguely on a framed picture of two teenage girls, but the action was clearly going on inside. I jumped in before the spark of optimism ignited prematurely.

"That's the good news. The bad news is that the D.A. thinks Townsend is the one who committed that string of rape-strangulations. She can only get an indictment on this one, but she'll do everything but show slides to suggest to the jury that he's the serial killer."

"She does and she'll have a mistrial. What about the autopsy?"

"I spoke to the D.A. We can have it as soon as she gets it."

He came straight forward with one elbow on the desk and the other hand snatching the phone out of its state of rest.

"She's playing games with you, sonny."

"Michael, Mr. Devlin. I prefer to be called Michael."

Or maybe I just thought it, while I watched him strangle the phone and punch numbers.

"This is Lex Devlin. Let me speak to Mrs. Lamb."

A pause, but a short one. She was not about to leave the

king on hold, even if he did ignore the "Ms." protocol.

"Angela, Lex Devlin. I'm representing Judge Townsend's son."

I could hear her heart drop across half a mile of Bell Tel cable.

"Be good enough to fax me the autopsy report. I'll need a full set of pictures too. You have my fax number."

Another pause for a tactical decision. Again, the king was not to be denied. Whatever she said amounted to "Yes."

Mr. Devlin wrapped it up with minimum pleasantries and shot me a look. "Don't let 'em stall you, sonny. The M.E. had *that* report finished before the sun came up. Probably delivered it in his pajamas. Bring it in as soon as it gets here."

I was back in five minutes with the report and a stack of photos of a young girl, undressed and beaten unmercifully from the waist up.

He scanned the pictures and winced at each new shot. He picked up the medical examiner's report and walked to the window, mumbling what he was reading. I picked the lowlights out of the copy I had made for myself.

Cause of death: strangulation.

. . . Contusions, the result of severe blows, as by a human fist, covering the abdomen, chest, and face, inflicted prior to death, . . . two ribs fractured . . . had been sexually assaulted . . . contusion and depression circling the throat . . . wool fibers found in depression as if garroted by loosely spun cord . . . fifteen centimeter circular contusion at back of neck with pressure fracture of first cervical vertebra . . .

Time of death: eleven P.M.

He was still grumbling when he caught up the phone and punched in more numbers. I thought I had become invisible until he glanced over and said, "Listen and learn, sonny."

There were the pat sounds of an official answering voice over the phone.

"Let me speak to the medical examiner."

More bureaucratic sounds. I wasn't surprised, since the Suffolk County M.E., Dr. Max Reinert, was known for the kind of arrogance only an entrenched institution can afford.

"Listen, dear. You walk through the swinging door and whisper two words into his pink little ears—'Lex Devlin.' "

My eyebrows must have been somewhere around my hairline, because he shrugged. "Sometimes you've got to call in old debts, Sonny. Remember that when a public official needs a favor."

He was back to the phone. "Max. Thanks. One question. How accurate is the time of death on the girl in the Townsend case?"

The baritone voice boomed through the phone like a speaker.

"Right on the money, Lex. Ten minutes either side."

"How?"

"Three good indicators. Body temperature. She was indoors at room temperature all evening till we got there. The state of rigor confirmed it. Contents of the stomach locked it in. I'd bet my next paycheck on it. More than that, your paycheck."

I saw the closest thing to a smile I could visualize on Devlin's features. "Good job, Max."

Mr. Devlin held the phone with his chin while he pressed the hang-up button with one hand and flipped the Rolodex with the other. He punched in enough numbers to get out of state.

"Dr. Mayhew, please. Lex Devlin in Boston."

Mr. Devlin hit the speaker-phone button and leaned back. A professional but softly feminine voice came over the speaker.

"Lex, how's my favorite crusader?"

"Damn few holy wars lately, Jean. I need you. Can you give me some time?"

If the pause was for indecision, there was none in the answer.

"When do I book the flight?"

That brought a real grin. "Soon. First a question. I've got a boy, eighteen years old, charged with the sadistic sex-murder of a young college girl. He confessed."

"So?"

"Three times in identical words. Says he was at a party, had a couple of drinks, and passed out. He woke up in his apartment much later. The only thing he recalls about the interim is this mesmerized, almost memorized confession. I saw it on videotape. He seems to believe it. A number of things don't square with the confession. He claims to have strangled the girl with a terrycloth belt. Says he did it from the front, since he could see her eyes and she fell backwards. He's firm on that. The M.E. says she was garroted with a cord that left *wool* fibers, probably from the back since there was a major contusion on the back of the neck and a broken cervical vertebra. The time's wrong too. He remembers being home by ten P.M. The M.E. is certain the time of death was ten minutes either side of eleven o'clock. What do you think?"

"I better come and see him. Was he on drugs that night?"

"He says no."

"Could a drug have been slipped to him?"

Lex looked at me. I nodded and whispered, "The first drink was brought to him by one of the kids at the party."

"Yes it could, Jean."

"There's a possibility the confession could have been suggested to him under a drug like Haldol, the so-called zombie drug. Your boy could have been set up to confess to someone else's doings. Has he been medically tested for drugs, especially the class that induce suggestibility?"

Mr. Devlin pointed a finger at me that got my feet in gear double-time.

"Even as we speak, Jean. Thanks. When can you get here?"

THE TRIAL WAS STANDING ROOM ONLY. I'VE ALWAYS thought that the state misses a bet by not charging admission. This one could have sold out Fenway Park.

Ms. Lamb bestrode the courtroom like a behemoth, to borrow a phrase. She played society's avenging angel as she led the medical examiner through his paces. She breezed over the facts that didn't square with the confession, and belabored the details of brutality. The clear and present hope was that the jurors would connect those details with the newspaper accounts of the other four murders without her risking a mistrial.

She put on the boy from the party who found the girl's body around midnight. He did not recall seeing Chip leave the party.

Next in the witness box was a boy by the name of Tom Keating who said that Chip came downstairs in a stupor and asked him for a ride home. He could not pinpoint the time.

Then the *pièce de résistance*, her one-way ticket to the governor's office—Chip's confession. First she played it in living color in video. Then she introduced it in permanent written form to accompany the jurors during their deliberations.

I was with Mr. Devlin at counsel table. When the prosecution rested, he stepped up to the plate, so to speak. He put Chip on the stand first, and actually asked him to repeat his confession, to the surprise and, I must say, delight of Ms. Lamb. She couldn't hear it too often. Chip went through it again—verbatim—in that same detached monotone.

Mr. Devlin next called Dr. Jean Mayhew. She was outstanding. He led her gently, but she knew where to go. She gave the jury a class on the suggestibility of confessions, especially when the subject is under the influence of a particular class of drugs.

"Dr. Mayhew, would you tell the jury why such a suggested confession would be convincing?"

She was the voice of scientific reason. "Because under the right conditions of suggestibility, the person is totally convinced of the truthfulness of the false confession. This is particularly true if a drug like Haldol is used. The subject can't be reasoned with or dissuaded."

"Thank you, Dr. Mayhew." *From the bottom of our hearts.*

MR. DEVLIN'S SUMMATION TO THE JURY WAS A *TOUR DE force.* He cut a mighty swath through Chip's confession with a recap of Dr. Mayhew's testimony, the finding of Dr. Burke of Mass General who tested Chip, at my request, and found traces of Haldol in his blood, and finally, a recitation of the inconsistencies between the medical examiner's findings and the confession—the timing of the death, the material used in the strangulation, and the position of the girl as facing away from the murderer during the strangulation. The evidence was circumstantial, but it seemed convincing to me.

Apart from the evidence itself, Mr. Devlin was Daniel Webster standing toe-to-toe with the Devil. He could have read from a box of Cheerios, and if I had been on the jury, I would have acquitted Adolf Eichmann. On the other hand, the members of the jury looked noncommittal.

By the time Ms. Lamb finished her strident closing harangue, imploring the jury to ignore apparent circumstantial inconsistencies and believe the defendant's voluntary and repeated confession, it was late in the day. The judge adjourned until the next morning for the charge to the jury and the retiring of the jurors to deliberate.

I started loading the briefcases to take them back to the office. Mr. Devlin was sitting beside me in a kind of funk. I chalked it up to the drain of his closing argument, until I heard him mumble through his hands, "Damn. It's not enough. It's not complete."

I reached for our set of the medical examiner's blown-up photos, when he took them out of my hand. He sat poring over them while I finished up.

Chip held his gangly cuffed hands out to Mr. Devlin before being led back to the sheriff's van for Charles Street.

"Whatever happens, Mr. Devlin, you gave me the best possible defense. You're beginning to convince me, even though I can still hear those words inside of me.... I'm really grateful."

He was no youngster, Mr. Devlin. The old war-horse used to be able to go all night after a performance like that. So went the stories. But now he was played out. I watched him sink back in the chair at counsel's table with his eyes closed.

He was still there when Ms. Lamb ran up to the court clerk and asked to see the judge in chambers. The clerk got permission and summoned Mr. Devlin and me to follow Ms. Lamb into chambers.

Judge Jeffreys had taken off the robe and was down to the suspenders. He waved us to seats from behind his desk.

"This couldn't wait till tomorrow, Angela?"

"Your Honor, I want to reopen for new evidence. This is critical. I just received it two minutes ago."

She laid a photograph on the desk and stood back like Prometheus placing fire at the feet of man. The judge cocked his glasses for a closer look. He handed it over to Mr. Devlin. I got third look. It was a candid shot of a smiling Chip Townsend roughhousing with a boy in a fraternity T-shirt who had his left arm locked around Chip's neck. The surroundings could be identified as the apartment where the party took place. It didn't take Columbo to spot the old school clock on the wall. In its unsubtle way, it was screaming eleven-thirty. No wonder Ms. Lamb had reached seventh heaven. The photo placed Chip at the party after the time of the girl's death. One of the pillars of our defense was his testimony that he was home by ten.

"I take it you can authenticate this photo, Angela."

"I can, Your Honor. One of the boys at the party was

taking candid shots that night. He just realized the importance of this one and rushed it in.''

The judge looked over his glasses at Mr. Devlin. He was unruffled, almost nonchalant, but looking into his eyes was like looking through the face of a fine watch at the meshing of intricate gears.

"Could I ask the worthy District Attorney if she spoke to this photographer before today? What's his name?''

"Charles Bingham. Yes, we've spoken before.''

"About the case?''

"Of course. I'd asked him if he could remember Townsend leaving the party. He couldn't. But this photo settles it.''

"Perhaps. When you first spoke to young Bingham, did you ask him to bring to your attention anything he later remembered about the case?''

"Certainly.''

"And therefore he brought in this picture. How did you hear about young Bingham in the first place?''

"The defendant gave his name as one of the people he knew at the party.''

"When?''

"When what?''

"When did the defendant give you his name?''

"He gave it to the police officer when he was arrested.''
His eyes were glowing like coals.

"That's interesting. What occasioned the arrest?''

"We got an anonymous tip that there had been a murder.''

"And that Townsend had committed it?''

"No. Just that he had been one of the male guests.''

Mr. Devlin settled back and looked at the judge. I may be wrong in thinking that a look that signified a single thought passed between them.

"Your Honor, I move to suppress the photo as evidence.''

A steel spring could have come through Ms. Lamb's chair without catapulting her to her feet in better time.

"That's absurd, Your Honor. On what grounds?"

The judge nodded to Mr. Devlin. "Would you care to illuminate, Lex?"

"As Your Honor knows, an anonymous tip that doesn't charge a crime is not sufficient to justify an arrest. The arrest was a violation of Mr. Townsend's constitutional rights. That arrest led to the defendant's telling the police about young Bingham, which in turn led to his bringing in the photograph. It is, in the poetic phrase of Mr. Justice Brennan, 'the fruit of the poisonous tree.' I move to exclude it."

The granting of Mr. Devlin's motion by the judge was the exit cue for Ms. Lamb, which she executed in what could best be described as a high dudgeon. She had gone from a lock on a guilty verdict back to a crap shoot. It was anybody's guess which way the jury would go on the evidence.

The photo sat on the desk. Since no one else seemed interested, I picked it up. This case had more whys and hows than a three-year-old.

THAT NIGHT, SOMETIME AFTER MIDNIGHT, I WAS IN THE company of a row of empty martini glasses at the upstairs bar of the Marliave. I was taking my two-thousandth look at the photo, when it grabbed me. The cold air on the dead run to the *Boston Globe* building chilled out the cobwebs. I was cold sober when I reached the photo lab.

The technician of technicians on the night staff was a former client with enough residual gratitude to do a drop-everything favor.

JUDGE JEFFREYS OPENED THE NEXT MORNING'S SESSION with the charge to the jury—an explanation of the law that applied to the case. I slid in beside Mr. Devlin partway through it. I had a bombshell, and I had to risk the sting of the court to whisper my discovery. The judge shot me a look that could have silenced Howard Cosell. Even Mr. Devlin gave me a silencing whack on the knee.

I sat there like a monkey on a barrel of rattlesnakes. But if I was edgy, I noticed that Chip Townsend was twice as agitated. Mr. Devlin was the calm between two storms.

When the charge ended and the jury left the room, Mr. Devlin shushed the both of us and led us to a vacant corner of the courtroom. He gave Chip the nod first. The boyish shyness had hardened, and his voice was an explosive hiss.

"There's supposed to be more evidence. Where's the picture?"

Mr. Devlin nodded. "I figured that was what was eating you." He looked at me. "And what have you got for us?"

I leaned in for secrecy. "I had a friend at the *Globe* do a blowup of this section of the picture. Since Chip was home at ten, the big clock on the wall showing eleven-thirty must have been a setup. They forgot one detail. Look at the watch on the wrist of the kid with his arm around Chip's neck. You can see in the blow-up. It says eight o'clock. That's probably the real time. This was rigged evidence. It proves that someone was trying to frame Chip."

I had an immediate seconder. Chip was leaning into both of our faces. "You've got to get the case reopened to get that in. I was framed."

Mr. Devlin looked Chip right in the eyes, but I could feel the fire two feet away.

"Listen to me, you little cockroach, you've played your last game with me. For starters, let's admit among us boys, you raped and killed that girl."

I looked to Chip for a denial. He was stone silent.

"I think you're a psychotic killer, kid. I think you killed four other girls and got away with it. I know you killed this one. I think you went upstairs with that girl and whatever it is that snaps in your mind went off. Only this time you got carried away in the wrong circumstances. You couldn't just walk away. Too many people knew you had gone upstairs with the girl. When they found the body, you knew they'd come looking for you. That's when you came up with that glassy-eyed confession that didn't quite tally with the facts. You fed it to the D.A., and she was so tickled to get it, she dropped the ball on the rest of the investigation. You even took a dose of Haldol, because you knew sooner or later I'd check you for it.''

Personally, I was blown away, but young Townsend didn't give an inch.

"That photo's got to get into evidence, Devlin.''

Mr. Devlin leaned closer, and the heat rose.

"That photo is as phony as you. You had your buddy deliver it so it'd be the last thing the jury'd see. Soon as I saw you and that clock and your pal's arm with the watch up there like a beacon in one cute package, I knew what you had in mind. You figured the D.A.'d bite like a trout, and she did. Since you had us primed to look for a frame-up, you knew we'd catch on to the difference in times. I'd expose the frame-up, and the jury'd acquit. Don't play boys' games with men, kid. I had it suppressed. The jury'll never see it.''

Chip was sputtering. "You can't keep out defense evidence!''

Mr. Devlin walked away. "I can when it amounts to perjury.''

I caught Mr. Devlin in the corridor. "You've got to tell me. How did you know he was guilty?''

His voice was back to normal. "That picture the M.E. took of the circular contusion on the back of the dead girl's neck. Two straight lines leading toward each other in the middle of the circle. That bothered me until yesterday afternoon when our grateful client shook hands with me. It perfectly matched the oars on the crest of his championship crew ring.''

Before he walked away, he actually smiled at me. "That was good work on the photo, sonny. You might be worth something yet.''

I recovered from the glow enough to yell after him, "What do you think the jury'll do?''

I saw the shoulders go up in a shrug. "Frankly, I think they'll nail him. We raised some smoke, but don't ever underestimate those twelve sweethearts in the jury box.

God bless them, they pay more attention to their instincts than to the lawyers.''

I turned to carry the bags back to the office and get on to other things, when his voice caught me.

"Hey, sonny."

He turned around on his way out the door.

"As soon as they come in with the guilty verdict, we file a motion for a new trial. This time we defend on insanity. At least he'll avoid the chair. Get on the research now. By the way, what's your first name?''

I've got to admit, it was a great day—despite the guilty verdict.

THE $2,000,000 DEFENSE

~

Harold Q. Masur

THE TRIAL HAD GONE WELL FOR THE PROSECUTION. Strand by strand, a web of guilt had been woven around the defendant, Lloyd Ashley. Now, late in the afternoon of the fifth day, District Attorney Herrick was tying up the last loose ends with his final witness.

Understandably, the case had made headlines. An avid public kept clamoring for more and more details, and the newspapers obligingly supplied whatever revelations they could find. For all the elements of a *cause célèbre* were present—a beautiful wife, allegedly unfaithful; a dashing Casanova, now dead; and a millionaire husband, charged with murder.

Beside Ashley at the counsel table sat his lawyer, Mark Robison, seemingly unconcerned by the drama unfolding before him. His lean face was relaxed, chin resting on the palm of his hand. To a casual observer he seemed preoccupied, almost disinterested; yet nothing would be further from the truth. Robison's mind was keenly attuned, ready to pounce on any error the district attorney might commit.

Defense counsel was a formidable opponent, as the district attorney well knew—they had both trained in the same school, Robison having served as an assistant prosecutor through two administrations.

In this capacity he had been tough and relentless, doing more than his share to keep the state prison at Ossining well populated.

As a muskrat takes to water, so Robison found his natural habitat in the courtroom. He had a commanding presence, the ego and voice of a born actor, and the quick, searching brain so essential to a skilled cross-examiner. He had, too, an instinct with jurors. Unerringly he would spot the most impressionable members of a panel, playing on their emotions and prejudices. And so, where his defenses were inadequate, he would often wind up with a hung jury.

But the Ashley case was more serious. Robison's defense was more than inadequate, it was virtually nonexistent.

Robison sat motionless, studying the prosecution's final witness.

James Keller, police department, specialist in ballistics, was a pale, heavy-set man, stolid and slow-spoken. District Attorney Herrick had taken him through the preliminaries, qualifying him as an expert, and was now extracting the final bit of testimony that should send Lloyd Ashley to eternity, the whine of a high-voltage electric current pounding in his ears.

The district attorney picked up a squat black pistol whose ownership by the accused had already been established. "And now, Mr. Keller," Herrick said, "I show you State's Exhibit B. Can you tell us what kind of gun this is?"

"Yes, sir. That is a 32 caliber Colt automatic, commonly known as a pocket model."

"Have you ever seen this gun before?"

"Yes, sir, I have."

"Under what circumstances?"

"It was handed to me in the performance of my duties as a ballistics expert to determine whether or not it had fired the fatal bullet."

"And did you make the tests?"

"I did."

"Will you tell the jury what you found."

Keller faced the twelve talesmen who were now leaning forward in their chairs. There were no women in the jury box—Robison had used every available challenge to keep them from being empaneled. It was his theory that men would be more sympathetic to acts of violence by a betrayed husband.

Keller spoke in a dry, somewhat pedantic voice. "I fired a test bullet to compare with the one recovered from the deceased. Both bullets had overall dimensions of three-tenths of an inch and a weight of seventy-four grams, placing them in a .32 caliber class. They both bore the imprint of six spiral grooves with a leftward twist which is characteristic of Colt firearms. In addition, every gun develops with usage certain personality traits of its own, and all these are impressed on the shell casing as it passes through the barrel. By checking the two bullets with a comparison microscope—"

Robison broke into Keller's monologue with a casual gesture.

"Your Honor, I think we can dispense with a long technical dissertation on the subject of ballistics. The defense concedes that Mr. Ashley's gun fired the fatal bullet."

The judge glanced at Herrick.

"Is the prosecution agreeable?"

Grudgingly, Herrick said, "The State has no desire to protract this trial longer than necessary."

Secretly, however, he was not pleased. Herrick preferred to build his case carefully and methodically, laying first the foundation, then each plank in turn, until the lid was finally clamped down, with no loophole for escape and no error that could be reversed on appeal. There were times, of course, when he might welcome a concession by the defense, but with Robison—well, you never knew; the man had to be watched.

When Robison resumed his seat, Lloyd Ashley turned to him, his eyes troubled. "Was that wise, Mark?" With hi life at stake, Ashley felt that every point should be hotly contested.

"It was never in dispute," Robison said, managing a smile of assurance.

But the smile had no effect, and seeing Ashley's face now, Robison felt a twist of compassion. How radically changed the man was! Ashley's usual arrogance had crumbled, his sarcastic tongue was now humble and beseeching. Not even his money, those vast sums solidly invested, could give him any sense of security.

Robison could not deny a certain feeling of responsibility for Ashley's plight. He had known Ashley for years, in a business way and socially. He could recall that day only two months ago when Ashley had come to him for advice, grim with repressed anger, suspecting his wife of infidelity.

"Have you any proof?" Robison had asked.

"I don't need any proof. This is something a man knows. She's been cold and untouchable."

"Do you want a divorce?"

"Never." The word had been charged with feeling. "I love Eve."

"Just what do you want me to do, Lloyd?"

"I want you to give me the name of a private detective. I'm sure you know someone I can trust. I'd like him to follow Eve, keep track of her movements. If he can identify the man for me, I'll know what to do."

Yes, Robison knew a reliable private detective—a lawyer sometimes needs the services of a trained investigator, to check the background of hostile witnesses whose testimony he might later want to impeach.

So Ashley retained the man and within a week had his report. The detective had trailed Eve Ashley to a rendez-vous with Tom Ward, an investment counselor in charge of Ashley's securities. He had watched them in obviously intimate conversations in an obscure cocktail lounge in the Village.

The one thing he had never anticipated, Robison told himself, was violence. Not that Ashley was a coward. But

Ashley's principal weapon in the past had been words—
sharp, barbed, insulting. When the call came through from
Police Headquarters that Ashley was being held for murder,
Robison had been genuinely shocked, and he had felt a
momentary pang of guilt. But Robison was not the kind of
man who would long condemn himself for lack of omni-
science. And Ashley, allowed one telephone call, demanded
that Robison appear for him.

At the preliminary hearing in Felony Court, Robison had
made a quick stab at getting the charge dismissed, pre-
senting Ashley's version with shrewdness and skill. The
whole affair had been an accident, Robison had maintained.
No premeditation, no malice, no intent to kill. Ashley had
gone to Ward's office and drawn his gun, brandishing it,
trying to frighten the man, to extract a promise that Ward
would stay away from Ashley's wife. He had been especially careful to check the safety catch, not to release it
before entering Ward's office.

But instead of suffering paralysis or pleading for mercy,
Ward had panicked, thrown himself at Ashley, and grap-
pled for the gun. It had fallen to the desk, Ashley swore,
and been accidentally discharged. He had been standing
over the body when Ward's secretary found them.

Hearing this version, the district attorney had scoffed,
promptly labeling it a bald fiction. The State, Herrick con-
tended, could prove motive, means, and opportunity. So the
magistrate had no choice.

Lloyd Ashley was bound over for action by the Grand
Jury which quickly returned an indictment for murder in
the first degree.

And now, in General Sessions, Judge Felix Cobb presiding, on the fifth day of testimony, Herrick was engaged in
destroying Ashley's last hope. He held up the gun so that
Keller and the jury could see it—a small weapon which
had erased a man's life in the twinkling of an eye.

He said, "You are acquainted with the operation of this
gun, Mr. Keller, are you not?"

"I am."

"In your opinion as a ballistics expert, could a gun of this type be accidentally discharged—with the safety catch on?"

"No, sir."

"You're certain of that?"

"Absolutely."

"Could it be discharged—with the safety on—if it were dropped from a height of several feet?"

"It could not."

"If it were slammed down on a hard surface?"

"No, sir."

"In all your experience—twenty years of testing and handling firearms—have you ever heard of any such incident."

"Not one, sir."

Herrick headed back to the prosecution table. "The defense may cross-examine."

"It is now five minutes to four," the judge said. "I think we can recess at this point." He turned to the jury. "You will remember my instructions, gentlemen. You are admonished not to discuss this case among yourselves, and not to permit anyone to discuss it in your presence. Do not form or express any opinions until all the evidence is before you. Court stands adjourned until ten o'clock tomorrow morning."

He straightened his black robes and strode off. Everyone else remained seated until a tipstaff had led the jurors through a side door. A court officer moved up and touched Ashley's shoulder.

Ashley turned to Robinson, his face drawn and tired. He had lost considerable weight during these last few weeks and the flaccid skin hung loose under his chin. His sunken eyes were veined and red, and a vagrant muscle kept twitching at the corner of his right temple.

"Tomorrow's the last day, isn't it, Mark?"

"Almost." Robison doubted if the whole defense would require more than a single session. "Except for the summation and the judge's charge."

The guard said, "Let's go, Mr. Ashley."

"Listen, Mark." There was sudden intensity in Ashley's voice. "I've got to talk to you. It—it's absolutely vital."

Robinson studied his client. "All right, Lloyd. I'll be up in about fifteen minutes."

Ashley left with the guard and disappeared through a door behind the judge's bench. A few spectators still lingered in the courtroom. Robison gathered his papers and notes, slid them into his brief case. He sat back, fingertips stroking his closed eyelids, still seeing Ashley's face. The man was terrified, and with considerable justification, Robison thought. Despite the judge's admonition to the jurors, advising them not to reach any decision, Robison's experience told him they had done just that.

He could read the signs. He could tell from the way they filed out, the way they averted their eyes, not looking at the defendant. Nobody really enjoys sending another human being to the electric chair. Ashley must have felt it too, this sense of doom.

When Robison reached the corridor, he saw Eve Ashley waiting at the south bank of elevators. She seemed small and lost, the very bones of her body cringing against themselves. Robison started forward, but she was swallowed up in the descending throng before he could reach her.

Eve's reaction had surprised him. She was taking it hard, ill with self-condemnation and remorse. He remembered her visit to his office directly after the murder. "I knew he was jealous," she said, her eyes full of pain, "but I never expected anything like this. Never." She kept clasping and unclasping her hands. "Oh, Mark, they'll send him to the chair! I know they will and it's all my fault."

He had spoken to her sharply. "Listen to me. You had no way of knowing. I want you to get hold of yourself. If you go to pieces, you won't be any good to yourself—or to Lloyd. It's not your fault."

"It *is* my fault." Her lips were trembling. "I should have known. Just look what I've done. Two men. Tom is already dead, and Lloyd soon will—"

"Now stop that!" He had gripped her shoulders.

"You must get him off," she cried fiercely. "Please, Mark. If you don't I'll never forgive myself."

"I'll do my best."

But he knew the odds. The State had a solid case. Motive, means, and opportunity . . .

The elevator took him down and he went around to the detention cells at the White Street entrance. After the usual routine he gained admittance to the counsel room, and a moment later Lloyd Ashley was brought in. They sat on opposite sides of the table, the board between them.

"All right, Mark." Ashley's clenched hands rested on the table. "I want the truth. How does it look?"

Robison shrugged. "The case isn't over. Nobody can tell what a jury will do."

"Stop kidding, Mark. I saw those men—I saw their faces."

Robison shrugged again.

"Look, Mark, you've been my lawyer for a long time. We've been through a lot of deals together. I've seen you operate. I know how your mind works. You're smart. You're resourceful. I have the utmost respect for your ability, but I—well, I . . ." He groped for words.

"Aren't you satisfied with the way I'm handling your defense?"

"I didn't say that, Mark."

"Don't you think I'm exploiting every possible angle?"

"Within legal limitations, yes. But I've seen you try cases before. I've watched you handle juries. And I've seen you pull some rabbits out of a hat. Now, all of a sudden, you're so damn scrupulous I hardly recognize the same man. Why, Mark? What's happened?"

"I can't find a single loophole, Lloyd, that's why. Not one crack in the State's case. My hands are tied."

"Untie them."

"How?" Robison asked quietly.

"Listen, Mark"—Ashley's fingers were gripping the edge of the table—"you know almost as much about my financial affairs as I do. You know how much money I inherited, how much I've made. As of now, I'm worth about four million dollars." He compressed his lips. "Maybe that's why Eve married me; I don't know. Anyway, it's a lot of loot and I'd like a chance to spend some of it. But I won't have that chance, not if they convict me."

Ashley moistened his lips, then went on: "Dead, the money will do me no good. Alive, I can do all I want to do on a lot less. If anybody can get me off the hook, even at this stage of the game, it's you. I don't know how, but I have a feeling—hunch, intuition, call it what you will. You can think of *something*. You've got the imagination. I know you can pull it off."

Robison felt a stir of excitement.

Ashley leaned forward. "Down the middle," he said, his voice hoarse, "An even split, Mark, of everything I own. Half for you, half for me. A two-million-dollar fee, Mark. You'll be financially independent for life. Just figure out an angle! I want an acquittal."

Robison said promptly, "Will you put that in writing, Lloyd?"

"Of course!"

Robison took a blank sheet of paper from his brief case. He wrote swiftly, in clear unmistakable language. He passed the paper to Ashley who scanned it briefly, reached for the pen, and scratched his signature. Robison, his fingers a trifle unsteady, folded the document and put it away.

"Have you any ideas, Mark?"

The lawyer sat motionless, his flat-cheeked face devoid of expression. He did have an idea, one that was not entirely new to him. He remembered, three nights ago, sitting bolt upright in bed, when the brainstorm suddenly struck him. He had considered the idea for a moment, weighed its possibilities, then putting his head back he had laughed aloud in the darkness.

It was ingenious, even amusing in a macabre way, but nothing he would actually use. Now, abruptly, his thinking had changed, all scruples gone. There was considerable per-

suasive power in a fee of $2,000,000. Men had committed
serious crimes—including murder—for much less.

Now the possibilities of his idea stood out, sharp and
clear and daring. There was no guarantee of success. He
would have to cope with certain imponderables—most of
them in the minds of twelve men, the twelve men in the
jury box.

"Leave it to me," Robison said, standing abruptly. "Relax, Lloyd. Try to get some sleep tonight." He swung toward the door with a peremptory wave at the guard.

The declining sun had cooled the air, and Robison
walked briskly, details of the plan churning in his mind.
Ethical? He would hardly call it that. But then Robison was
not often troubled by delicate moral considerations. As a
trial lawyer he'd been consistently successful. His voice
was a great asset: it could be gentle and sympathetic or
blistering and contemptuous. Neophytes around the Criminal Courts Building still talked about Robison's last case
as an assistant district attorney, remembering his savage
cross-examination of the defendant, a man accused of
armed robbery. He had won a conviction, and upon pro-
nouncement of a maximum sentence, the enraged defendant
had turned on him, swearing revenge. Later he had received
venomous, threatening letters from the man's relatives.

So Mark Robison had acquired a pistol permit. And each
year he had had it renewed. He always carried the permit
in his wallet.

His first stop was on Centre Street, not far from Police
Headquarters—at a small shop that specialized in firearms.
He examined the stock, carefully selected a Colt automatic,
pocket model, caliber .32, and a box of shells. The proprietor checked his permit and wrapped the package.

Robison then took a cab to his office. His secretary, Miss
Graham, paused in her typing to hand him a list of calls.
Seeing the abstracted look on his face, she did not bother
to ask him about the trial. He went on through to the inner
room.

It had recently been refurnished and Robison was pleased

with the effect. Hanging on the far wall, facing the desk, was a picture of the nine Justices of the United States Supreme Court. The extraordinary occurrence that now took place before these venerable gentlemen was probably unparalleled in all their collective histories.

Mark Robison unwrapped his package and balanced the gun for a moment in his hand. Then, without further hesitation, he inserted three bullets into the clip and rammed the clip into the butt. His jaw was set as he lifted the gun, aimed it at his left arm, slightly above the elbow, and pulled the trigger.

The echoing explosion left his ears ringing. Robison was no stoic. He felt the stab of pain, like a branding iron, and cried out. The next instant he gritted his teeth while his thumb reached for the safety catch and locked it into position.

A moment later the door burst open and Miss Graham's apprehensive face poked through. With sudden dismay she saw Robison's pallor and the widening stain on his sleeve. She stifled a scream.

"All right," Robison told her harshly. "It was an accident. Don't stand there gaping. Call a doctor. There's one down the hall."

Miss Graham fled. Her urgent story stopped whatever the doctor was doing and brought him on the double with his rumpled black bag.

"Well," he said, sparing the gun a brief look of distaste, "what have we here, another one of those didn't-know-it-was-loaded accidents?"

"Not quite," Robison said dryly.

"Here, let's get the coat off." The doctor helped him, then ripped the lawyer's shirt sleeve from cuff to shoulder, exposing the wound, and probed the inflamed area. The bullet had scooped out a shallow trench of flesh.

"Hmm," said the doctor. "Looks worse than it is. You're a lucky man, counselor. No muscles or arteries severed. Loss of tissue, yes, and some impairment of articulation—"

He reached into his bag and brought out some antiseptic. It burned Robison's arm like a flame. Then having dressed and bandaged the wound, the doctor stepped back to appraise his handiwork.

He looked faintly apologetic. "You know the law, counselor. Whenever a doctor is called in for the treatment of a gunshot wound, he is required to notify the police. I really have no choice."

Robison repressed a smile. Had the doctor been ignorant of the law, Robison would have immediately enlightened him. Most assuredly he *wanted* the police here. They were an essential part of his plan.

He could already picture the headlines: *Robison Accidentally Wounded. Defense Counsel Shot Making Test*—and the stories telling how he had tried to simulate the conditions that had existed in Tom Ward's office—by deliberately dropping a gun on his desk . . .

PROMPTLY AT TEN O'CLOCK THE FOLLOWING MORNING A court officer arose in Part III and intoned the ritual. "All rise, the Honorable Judge of the Court of General Sessions in and for the County of New York."

A door behind the bench opened and Justice Cobb emerged briskly, his black robe billowing behind him.

"Be seated, please," the attendant said, tapping his gavel. "This court is now in session."

The judge looked curiously at Robison, eyeing the wounded arm supported by a black-silk sling knotted around the lawyer's neck. "Call the witness," he said. James Keller was duly sworn and resumed his seat on the stand.

The twelve jurors bent forward, stirred by excitement and anticipation. District Attorney Herrick sat at the prosecution table, vigilant, wary. Robison smiled to himself, remembering the district attorney's tight-lipped greeting. Did Herrick suspect? Possibly.

"The defense may cross-examine," Judge Cobb said.

There was a murmur from the spectators as Robison

pushed erect. He half turned, letting everyone have a look at his wounded arm in its silken cradle. He saw Eve Ashley in the first row, her eyes eloquent with appeal.

Robison walked to the clerk's table and picked up Ashley's gun. Holding it, he advanced toward Keller and addressed the witness. "Now, Mr. Keller, if I remember correctly, you testified yesterday that you fired a test bullet from this gun, did you not?"

"Yes, sir, I did." Keller's tone was guarded.

"You wanted to prove that this gun and no other fired the fatal bullet."

"That is correct."

"I assume that you released the safety catch before making the test?"

"Naturally. Otherwise I would still be standing there in my laboratory pulling the trigger."

Someone in the courtroom tittered, and one of Herrick's assistants grinned. Keller's self-confidence mounted visibly.

Robison regarded him sternly. "This is hardly a moment for humor, Mr. Keller. You realize that your testimony may send an innocent man to the chair?"

Herrick's hand shot up. "I move that last remark be stricken."

"Yes," said the judge. "It will be stricken and the jury will disregard it."

"Then you're absolutely sure," Robison said, "that the safety catch must be released before the gun can be fired?"

"Positive."

"Are you equally positive that the safety catch on a gun of this type cannot be joggled loose under certain circumstances?"

Keller hesitated. "Well, yes, to the best of my knowledge."

"Have you ever made any such test?"

"What do you mean?"

"Did you ever load this gun—State's Exhibit B—and try dropping it on a hard surface?"

"I—I'm afraid not, sir."

"Even though you knew what the basis of our defense would be?"

Keller shifted uncomfortably and glanced at Herrick, but he found no help in the district attorney's expressionless face.

"Please answer the question." Robison's voice was no longer friendly.

"No, sir. I did not."

"Why, Mr. Keller? Why didn't you make such a test? Wouldn't it seem the obvious thing to do? Were you afraid it might confirm the defendant's story?"

"No, sir, not at all."

"Then why?"

Keller said lamely, "It just never occurred to me."

"It never occurred to you. I see. A man is accused of first degree murder; he is being tried for his life, facing the electric chair, and it never occurred to you to make that one simple test to find out if he might be telling the truth.

A flush rose from Keller's neck up to his cheeks. He sat silent, squirming in the witness chair.

"Let the record note that the witness did not answer," Robison said. "Now, sir, you testified yesterday that a gun of this type could never be discharged by dropping it on a hard surface, did you not?"

"With the safety catch on."

"Of course."

"I—yes, I believe I did."

"There is no doubt in your mind?"

Keller swallowed uncomfortably, glancing at Robison's arm. "Well . . . no."

"Let us see." Robison transferred the gun to his left hand, jutting out of the sling, its fingers slightly swollen. His right hand produced a .32 caliber shell from the pocket of his coat. His movements were awkward as he loaded the gun and jacked a shell into firing position. He stepped closer to the witness and started to offer the gun with his left hand, but he stopped short with a sudden grimace of pain. The expression was telling and dramatic. Then rue-fully he shifted the gun to his right hand and extended it to the witness.

In distinct, deliberate tones he said, "Now, Mr. Keller, will you please look at the safety device on State's Exhibit B and tell us if it is in the proper position to prevent fir-ing?"

"It is."

"Then will you kindly rise, sir? I would like you to prove to his Honor, and to these twelve jurors, and to the spectators in this courtroom, that the gun in question *cannot possibly be discharged by dropping it on the judge's dais.* Just lift it, if you please, or slap it down."

A murmur rustled through the courtroom as Herrick landed on both feet in front of the bench. The muscles around his jaw were contracted with anger. "I object, your Honor, This is highly irregular, a cheap grandstand play, inherently dangerous to every—" He caught himself, swal-lowing the rest of his sentence. His own words, uttered impulsively, had implied a possibility, however remote, that the gun might go off.

In contrast, Robison sounded calm and reasonable. "If it please the court, this witness made a statement under oath as a qualified expert. I am merely asking him to prove his own expert statement."

Judge Cobb spoke without pleasure. "Objection over-ruled."

"Go ahead, if you please, Mr. Keller," Robison said. "Demonstrate to the court and to the jury that State's Ex-hibit B could not *possibly* have been fired in the manner claimed by the defendant."

A hush fell over the courtroom as Keller rose. He lifted the gun slowly, and held it suspended over the bench, his face a mixture of anxiety and misgiving.

Robison held his breath as Keller's arm twitched. The judge, trying to look inconspicuous, started to slide down his chair, as if to minimize himself as a target.

"We're waiting," Robison said softly, clearly.

Beads of moisture formed along Keller's temples. Had he flexed his muscles? Had he lifted the gun a little higher? No one in the courtroom could be sure.

"Please proceed, Mr. Keller," Robison said, sharply now. "The court hasn't got all day."

Their eyes met and locked. Deliberately Robison rearranged his sling. Keller took a long breath, then without warning he dropped back into his seat. The gun hung loose between his knees.

A sigh of relief swelled in the courtroom.

The verdict, everyone conceded, was a foregone conclusion. Robison's closing speech was a model of forensic law, and the judge, charging the jury to be satisfied beyond a reasonable doubt, left them little choice. They were out for less than an hour before returning a verdict of Not Guilty.

Lloyd Ashley showed no jubilation—the strain had left him on the edge of nervous exhaustion. Robison touched his shoulder.

"All right, Lloyd. It's over. You're free now. Let's go back to my office. I believe we have some business to transact."

Ashley roused himself. "Yes, of course," he said with a stiff smile.

They got through the crowd, and hailed a cab. The closing speeches and the judge's charge had taken all afternoon, so it was growing dark when they reached Robison's office. He ushered the way into his private room and snapped on the light.

By way of celebration the lawyer produced a bottle and poured two drinks. Both men emptied their glasses in single gulps. Robison passed the humidor and snapped a lighter for his client. Ashley settled back, inhaling the rich smoke of a long, thin cigar.

"Well, Mark," he said, "I knew you could do it. You performed your share of the bargain. I suppose now you'd like me to fulfill mine."

Robison made a deprecating gesture.

"Have you a blank check?"

There was a pad of blank checks somewhere in the outer office, Robison knew. He kept it handy for clients who needed legal representation but who came to him with insufficient funds. He went out to the reception room, rummaged through a storage cabinet, and finally located the pad.

Lloyd Ashley had shifted chairs and was now seated behind Robison's desk. He accepted the blank check and Robison's pen. Without flicking an eyelash, he wrote out a check for $2,000,000.

"I said fifty-fifty, Mark. There may even be more coming to you. We'll know after my accountant goes over the books."

Robison held the check, his eyes transfixed by the string of figures. There was a faint throbbing in his wounded arm, but he didn't mind. Ashley's voice came back to him, sounding soft and strange.

"Oh, yes, Mark, there's more coming to you. Perhaps I can arrange to let you have it now."

Robison looked up and saw the .32 caliber automatic in Ashley's hand, his thumb on the safety catch.

"I found this in your desk," Ashley said. "It must be the gun you used last night. Ironic, isn't it, Mark? You now have the one thing that means more to you than anything else in this world—money—and you'll never be able to spend a penny of it."

Robison did not like the look in Ashley's eyes. "What are you talking about?"

"Remember that private detective you recommended? Funny thing, after that trouble with Ward I never had a chance to take him off the case. So he kept watching Eve all the time I was in jail. As a matter of fact, he brought me a report only two days ago. I don't suppose I have to tell you about it—who she's been seeing, who the other man really is."

Robison had gone white.

The gun in Ashley's hand was very steady. "You know, Mark, I feel you're almost as responsible for Ward's death as I am. After all, who persuaded Eve to use him as a decoy, so that you and she could be safe? It must have been you. Eve never had that much imagination."

Perspiration now bathed Robison's face and his voice went down to a whisper. "Wait, Lloyd, listen to me—"

"No, I'd rather not. You're too good at winning people over. I saw a demonstration of your powers in court today, remember? I've been planning on this for two days. Finding your gun merely accelerated the timetable. There's a kind of justice in this, I think. You forced me into killing the wrong man. Now I see no reason why I shouldn't kill the right one."

Of the two shots that rang out, Mark Robison heard only the first.

THE WITNESS FOR THE PROSECUTION

Agatha Christie

※

MR. MAYHERNE ADJUSTED HIS PINCE-NEZ AND CLEARED his throat with a little dry-as-dust cough that was wholly typical of him. Then he looked again at the man opposite him, the man charged with wilful murder.

Mr. Mayherne was a small man, precise in manner, neatly, not to say foppishly dressed, with a pair of very shrewd and piercing grey eyes. By no means a fool. Indeed, as a solicitor, Mr. Mayherne's reputation stood very high. His voice, when he spoke to his client, was dry but not unsympathetic.

"I must impress upon you again that you are in very grave danger, and that the utmost frankness is necessary."

Leonard Vole, who had been staring in a dazed fashion at the blank wall in front of him, transferred his glance to the solicitor.

"I know," he said hopelessly. "You keep telling me so. But I can't seem to realise yet that I'm charged with murder—*murder*. And such a dastardly crime too."

Mr. Mayherne was practical, not emotional. He coughed again, took off his pince-nez, polished them carefully, and replaced them on his nose. Then he said:

"Yes, yes, yes. Now, my dear Mr. Vole, we're going to

make a determined effort to get you off—and we shall succeed—we shall succeed. But I must have all the facts. I must know just how damaging the case against you is likely to be. Then we can fix upon the best line of defence.''

Still the young man looked at him in the same dazed, hopeless fashion. To Mr. Mayherne the case had seemed black enough, and the guilt of the prisoner assured. Now, for the first time, he felt a doubt.

"You think I'm guilty," said Leonard Vole, in a low voice. "But, by God, I swear I'm not! It looks pretty black against me, I know that. I'm like a man caught in a net—the meshes of it all round me, entangling me whichever way I turn. But I didn't do it, Mr. Mayherne, I didn't do it!''

In such a position a man was bound to protest his innocence. Mr. Mayherne knew that. Yet, in spite of himself, he was impressed. It might be, after all, that Leonard Vole was innocent.

"You are right, Mr. Vole," he said gravely. "The case does look very black against you. Nevertheless, I accept your assurance. Now, let us get to facts. I want you to tell me in your own words exactly how you came to make the acquaintance of Miss Emily French.''

"It was one day in Oxford Street. I saw an elderly lady crossing the road. She was carrying a lot of parcels. In the middle of the street she dropped them, tried to recover them, found a 'bus was almost on top of her and just managed to reach the curb safely, dazed and bewildered by people having shouted at her. I recovered her parcels, wiped the mud off them as best I could, retied the string of one, and returned them to her.''

"There was no question of your having saved her life?''

"Oh! dear me, no. All I did was to perform a common act of courtesy. She was extremely grateful, thanked me warmly, and said something about my manners not being those of most of the younger generation—I can't remember the exact words. Then I lifted my hat and went on. I never expected to see her again. But life is full of coincidences.

That very evening I came across her at a party at a friend's house. She recognised me at once and asked that I should be introduced to her. I then found out that she was a Miss Emily French and that she lived at Cricklewood. I talked to her for some time. She was, I imagine, an old lady who took sudden and violent fancies to people. She took one to me on the strength of a perfectly simple action which anyone might have performed. On leaving, she shook me warmly by the hand, and asked me to come and see her. I replied, of course, that I should be very pleased to do so, and she then urged me to name a day. I did not want particularly to go, but it would have seemed churlish to refuse, so I fixed on the following Saturday. After she had gone, I learned something about her from my friends. That she was rich, eccentric, lived alone with one maid and owned no less than eight cats.''

"I see," said Mr. Mayherne. "The question of her being well off came up as early as that?"

"If you mean that I inquired——" began Leonard Vole hotly, but Mr. Mayherne stilled him with a gesture.

"I have to look at the case as it will be presented by the other side. An ordinary observer would not have supposed Miss French to be a lady of means. She lived poorly, almost humbly. Unless you had been told the contrary, you would in all probability have considered her to be in poor circumstances—at any rate to begin with. Who was it exactly who told you that she was well off?"

"My friend, George Harvey, at whose house the party took place."

"Is he likely to remember having done so?"

"I really don't know. Of course it is some time ago now."

"Quite so, Mr. Vole. You see, the first aim of the prosecution will be to establish that you were in low water financially—that is true, is it not?"

Leonard Vole flushed.

"Yes," he said, in a low voice. "I'd been having a run of infernal bad luck just then."

"Quite so," said Mr. Mayherne again. "That being, as I say, in low water financially, you met this rich old lady and cultivated her acquaintance assiduously. Now if we are in a position to say that you had no idea she was well off, and that you visited her out of pure kindness of heart——"

"Which is the case."

"I dare say. I am not disputing the point. I am looking at it from the outside point of view. A great deal depends on the memory of Mr. Harvey. Is he likely to remember that conversation or is he not? Could he be confused by counsel into believing that it took place later?"

Leonard Vole reflected for some minutes. Then he said steadily enough, but with a rather paler face:

"I do not think that that line would be successful, Mr. Mayherne. Several of those present heard his remark, and one or two of them chaffed me about my conquest of a rich old lady."

The solicitor endeavoured to hide his disappointment with a wave of the hand.

"Unfortunate," he said. "But I congratulate you upon your plain speaking, Mr. Vole. It is to you I look to guide me. Your judgment is quite right. To persist in the line I spoke of would have been disastrous. We must leave that point. You made the acquaintance of Miss French, you called upon her, the acquaintanceship progressed. We want a clear reason for all this. Why did you, a young man of thirty-three, good-looking, fond of sport, popular with your friends, devote so much of your time to an elderly woman with whom you could hardly have anything in common?"

Leonard Vole flung out his hands in a nervous gesture.

"I can't tell you—I really can't tell you. After the first visit, she pressed me to come again, spoke of being lonely and unhappy. She made it difficult for me to refuse. She showed so plainly her fondness and affection for me that I was placed in an awkward position. You see, Mr. Mayherne, I've got a weak nature—I drift—I'm one of those people who can't say 'No.' And believe me or not, as you like, after the third or fourth visit I paid her I found myself getting genuinely fond of the old thing. My mother died when I was young, an aunt brought me up, and she too died before I was fifteen. If I told you that I genuinely enjoyed being mothered and pampered, I dare say you'd only laugh."

Mr. Mayherne did not laugh. Instead he took off his pince-nez again and polished them, a sign with him that he was thinking deeply.

"I accept your explanation, Mr. Vole," he said at last. "I believe it to be psychologically probable. Whether a jury would take that view of it is another matter. Please continue your narrative. When was it that Miss French first asked you to look into her business affairs?"

"After my third or fourth visit to her. She understood very little of money matters, and was worried about some investments."

Mr. Mayherne looked up sharply.

"Be careful, Mr. Vole. The maid, Janet Mackenzie, declares that her mistress was a good woman of business and transacted all her own affairs, and this is borne out by the testimony of her bankers."

"I can't help that," said Vole earnestly. "That's what she said to me."

Mr. Mayherne looked at him for a moment or two in silence. Though he had no intention of saying so, his belief in Leonard Vole's innocence was at that moment strengthened. He knew something of the mentality of elderly ladies. He saw Miss French, infatuated with the good-looking young man, hunting about for pretexts that should bring him to the house. What more likely than that she should plead ignorance of business, and beg him to help her with her money affairs? She was enough of a woman of the world to realise that any man is slightly flattered by such an admission of his superiority. Leonard Vole had been flattered. Perhaps, too, she had not been averse to letting this young man know that she was wealthy. Emily French had been a strongwilled old woman, willing to pay her price for what she wanted. All this passed rapidly through Mr. Mayherne's mind, but he gave no indication of it, and asked instead a further question.

"And you did handle her affairs for her at her request?"

"I did."

"Mr. Vole," said the solicitor, "I am going to ask you a very serious question, and one to which it is vital I should have a truthful answer. You were in low water financially. You had the handling of an old lady's affairs—an old lady who, according to her own statement, knew little or nothing of business. Did you at any time, or in any manner, convert to your own use the securities which you handled? Did you engage in any transaction for your own pecuniary advantage which will not bear the light of day?" He quelled the other's response. "Wait a minute before you answer. There are two courses open to us. Either we can make a feature of your probity and honesty in conducting her affairs whilst pointing out how unlikely it is that you would commit murder to obtain money which you might have obtained by such infinitely easier means. If, on the other hand, there is anything in your dealings which the prosecution will get hold of—if, to put it badly, it can be proved that you swindled the old lady in any way, we must take the line that you had no motive for the murder, since she was already a profitable source of income to you. You perceive the distinction. Now, I beg of you, take your time before you reply."

But Leonard Vole took no time at all.

"My dealings with Miss French's affairs were all perfectly fair and above board. I acted for her interests to the very best of my ability, as any one will find who looks into the matter."

"Thank you," said Mr. Mayherne. "You relieve my mind very much. I pay you the compliment of believing that you are far too clever to lie to me over such an important matter."

"Surely," said Vole eagerly, "the strongest point in my favour is the lack of motive. Granted that I cultivated the acquaintanceship of a rich old lady in the hopes of getting money out of her—that, I gather, is the substance of what you have been saying—surely her death frustrates all my hopes?''

The solicitor looked at him steadily. Then, very deliberately, he repeated his unconscious trick with his pince-nez. It was not until they were firmly replaced on his nose that he spoke.

''Are you not aware, Mr. Vole, that Miss French left a will under which you are the principal beneficiary?''

''What?'' The prisoner sprang to his feet. His dismay was obvious and unforced. ''My God! What are you saying? She left her money to me?''

Mr. Mayherne nodded slowly. Vole sank down again, his head in his hands.

''You pretend you know nothing of this will?''

''Pretend? There's no pretence about it. I knew nothing about it.''

''What would you say if I told you that the maid, Janet Mackenzie, swears that you *did* know? That her mistress told her distinctly that she had consulted you in the matter, and told you of her intentions?''

''Say? That she's lying! No, I go too fast. Janet is an elderly woman. She was a faithful watchdog to her mistress, and she didn't like me. She was jealous and suspicious. I should say that Miss French confided her intentions to Janet, and that Janet either mistook something she said, or else was convinced in her own mind that I had persuaded the old lady into doing it. I dare say that she believes herself now that Miss French actually told her so.''

''You don't think she dislikes you enough to lie deliberately about the matter?''

Leonard Vole looked shocked and startled.

''No, indeed! Why should she?''

''I don't know,'' said Mr. Mayherne thoughtfully. ''But she's very bitter against you.''

The wretched young man groaned again.

''I'm beginning to see,'' he muttered. ''It's frightful. I

made up to her, that's what they'll say, I got her to make a will leaving her money to me, and then I go there that night, and there's nobody in the house—they find her the next day—oh! my God, it's awful!''

"You are wrong about there being nobody in the house," said Mr. Mayherne. "Janet, as you remember, was to go out for the evening. She went, but about half-past nine she returned to fetch the pattern of a blouse sleeve which she had promised to a friend. She let herself in by the back door, went upstairs and fetched it, and went out again. She heard voices in the sitting-room, though she could not distinguish what they said, but she will swear that one of them was Miss French's and one was a man's.''

"At half-past nine," said Leonard Vole. "At half-past nine. . . .'' He sprang to his feet. "But then I'm saved—saved——''

"What do you mean, saved?" cried Mr. Mayherne, astonished.

"*By half-past nine I was at home again!* My wife can prove that. I left Miss French about five minutes to nine. I arrived home about twenty-past nine. My wife was there waiting for me. Oh! thank God—thank God! And bless Janet Mackenzie's sleeve pattern.''

In his exuberance, he hardly noticed that the grave expression of the solicitor's face had not altered. But the latter's words brought him down to earth with a bump.

"Who, then, in your opinion, murdered Miss French?''

"Why, a burglar, of course, as was thought at first. The window was forced, you remember. She was killed with a heavy blow from a crowbar, and the crowbar was found lying on the floor beside the body. And several articles were missing. But for Janet's absurd suspicions and dislike of me, the police would never have swerved from the right track.''

"That will hardly do, Mr. Vole," said the solicitor. "The things that were missing were mere trifles of no value, taken as a blind. And the marks on the window were not at all conclusive. Besides, think for yourself. You say you were no longer in the house by half-past nine. Who, then, was the man Janet heard talking to Miss French in the sittingroom? She would hardly be having an amicable conversation with a burglar?''

''No,'' said Vole. ''No——'' He looked puzzled and discouraged. ''But anyway,'' he added with reviving spirit, ''it lets me out. I've got an *alibi*. You must see Romaine—my wife—at once.''

''Certainly,'' acquiesced the lawyer. ''I should already have seen Mrs. Vole but for her being absent when you were arrested. I wired to Scotland at once, and I understand that she arrives back to-night. I am going to call upon her immediately I leave here.''

Vole nodded, a great expression of satisfaction settling down over his face.

''Yes, Romaine will tell you. My God! it's a lucky chance that.''

''Excuse me, Mr. Vole, but you are very fond of your wife?''

''Of course.''

''And she of you?''

''Romaine is devoted to me. She'd do anything in the world for me.''

He spoke enthusiastically, but the solicitor's heart sank a little lower. The testimony of a devoted wife—would it gain credence?

''Was there anyone else who saw you return at nine-twenty. A maid, for instance?''

''We have no maid.''

''Did you meet anyone in the street on the way back?''

''Nobody I knew. I rode part of the way in a 'bus. The conductor might remember.''

Mr. Mayherne shook his head doubtfully.

''There is no one, then, who can confirm your wife's testimony?''

''No. But it isn't necessary, surely?''

''I dare say not. I dare say not,'' said Mr. Mayherne

hastily. "Now there's just one thing more. Did Miss French know that you were a married man?"

"Oh, yes."

"Yet you never took your wife to see her. Why was that?"

For the first time, Leonard Vole's answer came halting and uncertain.

"Well—I don't know."

"Are you aware that Janet Mackenzie says her mistress believed you to be single, and contemplated marrying you in the future?"

Vole laughed.

"Absurd! There was forty years' difference in age between us."

"It has been done," said the solicitor drily. "The fact remains. Your wife never met Miss French?"

"No——" Again the constraint.

"You will permit me to say," said the lawyer, "that I hardly understand your attitude in the matter."

Vole flushed, hesitated, and then spoke.

"I'll make a clean breast of it. I was hard up, as you know. I hoped that Miss French might lend me some money. She was fond of me, but she wasn't at all interested in the struggles of a young couple. Early on, I found that she had taken it for granted that my wife and I didn't get on—were living apart. Mr. Mayherne—I wanted the money—for Romaine's sake. I said nothing, and allowed the old lady to think what she chose. She spoke of my being an adopted son to her. There was never any question of marriage—that must be just Janet's imagination."

"And that is all?"

"Yes—that is all."

Was there just a shade of hesitation in the words? The lawyer fancied so. He rose and held out his hand.

"Good-bye, Mr. Vole." He looked into the haggard young face and spoke with an unusual impulse. "I believe in your innocence in spite of the multitude of facts arrayed against you. I hope to prove it and vindicate you completely.''

Vole smiled back at him.

"You'll find the alibi is all right," he said cheerfully.

Again he hardly noticed that the other did not respond.

"The whole thing hinges a good deal on the testimony of Janet Mackenzie," said Mr. Mayherne. "She hates you. That much is clear."

"She can hardly hate me," protested the young man.

The solicitor shook his head as he went out.

"Now for Mrs. Vole," he said to himself.

He was seriously disturbed by the way the thing was shaping.

The Voles lived in a small shabby house near Paddington Green. It was to this house that Mr. Mayherne went.

In answer to his ring, a big slatternly woman, obviously a charwoman, answered the door.

"Mrs. Vole? Has she returned yet?"

"Got back an hour ago. But I dunno if you can see her."

"If you will take my card to her," said Mr. Mayherne quietly, "I am quite sure that she will do so."

The woman looked at him doubtfully, wiped her hand on her apron and took the card. Then she closed the door in his face and left him on the step outside.

In a few minutes, however, she returned with a slightly altered manner.

"Come inside, please."

She ushered him into a tiny drawing-room. Mr. Mayherne, examining a drawing on the wall, started up suddenly to face a tall pale woman who had entered so quietly that he had not heard her.

"Mr. Mayherne? You are my husband's solicitor, are you not? You have come from him? Will you please sit down?"

Until she spoke he had not realised that she was not English. Now, observing her more closely, he noticed the high cheekbones, the dense blue-black of the hair, and an occasional very slight movement of the hands that was distinctly foreign. A strange woman, very quiet. So quiet as to make one uneasy. From the very first Mr. Mayherne was conscious that he was up against something that he did not understand.

"Now, my dear Mrs. Vole," he began, "you must not give way——"

He stopped. It was so very obvious that Romaine Vole had not the slightest intention of giving way. She was perfectly calm and composed.

"Will you please tell me all about it?" she said. "I must know everything. Do not think to spare me. I want to know the worst" She hesitated, then repeated in a lower tone, with a curious emphasis which the lawyer did not understand: "I want to know the worst."

Mr. Mayherne went over his interview with Leonard Vole. She listened attentively, nodding her head now and then.

"I see," she said, when he had finished. "He wants me to say that he came in at twenty minutes past nine that night?"

"He did come in at that time?" said Mr. Mayherne sharply.

"That is not the point," she said coldly. "Will my saying so acquit him? Will they believe me?"

Mr. Mayherne was taken aback. She had gone so quickly to the core of the matter.

"That is what I want to know," she said. "Will it be enough? Is there anyone else who can support my evidence?"

There was a suppressed eagerness in her manner that made him vaguely uneasy.

"So far there is no one else," he said reluctantly.

"I see," said Romaine Vole.

She sat for a minute or two perfectly still. A little smile played over her lips.

The lawyer's feeling of alarm grew stronger and stronger.

"Mrs. Vole——" he began. "I know what you must feel——"

"Do you?" she said. "I wonder."

"In the circumstances——"

"In the circumstances—I intend to play a lone hand."

He looked at her in dismay.

"But, my dear Mrs. Vole—you are overwrought. Being so devoted to your husband——"

"I beg your pardon?"

The sharpness of her voice made him start. He repeated in a hesitating manner:

"Being so devoted to your husband——"

Romaine Vole nodded slowly, the same strange smile on her lips.

"Did he tell you that I was devoted to him?" she asked softly. "Ah! yes, I can see he did. How stupid men are! Stupid—stupid—stupid——"

She rose suddenly to her feet. All the intense emotion that the lawyer had been conscious of in the atmosphere was now concentrated in her tone.

"I hate him, I tell you! I hate him. I hate him. I hate him! I would like to see him hanged by the neck till he is dead."

The lawyer recoiled before her and the smouldering passion in her eyes.

She advanced a step nearer, and continued vehemently:

"Perhaps I *shall* see it. Supposing I tell you that he did not come in that night at twenty past nine, but at twenty past *ten?* You say that he tells you he knew nothing about the money coming to him. Supposing I tell you he knew all about it, and counted on it, and committed murder to get it? Supposing I tell you that he admitted to me that night when he came in what he had done? That there was blood on his coat? What then? Supposing that I stand up in court and say all these things?"

Her eyes seemed to challenge him. With an effort, he concealed his growing dismay, and endeavoured to speak in a rational tone.

"You cannot be asked to give evidence against your husband——"

"He is not my husband!"

The words came out so quickly that he fancied he had misunderstood her.

"I beg your pardon? I——"

"He is not my husband."

The silence was so intense that you could have heard a pin drop.

"I was an actress in Vienna. My husband is alive but in a madhouse. So we could not marry. I am glad now."

She nodded defiantly.

"I should like you to tell me one thing," said Mr. Mayherne. He contrived to appear as cool and unemotional as ever. "Why are you so bitter against Leonard Vole?"

She shook her head, smiling a little.

"Yes, you would like to know. But I shall not tell you. I will keep my secret. . . ."

Mr. Mayherne gave his dry little cough and rose.

"There seems no point in prolonging this interview," he remarked. "You will hear from me again after I have communicated with my client."

She came closer to him, looking into his eyes with her own wonderful dark ones.

"Tell me," she said, "did you believe—honestly—that he was innocent when you came here today?"

"I did," said Mr. Mayherne.

"You poor little man," she laughed.

"And I believe so still," finished the lawyer. "Goodevening, madam."

He went out of the room, taking with him the memory of her startled face.

"This is going to be the devil of a business," said Mr. Mayherne to himself as he strode along the street.

Extraordinary, the whole thing. An extraordinary woman. A very dangerous woman. Women were the devil when they got their knife into you.

What was to be done? That wretched young man hadn't

a leg to stand upon. Of course, possibly he did commit the crime. . . .

"No," said Mr. Mayherne to himself. "No—there's almost too much evidence against him. I don't believe this woman. She was trumping up the whole story. But she'll never bring it into court."

He wished he felt more conviction on the point.

THE POLICE COURT PROCEEDINGS WERE BRIEF AND DRAmatic. The principal witnesses for the prosecution were Janet Mackenzie, maid to the dead woman, and Romaine Heilger, Austrian subject, the mistress of the prisoner.

Mr. Mayherne sat in court and listened to the damning story that the latter told. It was on the lines she had indicated to him in their interview.

The prisoner reserved his defence and was committed for trial.

Mr. Mayherne was at his wits' end. The case against Leonard Vole was black beyond words. Even the famous K. C. who was engaged for the defence held out little hope.

"If we can shake that Austrian woman's testimony, we might do something," he said dubiously. "But it's a bad business."

Mr. Mayherne had concentrated his energies on one single point. Assuming Leonard Vole to be speaking the truth, and to have left the murdered woman's house at nine o'clock, who was the man Janet heard talking to Miss French at half-past nine?

The only ray of light was in the shape of a scapegrace nephew who had in bygone days cajoled and threatened his aunt out of various sums of money. Janet Mackenzie, the solicitor learned, had always been attached to this young man, and had never ceased urging his claims upon her mistress. It certainly seemed possible that it was this nephew who had been with Miss French after Leonard Vole left, especially as he was not to be found in any of his old haunts.

In all other directions, the lawyer's researches had been

negative in their result. No one had seen Leonard Vole entering his own house, or leaving that of Miss French. No one had seen any other man enter or leave the house in Cricklewood. All inquiries drew blank.

It was the eve of the trial when Mr. Mayherne received the letter which was to lead his thoughts in an entirely new direction.

It came by the six o'clock post. An illiterate scrawl, written on common paper and enclosed in a dirty envelope with the stamp stuck on crooked.

Mr. Mayherne read it through once or twice before he grasped its meaning.

"DEAR MISTER:
"Youre the lawyer chap wot acks for the young feller. If you want that painted foreign hussy showed up for wot she is an her pack of lies you come to 16 Shaw's Rents Stepney to-night It ull cawst you 2 hundred quid Arsk for Missis Mogson."

The solicitor read and re-read this strange epistle. It might, of course, be a hoax, but when he thought it over, he became increasingly convinced that it was genuine, and also convinced that it was the one hope for the prisoner. The evidence of Romaine Heilger damned him completely, and the line the defense meant to pursue, the line that the evidence of a woman who had admittedly lived an immoral life was not to be trusted, was at best a weak one.

Mr. Mayherne's mind was made up. It was his duty to save his client at all costs. He must go to Shaw's Rents.

He had some difficulty in finding the place, a ramshackle building in an evil-smelling slum, but at last he did so, and on inquiry for Mrs. Mogson was sent up to a room on the third floor. On this door he knocked, and getting no answer, knocked again.

At this second knock, he heard a shuffling sound inside, and presently the door was opened cautiously half an inch and a bent figure peered out.

Suddenly the woman, for it was a woman, gave a chuckle and opened the door wider.

"So it's you, dearie," she said, in a wheezy voice. "Nobody with you, is there? No playing tricks? That's right. You can come in—you can come in."

With some reluctance the lawyer stepped across the threshold into the small dirty room, with its flickering gas jet. There was an untidy unmade bed in a corner, a plain deal table and two rickety chairs. For the first time Mr. Mayherne had a full view of the tenant of this unsavoury apartment. She was a woman of middle age, bent in figure, with a mass of untidy grey hair and a scarf wound tightly round her face. She saw him looking at this and laughed again, the same curious, toneless chuckle.

"Wondering why I hide my beauty, dear? He, he, he. Afraid it may tempt you, eh? But you shall see—you shall see."

She drew aside the scarf and the lawyer recoiled involuntarily before the almost formless blur of scarlet. She replaced the scarf again.

"So you're not wanting to kiss me, dearie? He, he, I don't wonder. And yet I was a pretty girl once—not so long ago as you'd think, either. Vitriol, dearie, vitriol—that's what did that. Ah! but I'll be even with 'em——"

She burst into a hideous torrent of profanity which Mr. Mayherne tried vainly to quell. She fell silent at last, her hands clenching and unclenching themselves nervously.

"Enough of that," said the lawyer sternly. "I've come here because I have reason to believe you can give me information which will clear my client, Leonard Vole. Is that the case?"

Her eyes leered at him cunningly.

"What about the money, dearie?" she wheezed. "Two hundred quid, you remember."

"It is your duty to give evidence, and you can be called upon to do so."

"That won't do, dearie. I'm an old woman, and I know

nothing. But you give me two hundred quid, and perhaps I can give you a hint or two. See?"

"What kind of hint?"

"What should you say to a letter? A letter from *her*. Never mind how I got hold of it: That's my business. It'll do the trick. But I want my two hundred quid."

Mr. Mayherne looked at her coldly, and made up his mind.

"I'll give you ten pounds, nothing more. And only that if this letter is what you say it is."

"Ten pounds?" She screamed and raved at him.

"Twenty," said Mr. Mayherne, "and that's my last word."

He rose as if to go. Then, watching her closely, he drew out a pocketbook, and counted out twenty one-pound notes.

"You see," he said. "That is all I have with me. You can take it or leave it."

But already he knew that the sight of the money was too much for her. She cursed and raved impotently, but at last she gave in. Going over to the bed, she drew something out from beneath the tattered mattress.

"Here you are, damn you!" she snarled. "It's the top one you want."

It was a bundle of letters that she threw to him, and Mr. Mayherne untied them and scanned them in his usual cool, methodical manner. The woman, watching him eagerly, could gain no clue from his impassive face.

He read each letter through, then returned again to the top one and read it a second time. Then he tied the whole bundle up again carefully.

They were love letters, written by Romaine Heilger, and the man they were written to was not Leonard Vole. The top letter was dated the day of the latter's arrest.

"I spoke true, dearie, didn't I?" whined the woman. "It'll do for her, that letter?"

Mr. Mayherne put the letters in his pocket, then he asked a question.

"How did you get hold of this correspondence?"

"That's telling," she said with a leer. "But I know something more. I heard in court what that hussy said. Find out where *she* was at twenty past ten, the time she says she was at home. Ask at the Lion Road Cinema. They'll remember—a fine upstanding girl like that—curse her!"

"Who is the man?" asked Mr. Mayherne. "There's only a Christian name here."

The other's voice grew thick and hoarse, her hands clenched and unclenched. Finally she lifted one to her face.

"He's the man that did this to me. Many years ago now. She took him away from me—a chit of a girl she was then. And when I went after him—and went for him too—he threw the cursed stuff at me! And she laughed—damn her! I've had it in for her for years. Followed her, I have, spied upon her. And now I've got her! She'll suffer for this, won't she, Mr. Lawyer? She'll suffer?"

"She will probably be sentenced to a term of imprisonment for perjury," said Mr. Mayherne quietly.

"Shut away—that's what I want. You're going, are you? Where's my money? Where's that good money?"

Without a word, Mr. Mayherne put down the notes on the table. Then, drawing a deep breath, he turned and left the squalid room. Looking back, he saw the old woman crooning over the money.

He wasted no time. He found the cinema in Lion Road easily enough, and, shown a photograph of Romaine Heilger, the commissionaire recognized her at once. She had arrived at the cinema with a man some time after ten o'clock on the evening in question. He had not noticed her escort particularly, but he remembered the lady who had spoken to him about the picture that was showing. They stayed until the end, about an hour later.

Mr. Mayherne was satisfied. Romaine Heilger's evidence was a tissue of lies from beginning to end. She had evolved it out of her passionate hatred. The lawyer wondered whether he would ever know what lay behind that hatred. What had Leonard Vole done to her? He had seemed dumbfounded when the solicitor had reported her attitude to him.

He had declared earnestly that such a thing was incredible—yet it had seemed to Mr. Mayherne that after the first astonishment his protests had lacked sincerity.

He *did* know. Mr. Mayherne was convinced of it. He knew, but he had no intention of revealing the fact. The secret between those two remained a secret. Mr. Mayherne wondered if some day he should come to learn what it was.

The solicitor glanced at his watch. It was late, but time was everything. He hailed a taxi and gave an address.

"Sir Charles must know of this at once," he murmured to himself as he got in.

THE TRIAL OF LEONARD VOLE FOR THE MURDER OF EMILY French aroused widespread interest. In the first place the prisoner was young and good-looking, then he was accused of a particularly dastardly crime, and there was the further interest of Romaine Heilger, the principal witness for the prosecution. There had been pictures of her in many papers, and several fictitious stories as to her origin and history.

The proceedings opened quietly enough. Various technical evidence came first. Then Janet Mackenzie was called. She told substantially the same story as before. In cross-examination counsel for the defence succeeded in getting her to contradict herself once or twice over her account of Vole's association with Miss French; he emphasized the fact that though she had heard a man's voice in the sitting-room that night, there was nothing to show that it was Vole who was there, and he managed to drive home a feeling that jealousy and dislike of the prisoner were at the bottom of a good deal of her evidence.

Then the next witness was called.

"Your name is Romaine Heilger?"

"Yes."

"You are an Austrian subject?"

"Yes."

"For the last three years you have lived with the prisoner and passed yourself off as his wife?"

Just for a moment Romaine Heilger's eyes met those of

the man in the dock. Her expression held something curious and unfathomable.

"Yes."

The questions went on. Word by word the damning facts came out. On the night in question the prisoner had taken out a crowbar with him. He had returned at twenty minutes past ten, and had confessed to having killed the old lady. His cuffs had been stained with blood, and he had burned them in the kitchen stove. He had terrorised her into silence by means of threats.

As the story proceeded, the feeling of the court which had, to begin with, been slightly favourable to the prisoner, now set dead against him. He himself sat with downcast head and moody air, as though he knew he were doomed.

Yet it might have been noted that her own counsel sought to restrain Romaine's animosity. He would have preferred her to be more unbiased.

Formidable and ponderous, counsel for the defence arose.

He put it to her that her story was a malicious fabrication from start to finish, that she had not even been in her own house at the time in question, that she was in love with another man and was deliberately seeking to send Vole to his death for a crime he did not commit.

Romaine denied these allegations with superb insolence.

Then came the surprising denouement, the production of the letter. It was read aloud in court in the midst of a breathless stillness.

"Max, beloved, the Fates have delivered him into our hands! He has been arrested for murder—but, yes, the murder of an old lady! Leonard who would not hurt a fly! At last I shall have my revenge. The poor chicken! I shall say that he came in that night with blood upon him—that he confessed to me. I shall hang him, Max—and when he hangs he will know and realise that it was Romaine who sent him to his death. And then—happiness, Beloved! Happiness at last!"

THERE WERE EXPERTS PRESENT READY TO SWEAR THAT the handwriting was that of Romaine Heilger, but they were not needed. Confronted with the letter, Romaine broke down utterly and confessed everything. Leonard Vole had returned to the house at the time he said, twenty past nine. She had invented the whole story to ruin him.

With the collapse of Romaine Heilger, the case for the Crown collapsed also. Sir Charles called his few witnesses, the prisoner himself went into the box and told his story in a manly straightforward manner, unshaken by cross-examination.

The prosecution endeavoured to rally, but without great success. The judge's summing up was not wholly favourable to the prisoner, but a reaction had set in and the jury needed little time to consider their verdict.

"We find the prisoner not guilty."

Leonard Vole was free!

Little Mr. Mayherne hurried from his seat. He must congratulate his client.

He found himself polishing his pince-nez vigorously, and checked himself. His wife had told him only the night before that he was getting a habit of it. Curious things, habits. People themselves never knew they had them.

An interesting case—a very interesting case. That woman, now, Romaine Heilger.

The case was dominated for him still by the exotic figure of Romaine Heilger. She had seemed a pale, quiet woman in the house at Paddington, but in court she had flamed out against the sober background, flaunting herself like a tropical flower.

If he closed his eyes he could see her now, tall and vehement, her exquisite body bent forward a little, her right hand clenching and unclenching itself unconsciously all the time.

Curious things, habits. That gesture of hers with the hand was her habit, he supposed. Yet he had seen someone else do it quite lately. Who was it now? Quite lately——

He drew in his breath with a gasp as it came back to him. *The woman in Shaw's Rents. . . .*

He stood still, his head whirling. It was impossible—impossible——Yet, Romaine Heilger was an actress.

The K. C. came up behind him and clapped him on the shoulder.

"Congratulated our man yet? He's had a narrow shave, you know. Come along and see him."

But the little lawyer shook off the other's hand.

He wanted one thing only—to see Romaine Heilger face to face.

He did not see her until some time later, and the place of their meeting is not relevant.

"So you guessed," she said, when he had told her all that was in his mind. "The face? Oh! that was easy enough, and the light of that gas jet was too bad for you to see the make-up."

"But why—why—"

"Why did I play a lone hand?" She smiled a little, remembering the last time she had used the words.

"Such an elaborate comedy!"

"My friend—I had to save him. The evidence of a woman devoted to him would not have been enough—you hinted as much yourself. But I know something of the psychology of crowds. Let my evidence be wrung from me, as an admission, damning me in the eyes of the law, and a reaction in favour of the prisoner would immediately set in."

"And the bundle of letters?"

"One alone, the vital one, might have seemed like a—what do you call it?—put-up job."

"Then the man called Max?"

"Never existed, my friend."

"I still think," said little Mr. Mayherne, in an aggrieved manner, "that we could have got him off by the—er—normal procedure."

"I dared not risk it. You see you *thought* he was innocent——"

"And you *knew* it? I see," said little Mr. Mayherne.

"My dear Mr. Mayherne," said Romaine, "you do not see at all. I knew—he was guilty!"

THE EHRENGRAF
ALTERNATIVE

Lawrence Block

"WHAT'S MOST UNFORTUNATE," EHRENGRAF SAID, "IS that there seems to be a witness."

Evelyn Throop nodded in fervent agreement. "Mrs. Keppner," she said.

"Howard Bierstadt's housekeeper."

"She was devoted to him. She'd been with him for years."

"And she claims she saw you shoot him three times in the chest."

"I know," Evelyn Throop said. "I can't imagine why she would say something like that. It's completely untrue."

A thin smile turned up the corners of Martin Ehrengraf's mouth. Already he felt himself warming to his client, exhilarated by the prospect of acting in her defense. It was the little lawyer's great good fortune always to find himself representing innocent clients, but few of those clients were as singleminded as Miss Throop in proclaiming their innocence.

The woman sat on the edge of her iron cot with her shapely legs crossed at the ankle. She seemed so utterly in possession of herself that she might have been almost anywhere but in a jail cell, charged with the murder of her lover. Her age, according to the papers, was forty-six. Ehrengraf would have guessed her to be perhaps a dozen years younger. She was not rich—Ehrengraf, like most lawyers, did have a special fondness for wealthy clients—but she had excellent breeding. It was evident not only in her exquisite facial bones but in her positively ducal self-assurance.

"I'm sure we'll uncover the explanation of Mrs. Keppner's calumny," he said gently. "For now, why don't we go over what actually happened."

"Certainly. I was at my home that evening when Howard called. He was in a mood and wanted to see me. I drove over to his house. He made drinks for both of us and paced around a great deal. He was extremely agitated."

"Over what?"

"Leona wanted him to marry her. Leona Weybright."

"The cookbook writer?"

"Yes. Howard was not the sort of man to get married, or even to limit himself to a single relationship. He believed in a double standard and was quite open about it. He expected his women to be faithful while reserving the option of infidelity to himself. If one was going to be involved with Howard Bierstadt, one had to accept this."

"As you accepted it."

"As I accepted it," Evelyn Throop agreed. "Leona evidently pretended to accept it but could not, and Howard didn't know what to do about her. He wanted to break up with her but was afraid of the possible consequences. He thought she might turn suicidal and he didn't want her death on his conscience."

"And he discussed all of this with you."

"Oh, yes. He often confided in me about his relationship with Leona." Evelyn Throop permitted herself a smile. "I played a very important role in his life, Mr. Ehrengraf. I suppose he would have married me if there'd been any reason to do so. I was his true confidante. Leona was just one of a long string of mistresses."

Ehrengraf nodded. "According to the prosecution," he

said carefully, "you were pressuring him to marry you."

"That's quite untrue."

"No doubt." He smiled. "Continue."

The woman sighed. "There's not much more to say. He went into the other room to freshen our drinks. There was the report of a gunshot."

"I believe there were three shots."

"Perhaps there were. I can only remember the volume of the noise. It was so startling. I rushed in immediately and saw him on the floor, the gun by his outstretched hand. I guess I bent over and picked up the gun. I don't remember doing so, but I must have done because the next thing I knew I was standing there holding the gun." Evelyn Throop closed her eyes, evidently overwhelmed by the memory. "Then Mrs. Keppner was there—I believe she screamed, and then she went off to call the police. I just stood there for a while and then I guess I sat down in a chair and waited for the police to come and tell me what to do."

"And they brought you here and put you in a cell."

"Yes. I was quite astonished. I couldn't imagine why they would do such a thing, and then it developed that Mrs. Keppner had sworn she saw me shoot Howard."

Ehrengraf was respectfully silent for a moment. Then he said, "It seems they found some corroboration for Mrs. Keppner's story."

"What do you mean?"

"The gun," Ehrengraf said. "A .32 caliber revolver. I believe it was registered to you, was it not?"

"It was my gun."

"How did Mr. Bierstadt happen to have it?"

"I brought it to him."

"At his request?"

"Yes. When we spoke on the telephone, he specifically asked me to bring the gun. He said something about wanting to protect himself from burglars. I never thought he would shoot himself."

"But he did."

"He must have done. He was upset about Leona. Perhaps he felt guilty, or that there was no way to avoid hurting her."

"Wasn't there a paraffin test?" Ehrengraf mused. "As I recall, there were no nitrite particles found in Mr. Bierstadt's hand, which would seem to indicate he had not fired a gun recently."

"I don't really understand those tests," Evelyn Throop said. "But I'm told they're not absolutely conclusive."

"And the police gave you a test as well," Ehrengraf went on. "Didn't they?"

"Yes."

"And found nitrite particles in your right hand."

"Of course," Evelyn Throop said. "I'd fired the gun that evening before I took it along to Howard's house. I hadn't used it in the longest time, since I first practiced with it at a pistol range, so I cleaned it and to make sure it was in good operating condition I test-fired it before I went to Howard's."

"At a pistol range?"

"That wouldn't have been convenient. I just stopped at a deserted spot along a country road and fired a few shots."

"I see."

"I told the police all of this, of course."

"Of course. Before they gave you the paraffin test?"

"After the test, as it happens. The incident had quite slipped my mind in the excitement of the moment, but they gave me the test and said it was evident I'd fired a gun, and at that point I recalled having stopped the car and firing off a couple of rounds before continuing on to Howard's."

"Where you gave Mr. Bierstadt the gun."

"Yes."

"Whereupon he in due course took it off into another room and fired three shots into his heart," Ehrengraf murmured. "Your Mr. Bierstadt would look to be one of the most determined suicides in human memory."

"You don't believe me."

"But I do believe you," he said. "Which is to say that

I believe you did not shoot Mr. Bierstadt. Whether or not he did in fact die by his own hand is not, of course, something to which either you or I can testify.''

"How else could he have died?'' The woman's gaze narrowed. "Unless he really was genuinely afraid of burglars, and unless he did surprise one in the other room. But wouldn't I have heard sounds of a struggle? Of course, I was in another room a fair distance away, and there was music playing, and I did have things on my mind.''

"I'm sure you did.''

"And perhaps Mrs. Keppner saw the burglar shoot Howard, and then she fainted or something. I suppose that's possible, isn't it?''

"Eminently possible,'' Ehrengraf assured her.

"She might have come to when I had already entered the room and picked up the gun, and the whole incident could have been compressed in her mind. She wouldn't remember having fainted and so she might now actually believe she saw me kill Howard, while all along she saw something entirely different.'' Evelyn Throop had been looking off into the middle distance as she formulated her theory and now she focused her eyes upon the diminutive attorney. "It could have happened that way,'' she said, "couldn't it?''

"It could have happened precisely that way,'' Ehrengraf said. "It could have happened in any of innumerable ways. Ah, Miss Throop—'' and now the lawyer rubbed his small hands together ''—that's the whole beauty of it. There are any number of alternatives to the prosecution's argument, but of course they don't see them. Give the police a supposedly ironclad case and they look no further. It is not their task to examine alternatives. But it is our task, Miss Throop, to find not merely *an* alternative but the correct alternative, the ideal alternative. And in just that fashion we will make a free woman of you.''

"You seem very confident, Mr. Ehrengraf.''

"I am.''

"And prepared to believe in my innocence.''

"Unequivocally. Without question."

"I find that refreshing," Evelyn Throop said. "I even believe you'll get me acquitted."

"I fully expect to," Ehrengraf said. "Now let me see, is there anything else we have to discuss at present?"

"Yes."

"And what would that be?"

"Your fee," said Evelyn Throop.

BACK IN HIS OFFICE, SEATED BEHIND A DESK WHICH HE kept as untidy as he kept his own person immaculate, Martin H. Ehrengraf sat back and contemplated the many extraordinary qualities of his latest client. In his considerable experience, while clients were not invariably opposed to a discussion of his fees, they were certainly loathe to raise the matter. But Evelyn Throop, possessor of dove-grey eyes and remarkable facial bones, had proved an exception.

"My fees are high," Ehrengraf had told her, "but they are payable only in the event that my clients are acquitted. If you don't emerge from this ordeal scot-free, you owe me nothing. Even my expenses will be at my expense."

"And if I get off?"

"Then you will owe me one hundred thousand dollars. And I must emphasize, Miss Throop, that the fee will be due me however you win your freedom. It is not inconceivable that neither of us will ever see the inside of a courtroom, that your release when it comes will appear not to have been the result of my efforts at all. I will, nevertheless, expect to be paid in full."

The grey eyes looked searchingly into the lawyer's own. "Yes," she said after a moment. "Yes, of course. Well, that seems fair. If I'm released I won't really care how the end was accomplished, will I?"

Ehrengraf said nothing. Clients often whistled a different tune at a later date, but one could burn that bridge when one came to it.

"One hundred thousand dollars seems reasonable," the woman continued. "I suppose any sum would seem reasonable when one's life and liberty hangs in the balance. Of course, you must know I have no money of my own."

"Perhaps your family—"

She shook her head. "I can trace my ancestors back to William the Conqueror," she said, "and there were Throops who made their fortune in whaling and the China trade, but I'm afraid the money's run out over the generations. However, I shouldn't have any problem paying your fee."

"Oh?"

"I'm Howard's chief beneficiary," she explained. "I've seen his will and it makes it unmistakably clear that I held first place in his affections. After a small cash bequest to Mrs. Keppner for her loyal years of service, and after leaving his art collection—which, I grant you, *is* substantial— to Leona, the remainder comes to me. There may be a couple of cash bequests to charities but nothing that amounts to much. So while I'll have to wait for the will to make its way through probate, I'm sure I can borrow on my expectations and pay you your fee within a matter of days of my release from jail, Mr. Ehrengraf."

"A day that should come in short order," Ehrengraf said.

"That's your department," Evelyn Throop said, and smiled serenely.

Ehrengraf smiled now, recalling her smile, and made a little tent of his fingertips on the desktop. An exceptional woman, he told himself, and one on whose behalf it would be an honor to extend himself.

It was difficult, of course. Shot with the woman's own gun, and a witness to swear that she'd shot him. Difficult, certainly, but scarcely impossible.

The little lawyer leaned back, closed his eyes, and considered alternatives.

Some days later, Ehrengraf was seated at his desk reading the poems of William Ernest Henley, who had written so confidently of being the master of one's fate and the captain of one's soul. The telephone rang. Ehrengraf set his book down, located the instrument amid the desktop clutter, and answered it.

"Ehrengraf," said Ehrengraf.

He listened for a moment, spoke briefly in reply, and replaced the receiver. Smiling brightly, he started for the door, then paused to check his appearance in a mirror.

His tie was navy-blue, with a demure below-the-knot pattern of embroidered rams' heads. For a moment Ehrengraf thought of stopping at his house and changing it for his Caedmon Society necktie, one he'd taken to wearing on triumphal occasions. He glanced at his watch and decided not to squander the time.

Later, recalling the decision, he wondered if it hinted at prescience.

"QUITE REMARKABLE," EVELYN THROOP SAID. "Although I suppose I should have at least considered the possibility that Mrs. Keppner was lying. After all, I knew for a fact that she was testifying to something that didn't happen to be true. But for some reason I assumed it was an honest mistake on her part."

"One hesitates to believe the worst of people," Ehrengraf said.

"That's exactly it, of course. Besides, I rather took her for granted."

"So, it appears, did Mr. Bierstadt."

"And that was his mistake, wasn't it?" Evelyn Throop sighed. "Dora Keppner had been with him for years. Who would have guessed she'd been in love with him? Although I gather their relationship was physical at one point."

"There was a suggestion to that effect in the note she left."

"And I understand he wanted to get rid of her—to discharge her."

"The note seems to have indicated considerable mental disturbance," Ehrengraf said. "There were other jottings in a notebook found in Mrs. Keppner's attic bedroom. The impression seems to be that either she and her employer had been intimate in the past or that she entertained a fantasy to that effect. Her attitude in recent weeks apparently became less and less the sort proper to a servant, and either Mr. Bierstadt intended to let her go or she feared that he did and—well, we know what happened.''

"She shot him." Evelyn Throop frowned. "She must have been in the room when he went to freshen the drinks. I thought he'd put the gun in his pocket but perhaps he still had it in his hand. He would have set it down when he made the drinks and she could have snatched it up and shot him and been out of the room before I got there.'' The grey eyes moved to encounter Ehrengraf's. "She didn't leave any fingerprints on the gun.''

"She seems to have worn gloves. She was wearing a pair when she took her own life. A test indicated nitrite particles in the right glove.''

"Couldn't they have gotten there when she committed suicide?''

"It's unlikely," Ehrengraf said. "She didn't shoot herself, you see. She took poison.''

"How awful," Evelyn Throop said. "I hope it was quick.''

"Mercifully so," said Ehrengraf. Clearly this woman was the captain of her soul, he thought, not to mention master of her fate. Or ought it to be mistress of her fate?

And yet, he realized abruptly, she was not entirely at ease.

"I've been released," she said, "as is of course quite obvious. All charges have been dropped. A man from the district attorney's office explained everything to me.''

"That was considerate of him.''

"He didn't seem altogether happy. I had the feeling he didn't really believe I was innocent after all.''

"People believe what they wish to believe," Ehrengraf said smoothly. "The state's whole case collapses without their star witness, and after that witness has confessed to the crime herself and taken her life in the bargain, well, what does it matter what a stubborn district attorney chooses to believe?

"The important thing," Ehrengraf said, "is that you've been set free. You're innocent of all charges."

"Yes."

His eyes searched hers. "Is there a problem, Miss Throop?"

"There is, Mr. Ehrengraf."

"Dear lady," he began, "if you could just tell me—"

"The problem concerns your fee."

Ehrengraf's heart sank. Why did so many clients disappoint him in precisely this fashion? At the onset, with the sword of justice hanging over their throats, they agreed eagerly to whatever he proposed. Remove the sword and their agreeability went with it.

But that was not it at all.

"The most extraordinary thing," Evelyn Throop was saying. "I told you the terms of Howard's will. The paintings to Leona, a few thousand dollars here and there to various charities, a modest bequest to Mrs. Keppner—I suppose she won't get that now, will she?"

"Hardly."

"Well, that's something. Though it doesn't amount to much. At any rate, the balance is to go to me. The residue, after the bequests have been made and all debts settled and the state and federal taxes been paid, all that remains comes to me."

"So you explained."

"I intended to pay you out of what I received, Mr. Ehrengraf. Well, you're more than welcome to every cent I get. You can buy yourself a couple of hamburgers and a milkshake."

"I don't understand."

"It's the damned paintings," Evelyn Throop said. "They're worth an absolute fortune. I didn't realize how much he spent on them in the first place or how rapidly they appreciated in value. Nor did I have any idea how deeply mortgaged everything else he owned was. He had some investment reversals over the past few months and he'd taken out a second mortgage on his home and sold off stocks and other holdings. There's a little cash and a certain amount of equity in the real estate, but it'll take all of that to pay the estate taxes on the several million dollars' worth of paintings that go free and clear to that bitch Leona.''

"You have to pay the taxes?"

"No question about it," she said bitterly. "The estate pays the taxes and settles the debts. Then all the paintings go straight to America's favorite cook. I hope she chokes on them." Evelyn Throop sighed heavily, collected herself. "Please forgive the dramatics, Mr. Ehrengraf."

"They're quite understandable, dear lady."

"I didn't intend to lose control of myself in that fashion. But I feel this deeply. I know Howard had no intention of disinheriting me and having that woman get everything. It was his unmistakable intention to leave me the greater portion, and a cruel trick of fate has thwarted him in that purpose. Mr. Ehrengraf, I owe you one hundred thousand dollars. That was our agreement and I consider myself bound by it."

Ehrengraf made no reply.

"But I don't know how I can possibly pay you. Oh, I'll pay what I can, as I can, but I'm a woman of modest means. I couldn't honestly expect to discharge the debt in full within my lifetime."

"My dear Miss Throop." Ehrengraf was moved, and his hand went involuntarily to the knot of his necktie. "My dear Miss Throop," he said again, "I beg you not to worry yourself. Do you know Henley, Miss Throop?"

"Henley?"

"The poet," said Ehrengraf, and quoted:

" 'In the fell clutch of circumstance,
I have not winced nor cried aloud:
Under the bludgeonings of chance
My head is bloody, but unbowed.'

"William Ernest Henley, Miss Throop. Born 1849, died 1903. Bloody but unbowed, Miss Throop. 'I have not yet begun to fight.' That was John Paul Jones, Miss Throop, not a poet at all, a naval commander of the Revolutionary War, but the sentiment, dear lady, is worthy of a poet. 'Things are seldom what they seem, Skim milk masquerades as cream.' William Schwenk Gilbert, Miss Throop.''

"I don't understand."

"Alternatives, Miss Throop. Alternatives!" The little lawyer was on his feet, pacing, gesticulating with precision. "I tell you only what I told you before. There are always alternatives available to us."

The grey eyes narrowed in thought. "I suppose you mean we could sue to overturn the will," she said. "That occurred to me, but I thought you only handled criminal cases."

"And so I do."

"I wonder if I could find another lawyer who would contest the will on a contingency basis. Perhaps you know someone—"

"Ah, Miss Throop," said Ehrengraf, sitting back down and placing his fingertips together. "Contest the will? Life is too short for litigation. An unlikely sentiment for an attorney to voice, I know, but nonetheless valid for it. Put lawsuits far from your mind. Let us first see if we cannot find—" a smile blossomed on his lips "—the Ehrengraf alternative."

EHRENGRAF, A SHINE ON HIS BLACK WINGTIP SHOES AND a white carnation on his lapel, strode briskly up the cinder path from his car to the center entrance of the Bierstadt house. In the crisp autumn air, the ivy-covered brick mansion in its spacious grounds took on an aura suggestive of a college campus. Ehrengraf noticed this and touched his tie, a distinctive specimen sporting a half-inch stripe of royal-blue flanked by two narrower stripes, one of gold and the other of a particularly vivid green, all on a deep navy field. It was the tie he had very nearly worn to the meeting with his client some weeks earlier.

Now, he trusted, it would be rather more appropriate.

He eschewed the doorbell in favor of the heavy brass knocker, and in a matter of seconds the door swung inward. Evelyn Throop met him with a smile.

"Dear Mr. Ehrengraf," she said. "It's kind of you to meet me here. In poor Howard's home."

"Your home now," Ehrengraf murmured.

"Mine," she agreed. "Of course, there are legal processes to be gone through but I've been allowed to take possession. And I think I'm going to be able to keep the place. Now that the paintings are mine, I'll be able to sell some of them to pay the taxes and settle other claims against the estate. But let me show you around. This is the living room, of course, and here's the room where Howard and I were having drinks that night—"

"That fateful night," said Ehrengraf.

"And here's the room where Howard was killed. He was preparing drinks at the sideboard over there. He was lying here when I found him. And—"

Ehrengraf watched politely as his client pointed out where everything had taken place.

Then he followed her to another room where he accepted a small glass of Calvados.

For herself, Evelyn Throop poured a pony of Bénédictine.

"What shall we drink to?" she asked him.

To your spectacular eyes, he thought, but suggested instead that she propose a toast.

"To the Ehrengraf alternative," she said.

They drank.

"The Ehrengraf alternative," she said again. "I didn't know what to expect when we last saw each other. I thought you must have had some sort of complicated legal maneuver in mind, perhaps some way around the extortionate tax burden the government levies upon even the most modest inheritance. I had no idea the whole circumstances of poor Howard's murder would wind up turned utterly upside down.''

''It was quite extraordinary,'' Ehrengraf allowed.

''I had been astonished enough to learn that Mrs. Keppner had murdered Howard and then taken her own life. Imagine how I felt to learn that she *wasn't* a murderer and that she *hadn't* committed suicide but that she'd actually *herself* been murdered.''

''Life keeps surprising us,'' Ehrengraf said.

''And Leona Weybright winds up hoist on her own soufflé. The funny thing is that I was right in the first place. Howard *was* afraid of Leona, and evidently he had every reason to be. He'd apparently written her a note, insisting that they stop seeing each other.''

Ehrengraf nodded. ''The police found the note when they searched her quarters. Of course, she insisted she had never seen it before.''

''What else could she say?'' Evelyn Throop took another delicate sip of Bénédictine and Ehrengraf's heart thrilled at the sight of her pink tongue against the brim of the tiny glass. ''But I don't see how she can expect anyone to believe her. She murdered Howard, didn't she?''

''It would be hard to establish that beyond a reasonable doubt,'' Ehrengraf said. ''The supposition exists. However, Miss Weybright does have an alibi, and it might not be easily shaken. And the only witness to the murder, Mrs. Keppner, is no longer available to give testimony.''

''Because Leona killed her.''

Ehrengraf nodded. ''And that,'' he said, ''very likely *can* be established.''

''Because Mrs. Keppner's suicide note was a forgery.''

''So it would appear,'' Ehrengraf said. ''An artful forgery, but a forgery nevertheless. And the police seem to have found earlier drafts of that very note in Miss Weybright's desk. One was typed on the very machine at which she prepares her cookbook manuscripts. Others were written with a pen found in her desk, and the ink matched that on the note Mrs. Keppner purportedly left behind. Some of the drafts are in an imitation of the dead woman's handwriting, one in a sort of mongrel cross between the two women's penmanship, and one—evidently she was just trying to get the wording to her liking—was in Miss Weybright's own unmistakable hand. Circumstantial evidence, all of it, but highly suggestive.''

''And there was other evidence, wasn't there?''

''Indeed there was. When Mrs. Keppner's body was found, there was a glass on a nearby table, a glass with a residue of water in it. An analysis of the water indicated the presence of a deadly poison, and an autopsy indicated that Mrs. Keppner's death had been caused by ingesting that very substance. The police, combining two and two, concluded not illogically that Mrs. Keppner had drunk a glass of water with the poison in it.''

''But that's not how it happened?''

''Apparently not. Because the autopsy also indicated that the deceased had had a piece of cake not long before she died.''

''And the cake was poisoned?''

''I should think it must have been,'' Ehrengraf said carefully, ''because police investigators happened to find a cake with one wedge missing, wrapped securely in aluminum foil and tucked away in Miss Weybright's freezer. And that cake, when thawed and subjected to chemical analysis, proved to have been laced with the very poison which caused the death of poor Mrs. Keppner.''

Miss Throop looked thoughtful. ''How did Leona try to get out of that one?''

''She denied she ever saw the cake before and insisted she had never baked it.''

''And?''

''And it seems to have been prepared precisely according to an original recipe in her present cookbook-in-progress.''

''I suppose the book will never be published now.''

''On the contrary, I believe the publisher has tripled the initial print order.''

Ehrengraf sighed. ''As I understand it, the presumption

is that Miss Weybright was desperate at the prospect of losing the unfortunate Mr. Bierstadt. She wanted him, and if she couldn't have him alive she wanted him dead. But she didn't want to be punished for his murder, nor did she want to lose out on whatever she stood to gain from his will. By framing you for his murder, she thought she could increase the portion due her. Actually, the language of the will probably would not have facilitated this, but she evidently didn't realize it, any more than she realized that by receiving the paintings she would have the lion's share of the estate. In any event, she must have been obsessed with the idea of killing her lover and seeing her rival pay for the crime."

"How did Mrs. Keppner get into the act?"

"We may never know for certain. Was the housekeeper in on the plot all along? Did she actually fire the fatal shots and then turn into a false witness? Or did Miss Weybright commit the murder and leave Mrs. Keppner to testify against you? *Or* did Mrs. Keppner see what she oughtn't to have seen and then, after lying about you, try her hand at blackmailing Miss Weybright? Whatever the actual circumstances, Miss Weybright realized that Mrs. Keppner represented either an immediate or a potential hazard."

"And so Leona killed her."

"And had no trouble doing so." One might call it a piece of cake, Ehrengraf forbore to say. "At that point it became worth her while to let Mrs. Keppner play the role of murderess. Perhaps Miss Weybright became acquainted with the nature of the will and the estate itself and realized that she would already be in line to receive the greater portion of the estate, that it was not necessary to frame you. Furthermore, she saw that you were not about to plead guilty to a reduced charge or to attempt a Frankie-and-Johnny defense, as it were. By shunting the blame onto a dead Mrs. Keppner, she forestalled the possibility of a detailed investigation which might have pointed the finger of guilt in her own direction."

"My goodness," Evelyn Throop said. "It's quite extraordinary, isn't it?"

"It is," Ehrengraf agreed.

"And Leona will stand trial?"

"For Mrs. Keppner's murder."

"Will she be convicted?"

"One never knows what a jury will do," Ehrengraf said. "That's one reason I much prefer to spare my own clients the indignity of a trial."

He thought for a moment. "The district attorney might or might not have enough evidence to secure a conviction. Of course, more evidence might come to light between now and the trial. For that matter, evidence in Miss Weybright's favor might turn up."

"If she has the right lawyer."

"An attorney can often make a difference," Ehrengraf allowed. "But I'm afraid the man Miss Weybright has engaged won't do her much good. I suspect she'll wind up convicted of first-degree manslaughter or something of the sort. A few years in confined quarters and she'll have been rehabilitated. Perhaps she'll emerge from the experience with a slew of new recipes."

"Poor Leona," Evelyn Throop said, and shuddered delicately.

"Ah, well," Ehrengraf said. " 'Life is bitter,' as Henley reminds us in a poem. It goes on to say:

" 'Riches won but mock the old, unable years;
    Fame's a pearl that hides beneath a sea of tears;
    Love must wither, or must live alone and weep.
    In the sunshine, through the leaves, across the
        flowers,
    While we slumber, death approaches through the
        hours . . .
    Let me sleep.'

"Riches, fame, love—and yet we seek them, do we not? That will be one hundred thousand dollars, Miss Throop, and—Ah, you have the check all drawn, have you?" He accepted it from her, folded it, and tucked it into a pocket.

"It is rare," he said, "to meet a woman so businesslike and yet so unequivocally feminine. And so attractive."

There was a small silence. Then: "Mr. Ehrengraf? Would you care to see the rest of the house?"

"I'd like that," said Ehrengraf, and smiled his little smile.

THE CASE OF THE IRATE WITNESS

Erle Stanley Gardner

〰

THE EARLY-MORNING SHADOWS CAST BY THE MOUNTAINS still lay heavily on the town's main street as the big siren on the roof of the Jebson Commercial Company began to scream shrilly.

The danger of fire was always present, and at the sound, men at breakfast rose and pushed their chairs back from the table. Men who were shaving barely paused to wipe lather from their faces; men who had been sleeping grabbed the first available garments. All of them ran to places where they could look for the first telltale wisps of smoke.

There was no smoke.

The big siren was still screaming urgently as the men formed into streaming lines, like ants whose hill has been attacked. The lines all moved toward the Jebson Commercial Company.

There the men were told that the doors of the big vault had been found wide open. A jagged hole had been cut into one door with an acetylene torch.

The men looked at one another silently. This was the fifteenth of the month. The big, twice-a-month payroll, which had been brought up from the Ivanhoe National Bank the day before, had been the prize.

178

Frank Bernal, manager of the company's mine, the man who ruled Jebson City with an iron hand, arrived and took charge. The responsibility was his, and what he found was alarming.

Tom Munson, the night watchman, was lying on the floor in a back room, snoring in drunken slumber. The burglar alarm, which had been installed within the last six months, had been bypassed by means of an electrical device. This device was so ingenious that it was apparent that, if the work were that of a gang, at least one of the burglars was an expert electrician. Ralph Nesbitt, the company account-ant, was significantly silent. When Frank Bernal had been appointed manager a year earlier, Nesbitt had pointed out that the big vault was obsolete.

Bernal, determined to prove himself in his new job, had avoided the expense of tearing out the old vault and in-stalling a new one by investing in an up-to-date burglar alarm and putting a special night watchman on duty.

Now the safe had been looted of $100,000 and Frank Bernal had to make a report to the main office in Chicago, with the disquieting knowledge that Ralph Nesbitt's memo stating that the antiquated vault was a pushover was at this moment reposing in the company files.

SOME DISTANCE OUT OF JEBSON CITY, PERRY MASON, THE famous trial lawyer, was driving fast along a mountain road. He had planned a weekend fishing trip for a long time, but a jury which had waited until midnight before reaching its verdict had delayed Mason's departure and it was now 8:30 in the morning.

His fishing clothes, rod, wading boots, and creel were all in the trunk. He was wearing the suit in which he had stepped from the courtroom, and having driven all night he was eager for the cool, piny mountains.

A blazing red light, shining directly at him as he rounded a turn in the canyon road, dazzled his road-weary eyes. A sign, *STOP—POLICE*, had been placed in the middle of the road. Two men, a grim-faced man with a .30–30 rifle in his hands and a silver badge on his shirt and a uniformed motorcycle officer, stood beside the sign.

Mason stopped his car.

The man with the badge, deputy sheriff, said, "We'd better take a look at your driving license. There's been a big robbery at Jebson City."

"That so?" Mason said. "I went through Jebson City an hour ago and everything seemed quiet."

'Where you been since then?''

"I stopped at a little service station and restaurant for breakfast."

"Let's take a look at your driving license."

Mason handed it to him.

The man started to return it, then looked at it again. "Say," he said, "you're Perry Mason, the big criminal lawyer!"

"Not a criminal lawyer," Mason said patiently, "a trial lawyer. I sometimes defend men who are accused of crime."

"What are you doing up in this country?"

"Going fishing."

The deputy looked at him suspiciously. "Why aren't you wearing your fishing clothes?"

"Because," Mason said, and smiled, "I'm not fishing."

"You said you were going fishing."

"I also intend," Mason said, "to go to bed tonight. According to you, I should be wearing my pajamas."

The deputy frowned. The traffic officer laughed and waved Mason on.

The deputy nodded at the departing car. "Looks like a live clue to me," he said, "but I can't find it in that conversation."

"There isn't any," the traffic officer said.

The deputy remained dubious, and later on, when a news-hungry reporter from the local paper asked the deputy if he knew of anything that would make a good story, the deputy said that he did.

And that was why Della Street, Perry Mason's confidential secretary, was surprised to read stories in the metropolitan papers stating that Perry Mason, the noted trial lawyer, was rumored to have been retained to represent the person or persons who had looted the vault of the Jebson Commercial Company. All this had been arranged, it would seem, before Mason's "client" had even been apprehended.

WHEN PERRY MASON CALLED HIS OFFICE BY LONG-distance the next afternoon, Della said, "I thought you were going to the mountains for a vacation."

"That's right. Why?"

"The papers claim you're representing whoever robbed the Jebson Commercial Company."

"First I've heard of it," Mason said. "I went through Jebson City before they discovered the robbery, stopped for breakfast a little farther on, and then got caught in a road-block. In the eyes of some officious deputy, that seems to have made me an accessory after the fact."

"Well," Della Street said, "they've caught a man by the name of Harvey L. Corbin, and apparently have quite a case against him. They're hinting at mysterious evidence which won't be disclosed until the time of trial."

"Was he the one who committed the crime?" Mason asked.

"The police think so. He has a criminal record. When his employers at Jebson City found out about it, they told him to leave town. That was the evening before the robbery."

"Just like that, eh?" Mason asked.

"Well, you see, Jebson City is a one-industry town, and the company owns all the houses. They're leased to the employees. I understand Corbin's wife and daughter were told they could stay on until Corbin got located in a new place, but Corbin was told to leave town at once. You aren't interested, are you?"

"Not in the least," Mason said, "except that when I

drive back I'll be going through Jebson City, and I'll probably stop to pick up the local gossip.''

"Don't do it," she warned. "This man Corbin has all the earmarks of being an underdog, and you know how you feel about underdogs.''

A quality in her voice made Perry suspicious. "You haven't been approached, have you, Della?''

"Well," she said, "in a way. Mrs. Corbin read in the papers that you were going to represent her husband, and she was overjoyed. It seems that she thinks her husband's implication in this is a raw deal. She hadn't known anything about his criminal record, but she loves him and is going to stand by him.''

"You've talked with her?" Mason asked.

"Several times. I tried to break it to her gently. I told her it was probably nothing but a newspaper story. You see, Chief, they have Corbin dead to rights. They took some money from his wife as evidence. It was part of the loot.''

"And she has nothing?''

"Nothing. Corbin left her forty dollars, and they took it all as evidence.''

"I'll drive all night," he said. "Tell her I'll be back tomorrow.''

"I was afraid of that," Della Street said. "Why did you have to call up? Why couldn't you have stayed up there fishing? Why did you have to get your name in the papers?''

Mason laughed and hung up.

PAUL DRAKE, OF THE DRAKE DETECTIVE AGENCY, came in and sat in the big chair in Mason's office and said, "You have a bear by the tail, Perry.''

"What's the matter, Paul? Didn't your detective work in Jebson City pan out?''

"It panned out all right, but the stuff in the pan isn't what you want, Perry," Drake explained.

"How come?''

"Your client's guilty.''

"Go on," Mason said.

"The money he gave his wife was some of what was stolen from the vault."

"How do they know it was the stolen money?" Mason asked.

Drake pulled a notebook from his pocket. "Here's the whole picture. The plant manager runs Jebson City. There isn't any private property. The Jebson company controls everything."

"Not a single small business?"

Drake shook his head. "Not unless you want to consider garbage collecting as small business. An old coot by the name of George Addey lives five miles down the canyon; he has a hog ranch and collects the garbage. He's supposed to have the first nickel he ever earned. Buries his money in cans. There's no bank nearer than Ivanhoe City."

"What about the burglary? The men who did it must have moved in acetylene tanks and—"

"They took them right out of the company store," Drake said. And then he went on: "Munson, the watchman, likes to take a pull out of a flask of whiskey along about midnight. He says it keeps him awake. Of course, he's not supposed to do it, and no one was supposed to know about the whiskey, but someone did know about it. They doped the whiskey with a barbiturate. The watchman took his usual swig, went to sleep, and stayed asleep."

"What's the evidence against Corbin?" Mason asked.

"Corbin had a previous burglary record. It's a policy of the company not to hire anyone with a criminal record. Corbin lied about his past and got a job. Frank Bernal, the manager, found out about it, sent for Corbin about 8 o'clock the night the burglary took place, and ordered him out of town. Bernal agreed to let Corbin's wife and child stay on in the house until Corbin could get located in another city. Corbin pulled out in the morning, and gave his wife this money. It was part of the money from the burglary."

"How do they know?" Mason asked.

"Now there's something I don't know," Drake said. "This fellow Bernal is pretty smart, and the story is that he can prove Corbin's money was from the vault."

Drake paused, then continued: "The nearest bank is at Ivanhoe City, and the mine pays off in cash twice a month. Ralph Nesbitt, the cashier, wanted to install a new vault. Bernal refused to okay the expense. So the company has ordered both Bernal and Nesbitt back to its main office at Chicago to report. The rumor is that they may fire Bernal as manager and give Nesbitt the job. A couple of the directors don't like Bernal, and this thing has given them their chance. They dug out a report Nesbitt had made showing the vault was a pushover. Bernal didn't act on that report." He sighed and then asked, "When's the trial, Perry?"

"The preliminary hearing is set for Friday morning. I'll see then what they've got against Corbin."

"They're laying for you up there," Paul Drake warned. "Better watch out, Perry. That district attorney has something up his sleeve, some sort of surprise that's going to knock you for a loop."

IN SPITE OF HIS LONG EXPERIENCE AS A PROSECUTOR, VERnon Flasher, the district attorney of Ivanhoe County, showed a certain nervousness at being called upon to oppose Perry Mason. There was, however, a secretive assurance underneath that nervousness.

Judge Haswell, realizing that the eyes of the community were upon him, adhered to legal technicalities to the point of being pompous both in rulings and mannerisms.

But what irritated Perry Mason was in the attitude of the spectators. He sensed that they did not regard him as an attorney trying to safeguard the interests of a client, but as a legal magician with a cloven hoof. The looting of the vault had shocked the community, and there was a tightlipped determination that no legal tricks were going to do Mason any good *this* time.

Vernon Flasher didn't try to save his surprise evidence

for a whirlwind finish. He used it right at the start of the case.

Frank Bernal, called as a witness, described the location of the vault, identified photographs, and then leaned back as the district attorney said abruptly, "You had reason to believe this vault was obsolete?"

"Yes, sir."

"It had been pointed out to you by one of your fellow employees, Mr. Ralph Nesbitt?"

"Yes, sir."

"And what did you do about it?"

"Are you," Mason asked in some surprise, "trying to cross-examine your own witness?"

"Just let him answer the question, and you'll see," Flasher replied grimly.

"Go right ahead and answer," Mason said to the witness.

Bernal assumed a more comfortable position. "I did three things," he said, "to safeguard the payrolls and to avoid the expense of tearing out the old vault and installing a new vault in its place."

"What were those three things?"

"I employed a special night watchman; I installed the best burglar alarm money could buy; and I made arrangements with the Ivanhoe National Bank, where we have our payrolls made up, to list the number of each twenty-dollar bill which was a part of each payroll."

Mason suddenly sat up straight.

Flasher gave him a glance of gloating triumph. "Do you wish the court to understand, Mr. Bernal," he said smugly, "that you have the numbers of the bills in the payroll which was made up for delivery on the fifteenth?"

"Yes, sir. Not *all* the bills, you understand. That would have taken too much time, but I have the numbers of all the twenty-dollar bills."

"And who recorded those numbers?" the prosecutor asked.

"The bank."

"And do you have that list of numbers with you?"

"I do. Yes, sir." Bernal produced a list. "I felt," he said, glancing coldly at Nesbitt, "that these precautions would be cheaper than a new vault."

"I move the list be introduced in evidence," Flasher said.

"Just a moment," Mason objected.

"I have a couple of questions. You say this list is not in your handwriting, Mr. Bernal?"

"Yes, sir."

"Whose handwriting is it, do you know?" Mason asked.

"The assistant cashier of the Ivanhoe National Bank."

"Oh, all right," Flasher said. "We'll do it the hard way, if we have to. Stand down, Mr. Bernal, and I'll call the assistant cashier."

Harry Reedy, assistant cashier of the Ivanhoe Bank, had the mechanical assurance of an adding machine. He identified the list of numbers as being in his handwriting. He stated that he had listed the numbers of the twenty-dollar bills and put that list in an envelope which had been sealed and sent up with the money for the payroll.

"Cross-examine," Flasher said.

Mason studied the list. "These numbers are all in your handwriting?" he asked Reedy.

"Yes, sir."

"Did you yourself compare the numbers you wrote down with the numbers on the twenty-dollar bills?"

"No, sir. I didn't personally do that. Two assistants did that. One checked the numbers as they were read off, one as I wrote them down."

"The payrolls are for approximately a hundred thousand dollars, twice each month?"

"That's right. And ever since Mr. Bernal took charge, we have taken this means to identify payrolls. No attempt is made to list the bills in numerical order. The serial numbers are simply read off and written down. Unless a robbery occurs, there is no need to do anything further. In the event of a robbery, we can reclassify the numbers and list the bills in numerical order.''

"These numbers are in your handwriting—every number?"

"Yes, sir. More than that, you will notice that at the bottom of each page I have signed my initials.''

"That's all,'' Mason said.

"I now offer once more to introduce this list in evidence,'' Flasher said.

"So ordered,'' Judge Haswell ruled.

"My next witness is Charles J. Oswald, the sheriff,'' the district attorney announced.

The sheriff, a long, lanky man with a quiet manner, took the stand. "You're acquainted with Harvey L. Corbin, the defendant in this case?'' the district attorney asked.

"I am.''

"Are you acquainted with his wife?''

"Yes, sir.''

"Now, on the morning of the fifteenth of this month, the morning of the robbery at the Jebson Commercial Company, did you have any conversation with Mrs. Corbin?''

"I did. Yes, sir.''

"Did you ask her about her husband's activities the night before?''

"Just a moment,'' Mason said. "I object to this on the ground that any conversation the sheriff had with Mrs. Corbin is not admissible against the defendant, Corbin; furthermore, that in this state a wife cannot testify against her husband. Therefore, any statement she might make would be an indirect violation of that rule. Furthermore, I object on the ground that the question calls for hearsay.''

Judge Haswell looked ponderously thoughtful, then said, "It seems to me Mr. Mason is correct.''

"I'll put it this way, Mr. Sheriff,'' the district attorney said. "Did you, on the morning of the fifteenth, take any money from Mrs. Corbin?''

"Objected to as incompetent, irrelevant, and immaterial,'' Mason said.

"Your Honor," Flasher said irritably, "that's the very gist of our case. We propose to show that two of the stolen twenty-dollar bills were in the possession of Mrs. Corbin."

Mason said, "Unless the prosecution can prove the bills were given to Mrs. Corbin by her husband, the evidence is inadmissible."

"That's just the point," Flasher said. "Those bills *were* given to her by the defendant."

"How do you know?" Mason asked.

"She told the sheriff so."

"That's hearsay," Mason snapped.

Judge Haswell fidgeted on the bench. "It seems to me we're getting into a peculiar situation here. You can't call the wife as a witness, and I don't think her statement to the sheriff is admissible."

"Well," Flasher said desperately, "in this state, Your Honor, we have a community-property law. Mrs. Corbin had this money. Since she is the wife of the defendant, it was community property. Therefore, it's partially his property."

"Well now, there," Judge Haswell said, "I think I can agree with you. You introduce the twenty-dollar bills. I'll overrule the objection made by the defense."

"Produce the twenty-dollar bills, Sheriff," Flasher said triumphantly.

The bills were produced and received in evidence.

"Cross-examine," Flasher said curtly.

"No questions of this witness," Mason said, "but I have a few questions to ask Mr. Bernal on cross-examination. You took him off the stand to lay the foundation for introducing the bank list, and I didn't have an opportunity to cross-examine him."

"I beg your pardon," Flasher said. "Resume the stand, Mr. Bernal."

His tone, now that he had the twenty-dollar bills safely introduced in evidence, had a gloating note to it.

Mason said, "This list which has been introduced in evidence is on the stationery of the Ivanhoe National Bank?"

"That's right. Yes, sir."

"It consists of several pages, and at the end there is the signature of the assistant cashier?"

"Yes, sir."

"And each page is initialed by the assistant cashier?"

"Yes, sir."

"This was the scheme which you thought of in order to safeguard the company against a payroll robbery?"

"Not to safeguard the company against a payroll robbery, Mr. Mason, but to assist us in recovering the money in the event there was a holdup."

"This was your plan to answer Mr. Nesbitt's objections that the vault was an outmoded model?"

"A part of my plan, yes. I may say that Mr. Nesbitt's objections had never been voiced until I took office. I felt he was trying to embarrass me by making my administration show less net returns than expected." Bernal tightened his lips and added, "Mr. Nesbitt had, I believe, been expecting to be appointed manager. He was disappointed. I believe he still expects to be manager."

In the spectators' section of the courtroom, Ralph Nesbitt glared at Bernal.

"You had a conversation with the defendant on the night of the fourteenth?" Mason asked Bernal.

"I did. Yes, sir."

"You told him that for reasons which you deemed sufficient you were discharging him immediately and wanted him to leave the premises at once?"

"Yes, sir. I did."

"And you paid him his wages in cash?"

"Mr. Nesbitt paid him in my presence, with money he took from the petty-cash drawer of the vault."

"Now, as part of the wages due him, wasn't Corbin given these two twenty-dollar bills which have been introduced in evidence?"

Bernal shook his head. "I had thought of that," he said, "but it would have been impossible. Those bills weren't available to us at that time. The payroll is received from the bank in a sealed package. Those two twenty-dollar bills were in that package.''

''And the list of the numbers of the twenty-dollar bills?''

''That's in a sealed envelope. The money is placed in the vault. I lock the list of numbers in my desk.''

''Are you prepared to swear that neither you nor Mr. Nesbitt had access to these two twenty-dollar bills on the night of the fourteenth?''

''That is correct.''

''That's all,'' Mason said. ''No further cross-examination.''

''I now call Ralph Nesbitt to the stand,'' District Attorney Flasher said. ''I want to fix the time of these events definitely, Your Honor.''

''Very well,'' Judge Haswell said. ''Mr. Nesbitt, come forward.''

Ralph Nesbitt, after answering the usual preliminary questions, sat down in the witness chair.

''Were you present at a conversation which took place between the defendant, Harvey L. Corbin, and Frank Bernal on the fourteenth of this month?'' the district attorney asked.

''I was. Yes, sir.''

''What time did that conversation take place?''

''About 8 o'clock in the evening.''

''And, without going into the details of that conversation, I will ask you if the general effect of it was that the defendant was discharged and ordered to leave the company's property?''

''Yes, sir.''

''And he was paid the money that was due him?''

''In cash. Yes, sir. I took the cash from the safe myself.''

''Where was the payroll then?''

''In the sealed package in a compartment in the safe. As cashier, I had the only key to that compartment. Earlier in the afternoon I had gone to Ivanhoe City and received the sealed package of money and the envelope containing the list of numbers. I personally locked the package of money in the vault.''

"And the list of numbers?"

"Mr. Bernal locked that in his desk."

"Cross-examine," Flasher said.

"No questions," Mason said.

"That's our case, Your Honor," Flasher observed.

"May we have a few minutes indulgence?" Mason asked Judge Haswell.

"Very well. Make it brief," the judge agreed.

Mason turned to Paul Drake and Della Street. "Well, there you are," Drake said. "You're confronted with the proof, Perry."

"Are you going to put the defendant on the stand?" Della Street asked.

Mason shook his head. "It would be suicidal. He has a record of a prior criminal conviction. Also, it's a rule of law that if one asks about any part of a conversation on direct examination, the other side can bring out all the conversation. That conversation, when Corbin was discharged, was to the effect that he had lied about his past record. And I guess there's no question that he did."

"And he's lying now," Drake said. "This is one case where you're licked. I think you'd better cop a plea, and see what kind of a deal you can make with Flasher."

"Probably not any," Mason said. "Flasher wants to have the reputation of having given me a licking—wait a minute, Paul. I have an idea."

Mason turned abruptly, walked away to where he could stand by himself, his back to the crowded courtroom.

"Are you ready?" the judge asked.

Mason turned. "I am quite ready, Your Honor. I have one witness whom I wish to put on the stand. I wish a subpoena *duces tecum* issued for that witness. I want him to bring certain documents which are in his possession."

"Who is the witness, and what are the documents?" the judged asked.

Mason walked quickly over to Paul Drake. "What's the

name of that character who has the garbage-collecting business," he said softly, "the one who has the first nickel he'd ever made?"

"George Addey."

The lawyer turned to the judge. "The witness that I want is George Addey, and the documents that I want him to bring to court with him are all the twenty-dollar bills that he has received during the past sixty days."

"Your Honor," Flasher protested, "this is an outrage. This is making a travesty out of justice. It is exposing the court to ridicule."

Mason said, "I give Your Honor my assurance that I think this witness is material, and that the documents are material. I will make an affidavit to that effect if necessary. As attorney for the defendant, may I point out that if the court refuses to grant this subpoena, it will be denying the defendant due process of law."

"I'm going to issue the subpoena," Judge Haswell said, testily, "and for your own good, Mr. Mason, the testimony had better be relevant."

GEORGE ADDEY, UNSHAVEN AND BRISTLING WITH INDIGNATION, held up his right hand to be sworn. He glared at Perry Mason.

"Mr. Addey," Mason said, "you have the contract to collect garbage from Jebson City?"

"I do."

"How long have you been collecting garbage there?"

"For over five years, and I want to tell you—"

Judge Haswell banged his gavel. "The witness will answer questions and not interpolate any comments."

"I'll interpolate anything I dang please," Addey said.

"That'll do," the judge said. "Do you wish to be jailed for contempt of court, Mr. Addey?"

"I don't want to go to jail, but I—"

"Then you'll remember the respect that is due the court," the judge said. "Now you sit there and answer questions. This is a court of law. You're in this court as a citizen, and I'm here as a judge, and I propose to see that the respect due to the court is enforced." There was a moment's silence while the judge glared angrily at the witness. "All right, go ahead, Mr. Mason," Judge Haswell said.

Mason said, "During the thirty days prior to the fifteenth of this month, did you deposit any money in any banking institution?"

"I did not."

"Do you have with you all the twenty-dollar bills that you received during the last sixty days?"

"I have, and I think making me bring them here is just like inviting some crook to come and rob me and—"

Judge Haswell banged with his gavel. "Any more comments of that sort from the witness and there will be a sentence imposed for contempt of court. Now you get out those twenty-dollar bills, Mr. Addey, and put them right up here on the clerk's desk."

Addey, mumbling under his breath, slammed a roll of twenty-dollar bills down on the desk in front of the clerk.

"Now," Mason said, "I'm going to need a little clerical assistance. I would like to have my secretary, Miss Street, and the clerk help me check through the numbers on these bills. I will select a few at random."

Mason picked up three of the twenty-dollar bills and said, "I am going to ask my assistants to check the list of numbers introduced in evidence. In my hand is a twenty-dollar bill that has the number L 07083274 A. Is that bill on the list? The next bill that I pick up is number L 07579190 A. Are any of those bills on the list?"

The courtroom was silent. Suddenly, Della Street said, "Yes, here's one that's on the list—bill number L 07579190 A. It's on the list, on page eight."

"What?" the prosecutor shouted.

"Exactly," Mason said, smiling. "So, if a case is to be made against a person merely because he has possession of the money that was stolen on the fifteenth of this month, then your office should prefer charges against this witness, George Addey, Mr. District Attorney."

Addey jumped from the witness stand and shook his fist in Mason's face. "You're a cockeyed liar!" he screamed. "There ain't a one of those bills but what I didn't have it before the fifteenth. The company cashier changes my money into twenties, because I like big bills. I bury 'em in cans, and I put the date on the side of the can."

"Here's the list," Mason said. "Check it for yourself."

A tense silence gripped the courtroom as the judge and the spectators waited.

"I'm afraid I don't understand this, Mr. Mason," Judge Haswell said, after a moment.

"I think it's quite simple," Mason said. "And I now suggest the court take a recess for an hour and check these other bills against this list. I think the district attorney may be surprised."

And Mason sat down and proceeded to put papers in his brief case.

DELLA STREET, PAUL DRAKE, AND PERRY MASON WERE sitting in the lobby of the Ivanhoe Hotel.

"When are you going to tell us?" Della Street asked fiercely. "Or do we tear you limb from limb? How could the garbage man have—?"

"Wait a minute," Mason said. "I think we're about to get results. Here comes the esteemed district attorney, Vernon Flasher, and he's accompanied by Judge Haswell."

The two strode over to Mason's group and bowed with cold formality.

Mason got up.

Judge Haswell began in his best courtroom voice. "A most deplorable situation has occurred. It seems that Mr. Frank Bernal has—well—"

"Been detained somewhere," Vernon Flasher said.

"Disappeared," Judge Haswell said. "He's gone."

"I expected as much," Mason said.

"Now will you kindly tell me just what sort of pressure you brought to bear on Mr. Bernal to—?"

"Just a moment, Judge," Mason said. "The only pressure I brought to bear on him was to cross-examine him."

"Did you know that there had been a mistake in the dates on those lists?"

"There was no mistake. When you find Bernal, I'm sure you will discover there was a deliberate falsification. He was short in his accounts, and he knew he was about to be demoted. He had a desperate need for a hundred thousand dollars in ready cash. He had evidently been planning this burglary, or, rather, this embezzlement, for some time. He learned that Corbin had a criminal record. He arranged to have these lists furnished by the bank. He installed a burglar alarm, and, naturally, knew how to circumvent it. He employed a watchman he knew was addicted to drink. He only needed to stage his coup at the right time. He fired Corbin and paid him off with bills that had been recorded by the bank on page eight of the list of bills *in the payroll on the first of the month*.

"Then he removed page eight from the list of bills contained in the payroll *of the fifteenth*, before he showed it to the police, and substituted page eight of the list for the *first of the month* payroll. It was that simple.

"Then he drugged the watchman's whiskey, took an acetylene torch, burned through the vault doors, and took all the money."

"May I ask how you knew all this?" Judge Haswell demanded.

"Certainly," Mason said. "My client told me he received those bills from Nesbitt, who took them from the petty-cash drawer in the safe. He also told the sheriff that. I happened to be the only one who believed him. It sometimes pays, Your Honor, to have faith in a man, even if he has made a previous mistake. Assuming my client was innocent, I knew either Bernal or Nesbitt must be guilty. I then realized that only Bernal had custody of the *previous* lists of numbers.

"As an employee, Bernal had been paid on the first of the month. He looked at the numbers on the twenty-dollar bills in his pay envelope and found that they had been listed on page eight of the payroll for the first.

"Bernal only needed to abstract all twenty-dollar bills from the petty-cash drawer, substitute twenty-dollar bills from his own pay envelope, call in Corbin, and fire him. His trap was set.

"I let him know I knew what had been done by bringing Addey into court and proving my point. Then I asked for a recess. That was so Bernal would have a chance to skip out. You see, flight may be received as evidence of guilt. It was a professional courtesy to the district attorney. It will help him when Bernal is arrested."

ROUGH JUSTICE

~

Michael Gilbert

IT WAS A FINE MORNING IN EARLY OCTOBER WHEN DE-
tective Inspector Patrick Petrella became Detective Chief
Inspector Petrella. The promotion had been expected for
some time, but it was nevertheless agreeable when a copy
of District Orders and a friendly note of congratulation
from Chief Superintendent Watterson arrived together on
Petrella's desk at Patton Street Police Station.

He had been six months in Q Division and had been
carrying out a mental stocktaking. A few successes, a lot
of routine work done without discredit, one or two un-
doubted flops. One of the worst had been his failure to
secure the conviction of Arthur Bond. If ever anyone
should have been found guilty and jailed—

"A Mr. Bond asking for you," said Constable Lampier,
projecting his untidy head of hair round the door. Lampier
was the newest, youngest, least efficient, and most cheerful
of the constables at Patton Street. Repeated orders from
Sergeant Gwilliam to smarten himself up generally and for
God's sake get his hair cut had had only a superficial effect.
Like brushing a puppy which immediately goes out and
chases a cat through a thorn bush.

"Mr. *Who*?"

"Bond. He's the geezer who keeps that garage. The one we didn't make it stick with that time—"

"All right, all right," said Petrella. "Don't let's conduct a postmortem. Just show him in."

Mr. Bond was not one of his favorite people. He had a big white face, a lower lip which turned down like the spout of a jug, and a voice which grated more when he tried to be friendly than when he was in his normal mood of oily arrogance. On this occasion he was making no attempt to be agreeable.

He said, "You've got no right to say the things you've been saying about me. I'm telling you, I'm not standing for it."

"If you'd explain what you're talking about."

"I'll explain, all right."

He opened his briefcase and threw a document onto the table. It was a photocopy, and to Petrella's astonishment it was a copy of a report he had himself written the day before.

He said, "Where on earth did you get that?"

"Never mind where I got it. You got no right to say those things."

"I do mind where you got it. And I insist on an explanation."

"If you want an explanation, ask the editor of the *Courier*."

"I certainly will ask him," said Petrella grimly, "and I hope he's got an explanation, because if he hasn't, he's going to be in trouble."

"The person who's going to be in trouble," said Mr. Bond, his lower lip quivering with some indefinable emotion, "is you. This is libelous. I've got my rights. I'm going to take this to court. You can't go around ruining people's characters. You know that."

"If you produce this document in court you realize you'll have to explain exactly how you got hold of it."

"No difficulty. The editor gave it to me."

"Then he'll have to explain."

"You don't seem to realize," snarled Mr. Bond, "it isn't him or me who's in trouble. It's you."

When he had gone Petrella telephoned Sergeant Gwilliam. He said, "Yesterday I sent a batch of confidentials by hand to Central. Find out who took them, and send him up."

Five minutes later the untidy topknot of Constable Lampier made a second appearance round his door.

"So it was you, was it?" said Petrella.

"That's right, sir."

"Then perhaps you'll explain how one of the documents got into the hands of the editor of the local paper."

"Lost the wallet, sir."

"You *lost* it?"

"Had it taken."

"Explain."

"Went up by tube. Victoria Line from Stockwell. The train was very crowded."

Petrella considered the matter. So far there was an element of plausibility in it. Junior constables on routine errands usually traveled by public transport and, as he knew himself, the Victoria Line could be crowded.

He said, "What actually happened?"

"I don't really know," said Lampier unhappily. "The car was full. I was standing near the door. I put the wallet down on the floor, by my foot. When I got to Victoria it was gone. I made a fuss, but it wasn't any use. Someone must have slid out with it the station before."

"Why didn't you report it?"

"I did, sir. That afternoon when I got back. To Sergeant Cove."

Petrella was on the point of telephoning for Sergeant Cove when he spotted the report. It was at the bottom of his In tray. He had been so pleased with reading about his own promotion that he hadn't got down to it.

THE EDITOR OF THE STOCKWELL AND CLAPHAM *COURIER* was an elderly man with a face like a bloodhound's. Petrella knew him of old as a nurser of grudges and no friend of authority. The editor said, "The papers were dropped in here by hand this morning. We get a crowd of people in and out of the front office. No one noticed this one in particular. If they're yours you'd better have them."

He pushed across a bundle of papers. Petrella picked them up and looked through them. As far as he could see they were all there. He said, "Was there a covering letter?"

"There was."

"May I see it?"

The editor hesitated. Then he said, "I don't see why not."

The letter was typewritten. It said: "Dear Editor, I picked these up in a pub in Victoria Street this afternoon. I think they might interest you, particularly the stuff about Mr. Bond."

The note was unsigned.

"These are official documents," said Petrella. "You should have sent them straight back."

"How was I to know? They're not marked 'Top Secret.' "

"They're on official paper."

"Doesn't mean a thing. Anyone can get hold of notepaper."

"If you didn't know, why didn't you ring up and find out?"

"Why should I go out of my way to help the police? What have they ever done to help me?"

It was an outlook Petrella had heard expressed before, though never quite so baldly.

"All right," he said. "I agree there was no actual obligation on your part to do anything. So why did you have one particular document copied and sent to Mr. Bond?"

"Mr. Bond happens to be a friend of mine," said the editor. "I thought he ought to know about it."

"AND THAT'S THE WHOLE STORY?" SAID COMMANDER Abel.

"That's it, sir."

"Tell me about the previous case involving Bond."

"We'd heard a lot of talk about that particular garage. People put their cars in to have a tire changed and when they came to pick up the cars found the engine taken down and half a dozen other things apparently needing to be put right. And straight overcharging for any job that was done. It's difficult to prove.

"Then we thought we had got something that would stand up. This man, Mr. Ferris, put his car in for an M.O.T. test. When he went to fetch it he got a bill for nearly one hundred pounds. The point was, he'd just had the car overhauled by a garage in Southend, where he'd been staying. A complete five-thousand-mile test. He lodged an official complaint. We had to take it up."

"But you couldn't make it stick."

"No, sir."

"Why not?"

"Bond had it all lined up. One of his mechanics gave evidence. A real old villain. Blinded the bench with science. Our Mr. Fairbrother's a good magistrate, but he's not a motorist. Invoices for spare parts, all in order. Work sheets showing time spent on the overhaul. If a car came in for a test it had to be made roadworthy, didn't it? He'd told the gentleman that. The gentleman had agreed. The job had been done. Here was the evidence all in order."

"Then what went wrong?"

"The whole thing went wrong," said Petrella slowly. "The mechanic was in it, of course. He made up his own time sheets. The spare parts were bought for cash, from car breakers though-out the Borough—the sort of people who keep no records. The invoices themselves were dirty little scraps of paper. And I fancy most of them had been altered."

While Commander Abel was considering the matter the third man present spoke. Mr. Samson was the senior legal adviser to the Metropolitan Police. He said, "I'm afraid there's no doubt about it. If Bond starts an action for libel, you've got something to answer.''

''But surely,'' said Abel, ''a report like this is privileged.''

''Qualified privilege.''

''What does that mean?''

''It can be set aside by proof of malice.''

''And just how would they prove that?''

''They'd say that this officer was so annoyed about Bond getting off last time that he made entirely unjustified allegations against him in a report. If the report had never gone outside Scotland Yard, it wouldn't have mattered. But it did. It was published to third parties.''

''That's something that wants looking into too,'' said Abel grimly.

''YOU'RE SURE YOU DID HAVE THAT BAG STOLEN?'' SAID Petrella.

''Dead-sure, sir,'' said Lampier. ''It happened just like I told you.''

''You didn't leave it in a pub in Victoria Street?''

''Certainly not, sir.''

Petrella examined the untidy young man critically. It was a long time since he had walked a beat himself. He tried to think himself back to those days. Lampier would have got to Victoria Station at about one o'clock. He probably hadn't had any lunch before he started. Would he have stopped at a pub for a drink and a sandwich? It was perfectly possible. Was Lampier a liar? That was possible too. Was it any use pressing him further? Petrella thought not. There came a moment when policemen had to believe one another.

Petrella said, ''That's all right, Lampier. I just wanted to be clear about it.''

Lampier, as he was going, stopped for a moment by the door and said, ''Is anyone going to make trouble, sir, about that paper?''

''If they do, we'll get over it,'' said Petrella.

He managed to say it confidently, but it was a confidence he was far from feeling.

THE NEXT THREE MONTHS WERE NOT PLEASANT. ROUTINE work continued. No one said anything. Even the Stockwell and Clapham *Courier* was muted. There was a brief paragraph to the effect that a local businessman, a Mr. Bond, had issued a writ claiming damages against a police officer.

Petrella had two more conferences with the legal Mr. Samson and could feel lapping around him, like the serpents about Laocoon, the strangling coils of the law. He knew enough about the processes of the civil courts to realize that no public servant came entirely clean out of that particular mud bath.

It was toward the end of the third conference that something really alarming occurred. He began to detect, in the measured utterances of the lawyer, a suggestion that the matter might be settled out of court—a payment to solace Mr. Bond's wounded feelings and an apology in open court.

"My client wishes it to be understood that there is no truth whatever in the statements made about the plaintiff. The plaintiff is a man of excellent character." Like hell he was! Bond was a crook. A successful crook, but a crook nonetheless. The thought of crawling to him made Petrella wince.

"We're in a cleft stick," said Mr. Samson. "If we plead fair comment, we've got to show that what you said was fair. And that really means proving the charges against Bond, which was something you couldn't do in court, and certainly couldn't do now. We can run the defense of qualified privilege, but that lets them bring in all the arguments that you were prejudiced against Bond, that you didn't like him, and were angry that he'd got off."

"Which is true," said Petrella. "But it wasn't my reason for writing the report."

"If you're as candid as that when you give evidence," said Mr. Samson drily, "the case is lost before we begin."

• • •

IT WAS A FEW DAYS AFTER THIS UNHAPPY INTERVIEW THAT Constable Lampier brought Nurse Fearing to see Petrella. She was a middle-aged woman with an air of professional competence about her that was explained when he recognized her as the most senior and respected of the local District Nurses. She said, "I rely on my little car, Inspector. If it goes wrong it has to be put right. I've been driving for forty years. I know a lot about cars, and I know that this garage swindled me. The man must be brought to book."

Petrella listened, fascinated. A lifetime of dealing with nervous young mothers and panic-stricken young fathers had endowed her with a calm authority which brooked no argument. He said, "It isn't going to be at all easy, Mrs. Fearing. I hardly think you realize just how awkward it is."

"I've heard about the other case," said Nurse Fearing. "And all the lies this man, Bond, told. How anyone could get up in court and say things like that passes my comprehension, but then, I'm old-fashioned."

"All the same—" said Petrella. And this was all he did manage to say. For the next ten minutes it was Nurse Fearing who did the talking.

"I CAN'T STOP YOU," SAID CHIEF SUPERINTENDENT WATterson. He sounded worried. "A member of the public has made a complaint. We're bound to follow it up. There's *prima facie* evidence. But I need hardly tell you—"

"That's all right," said Petrella. "I understand the position. If we lose this one we're sunk. Another unsuccessful prosecution. Further proof that I'm prejudiced. Right?"

"If you don't get home this time," said Watterson, "we shall have to settle the libel case on their terms. And that won't do your prospects any good at all."

"You're understating the case," said Petrella. "I won't have any prospects left."

"Are you going to handle it yourself?"

"I may be foolish, but I'm not that foolish. I'm getting Mr. Tasker to handle it."

Mr. Tasker was a local solicitor who did a lot of police-court work, appearing both for and against the police.

"Tasker's good," said Watterson. "But he can't fight unless you give him some ammunition."

"We shall do our best," said Petrella.

He sounded, thought Watterson, unaccountably cheerful for a man who has placed his own head on the block.

COUNSEL FOR THE DEFENSE SAID, "I ONLY PROPOSE TO call one more witness, sir. You have heard Mr. Bond and seen the documents he produced. In the ordinary way I should have submitted that this evidence was conclusive. The solicitor appearing for the police challenged it—"

Mr. Tasker smiled blandly.

"—but was quite unable to shake it. Mr. Bond told us that he himself had purchased the new distributor—"

"Not new, reconditioned," said Mr. Tasker without troubling to get up.

"I beg your pardon," said Counsel with elaborate politeness, but a slight flush of annoyance. "I should have said the reconditioned distributor and the new set of points. He also supervised the work, which was actually carried out by his mechanic, whom I am now calling. If he corroborates the evidence already given, I think you will agree that this effectively disposes of the charges which the police"—here Counsel swiveled round and stared at Petrella who was seated beside Mr. Tasker—"the police have seen fit to bring for the second time in three months against my client. I hesitate to use the word persecution, but in the circumstances—"

"I think we'd better hear your witness first," said the magistrate mildly.

"If you please. Call Mr. Ardingly. Now, Mr. Ardingly, I will ask you if you recall effecting certain repairs to an Austin 1100 motorcar on December 28 of last year—"

Mr. Ardingly, who looked about 17, had blue eyes, curly hair, and a shy smile, said he certainly remembered fixing a distributor to the car in question. Yes, he had done the work himself. Yes, he had filled in the time sheets which were shown to him. Yes, that was his signature at the bottom. After about five minutes Counsel sat down with a satisfied smile.

Mr. Tasker rose slowly to his feet. He said, "Mr. Ardingly, this time sheet shows a record of six hours of work on this motorcar on December 28 and an additional three hours on December 29. Did you actually do that amount of work?"

"Nine hours to put on a new distributor," said Mr. Ardingly in tones of surprise. "Not likely."

"Then if it didn't take you nine hours," said Mr. Tasker with a look at Mr. Bond, whose white face had turned even whiter, "why did you put down that number of hours on the sheet?"

"I put down what the guv'nor told me to put down."

"It's a lie," screamed Mr. Bond, leaping up.

"I must ask you to warn your client to behave himself," said the magistrate. "If he does not do so, I will have him taken out of the court and held in custody."

Mr. Bond subsided slowly.

"Now, Mr. Ardingly," said Mr. Tasker. "About the distributor. The reconditioned distributor, which Mr. Bond has told us he purchased from Acme Spares—"

"That's quite right. I went and fetched it for him myself. I slipped them a quid."

"One pound!" said Mr. Tasker in beautifully simulated surprise, peering at the paper he held in his hand. "But this invoice for the distributor is for twelve pounds and fifty pence."

"You know how it is," said Mr. Ardingly with an engaging smile. "They always add on a bit."

"Very satisfactory," said Superintendent Watterson grimly. "Guilty as charged. Papers sent to the Director of Public Prosecutions. Charges of perjury pending against Bond. He can hardly continue his libel action against you. Would you mind explaining how you fixed it?"

"Fixed it?" said Petrella.

"You're not in court now. The truth, the whole truth, and nothing but the truth. How much did you pay Ardingly?"

Petrella looked genuinely shocked. "I should never have dreamed of doing such a thing. Besides, it was quite unnecessary. The boy loathed Bond. He's a nasty old man, and had already made a pass at him."

"And how did you find that out?"

"He's Constable Lampier's cousin."

"I see," said Watterson. As, indeed, he was beginning to do. "No relation of Nurse Fearing, I suppose."

"He was one of her babies."

"Quite a coincidence."

"Not really. She's delivered half of the Borough in her time."

"I suppose there's a moral to it."

"The moral," said Petrella smugly, "is always trust your own staff."

INTERROGATION

⌇⌇⌇

Jeffery Deaver

"HE'S IN THE LAST ROOM."

The man nodded to the sergeant and continued down the long corridor, grit underfoot. The walls were yellow cinder block, but the hallway reminded him of an old English prison, bricky and sootwashed.

As he approached the room, he heard a bell somewhere nearby, a delicate ringing. He used to come here regularly but hadn't been in this portion of the building for months. The sound wasn't familiar, and despite the cheerful jingling, it was oddly unsettling.

He was halfway down the hallway when the sergeant called, "Captain?"

He turned.

"That was a good job you guys did. Getting him, I mean."

Boyle, a thick file under his arm, nodded and continued down the windowless corridor to Room I-7.

What he saw through the square window: a benign-looking man of about forty, not big, not small, thick hair shot with gray. His amused eyes were on the wall, also cinder block. His slippered feet were chained, his hands, too, the silvery links looped through a waist bracelet.

Boyle unlocked and opened the door. The man grinned, looked the detective over.

"Hello, James," Boyle said.

After a lengthy pause the prisoner said, "So you're him."

Boyle looked at the lean face, with a one-or two-days' growth of salt-and-pepper beard, the eyes blue as Delft china. The detective had been tracking down and putting away murderers for nineteen years. He saw in James Kit Phelan's face what he always saw in such men and women at times like this. Insolence, anger, pride, fear.

But something was missing, Boyle decided. What? Yeah, that was it. Behind the eyes of most prisoners sitting in interrogation rooms was a pool of bewilderment. In James Phelan this was absent.

Boyle dropped the file on the table. Flipped through it quickly.

"You're the one," Phelan muttered. "The one finally got me."

"Oh, I don't deserve all the credit, James. We had a lotta folks out looking for you."

"But the word is they wouldn't've kept going you hadn't been riding their tails. No sleep for your boys and girls's what I heard."

Boyle, a captain and the head of Homicide, had overseen the Granville Park murder task force of five men and women working full time—and dozens of others working part time (though everyone seemed to have logged at least ten, twelve hours a day). Still, Boyle hadn't testified in court, had never had a conversation with Phelan before to-day, never seen him up close. He expected to find the man looking very ordinary. Boyle was surprised to see another quality in the blue eyes. Something indescribable. There'd been no trace of this in the confession tape. What was it?

Before Boyle could nail down what he sensed, James Phelan's eyes grew enigmatic once again as he studied the detective's sports clothes. Jeans, Nikes, a purple Izod shirt. Phelan wore an orange jumpsuit.

Anyway, what it was, I killed her.

"That's a one-way mirror, ain't it?"

"Yes."

"Who's behind there?" The man peered at the dim mirror, never once, Boyle noticed, glancing at his own reflection.

"We sometimes bring witnesses in to check out suspects. But there's nobody there now. Don't need 'em, do we?"

Phelan sat back in the blue fiberglass chair. Boyle opened his notebook, took out a Bic pen. Boyle outweighed the prisoner by forty pounds, most of it muscle, and Phelan's shackles were short-linked to keep his hands and legs close to his body. Still, Boyle set the pen far out of the man's reach.

Anyway, what it was . . .

"I've been asking to see you for almost a month," Boyle said amiably. "You haven't agreed to a meeting until now."

Sentencing was on Monday, and after the judge pronounced one of the two sentences he was deciding upon at this very moment—life imprisonment or death by lethal injection—James Kit Phelan would be permanently giving up the county's hospitality for the state's.

" 'Meeting,' " Phelan repeated. He seemed amused. "Wouldn't 'interrogation' be more like it? That's whatcha got in mind, right?"

"You've confessed, James. Why would I want to interrogate you?"

"Dunno. Why'd you put in, let's see, was it something like a dozen phone calls to my lawyer over the past coupla months wanting to 'meet' with me?"

"Just some loose ends on the case. Nothing important."

In fact, Boyle struggled to keep his excitement hidden. He'd despaired of ever having a chance to talk to Boyle face to face; the longer the captain's requests had gone unanswered, the more he brooded that he'd never learn what he was desperate to know. Today was Saturday, and only an hour ago he'd been packing up turkey sandwiches for a picnic with the family when the phone had rung with a call from Phelan's lawyer. He'd sent Judith and the kids on ahead and sped to the county lockup at ninety miles per hour.

Nothing important . . .

"I didn't want to see you 'fore this," Phelan said slowly, " 'cause I was thinking maybe you just wanted to, you know, gloat."

Boyle shook his head goodnaturedly. But he also admitted to himself that he certainly had something to gloat about. When there'd been no arrest immediately following the murder, the case had quickly turned sour, and it had turned personal. Chief of Homicide Boyle versus the elusive, unknown killer. The contest between the two adversaries escalated, became a raging battle. First in the tabloids, then in the police department and—finally, insidiously—in Boyle's mind. Still taped up behind his desk was the front page of the *Post*, which showed a picture of dark-haired, swarthy Boyle glaring at the camera from the right-hand side of the paper while the artist's composite of Anna Devereaux's killer gazed outward from the left. The two pieces of art were separated by a bold, black VS., and the detective's was by far the scarier image.

Boyle remembered the press conference held six months to the day after the murder in which he promised the people of the town of Granville that, though the investigation had bogged down, the police weren't giving up hope and that the killer would be caught. Boyle had concluded, "That man is *not* getting away. There's only one way this's going to end. Not in a draw. In a checkmate." The comment—which a few months later became an embarrassing reminder of his failure—had, at last, been validated. The headline of every newspaper story about Phelan's arrest read, of course, *CHECKMATE!*

There was a time when Boyle would have taken the high ground and sneered down the suggestion that he was gloating over a fallen enemy. But now he wondered. Phelan had for no apparent reason killed a defenseless woman and had eluded the police for almost a year. It had been the hardest case Boyle had ever run, and he'd despaired many times of ever finding the perp. But by God, he'd finally won. Yes, yes, maybe there was a part of him that had come here today for the purpose of gazing down at his trophy.

. . . I killed her. . . . And there's nothing else I have to say.

"I just have a few questions to ask you," Boyle said. "Do you mind?"

"Talking about it? Guess not. It's kinda boring, though, you ask me. Ain't that the truth about the past? Boring."

"Sometimes."

"That's not much of an answer. The past. Is. Boring. Hey, you ever shot anybody?"

Boyle had. Twice. And killed them both. "We're here to talk about you."

"I'm here 'cause I got caught. *You're* here to talk about me."

Phelan slouched in the chair. The chains clinked softly. It reminded him of the bell he'd heard when he entered the interrogation room corridor.

Boyle looked down at the open file.

"So what do you want to know?" Phelan asked.

"Only one thing," Boyle said, caressing the battered manila folder. "Why'd you kill her?"

" 'WHY?' " PHELAN REPEATED SLOWLY. "YEAH, EVERY-body asked me about the motive. Now, motive's a big word. A ten dollar word, my father'd say. But 'why?' That cuts right to the chase."

"And the answer is?"

"Why's it so important?"

It wasn't. Not legally. You only need to establish motive if the case is going to trial or if the confession is uncorroborated or unsupported by physical evidence. But it had been Phelan's fingerprints that were found at the crime scene, and the DNA testing verified that Phelan's skin was the tissue dug from beneath Anna Devereaux's perfect dusty-rose polished fingernails. The judge accepted the confession without any state presentation of motive, though even he had suggested to the prisoner that he have the decency to explain why he'd committed this terrible crime. Phelan had remained silent, unemotional, and let the judge read him the guilty verdict.

"We just want to complete the report," Boyle said casually.

" 'Complete the report,' " Phelan mocked. "If that ain't some bureaucratic crap, I don't know what is."

In fact Boyle wanted the answer for a personal, not professional, reason. So he could get some sleep. The mystery of why this drifter and petty criminal had killed the thirty-six-year-old wife and mother had been growing in his mind like a deadly tumor. In the past week alone—when it looked like Phelan was going down to Katona maximum security without ever agreeing to meet Boyle—the captain had wakened abruptly three times, sweating, plagued by what he called Phelanmares. The dreams had nothing to do with Anna Devereaux's murder; they were a series of gut-wrenching scenes in which the prisoner was whispering something to Boyle, words that the detective was desperate to hear but could not.

"Makes no difference in the world to us or you at this point," Boyle said evenly. "But we just want to know."

" 'We?' " the prisoner asked coyly, and Boyle felt he'd been caught at something. Phelan continued, "Suppose you folks have some theories."

"Not really."

"No?"

Phelan swung the chain against the table and kept looking the captain over. Boyle was uncomfortable. Prisoners swore at him all the time. Occasionally they spit at him, and some even attacked him. But Phelan just had that curious expression on his face—what the hell did it mean?—and adjusted his smile. He kept studying Boyle.

"That's a weird sound, ain't it, captain? The chain. Hey, you like horror films?"

"Some. Not the gory ones."

Three ringing taps. Phelan laughed. "Good sound effects for a Stephen King movie, don'tcha think? Or Clive Barker. Chains at night."

"How 'bout if we go through the facts again? What happened. Might refresh your memory."

"You mean my confession? Why not? Haven't seen it since the trial."

"I don't have the video. How 'bout if I just read the transcript?"

"I'm all ears."

"ON SEPTEMBER THIRTEENTH YOU WERE IN THE TOWN OF Granville. You were riding a stolen Honda Nighthawk motorcycle."

"That's about right."

Boyle lowered his head and in his best jury-pleasing baritone read from the transcript, " 'I was riding around just, you know, seeing what was there. And I heard they had this fair or festival or something, and I kept hearing this music when I cut back the throttle. And I followed it to this park in the middle of town.

" 'There was pony rides and all kinds of food and crafts and stuff like that. Okay, so I park the bike and go looking at what they got. Only it was boring, so I walked off along this little river, and before I went too far, it went into this forest and I seen a flash of white or color or something, I don't remember what. And I went closer, and there was this woman sitting on a log, looking at the river. I remembered her from town. She worked in some charity store downtown. You know, where they donate stuff and sell it and the money goes to a hospital or something. I thought her name was Anne or Annie or Anna or something.' "

Anna Devereaux. . . .

" 'She was having a cigarette, like she'd snuck off to have one, like she'd promised everybody she wasn't going to but had to have one. The first thing she did when she heard me come up was drop the cigarette on the ground and crush it out. Without even looking at me first. Then she did and looked pretty freaked. I go, "Hey." She nodded and said something I couldn't hear and looked at her watch, like she had someplace she really had to be. Right. She started to walk away. And when she passed me, I hit her hard in the neck, and she fell down. Then I sat on her and grabbed this scarf she was wearing and pulled it real tight and I squeezed until she stopped moving, then I still kept squeezing. The cloth felt good on my wrists. I got off her, found the cigarette. It was still burning. I finished it and walked back to the fair. I got a snow cone. It was cherry. And got on my bike and left.

" 'Anyway, what it is, I killed her. I took that pretty blue scarf in my hands and killed her with it. And there's nothing else I have to say.' "

Boyle'd heard similar words hundreds of times. He now felt something he hadn't for years. An icy shiver down his spine.

"So that's about it, James?"

"Yeah. That's all true. Every word."

"You know," Boyle began, "I've been through the confession with a magnifying glass, I've been through your statements to the detectives, I watched the interview, the one you did with that TV reporter . . ."

"She was a fox."

"But you never said a word about motive."

The ringing again. The waist chain, swinging like a pendulum against the metal table leg.

"Why'd you kill her, James?" Boyle whispered.

Phelan shook his head. "I don't exactly . . . it's all muddy."

"You must've thought about it some."

Phelan laughed. "Hell, I thought about it tons. I spent days talking it over with . . ." He stopped talking abruptly.

"Who?"

"Just this friend. Nobody—"

"Who was he?" Boyle asked quickly. His detective instinct had taken over and was trying to run to ground an escaping fact.

"Didn't have nothing to do with what happened."

"He harbored you." Boyle fell into cop-speak before he reminded himself to be more conversational.

"Just a guy. He's a biker. He put me up for a few months."

Boyle knew he'd never get the name. He was afraid Phelan would stonewall if pushed. He let it go.

Phelan continued, "Anyway, what it was, him and me, we'd pass a bottle around and spend days talking 'bout it. See, he's a tough son of a bitch. He's hurt people in his day. But it was always 'cause they crossed him. Or for money. Or something like that. He couldn't figure out why I'd just up and kill that lady."

"Well?"

"We didn't come up with no answers. I'm just telling you that it ain't like I didn't think about it."

"So you drink some, do you, James?"

"Yeah. But I wasn't drinking that day. Nothing but lemonade."

"How well did you know her? Anna Devereaux?"

"Know her? I didn't know her."

"I thought you said you did." Boyle looked down at the confession.

"I said I'd *seen* her. Same as I seen the pope on TV one time. And Julia Roberts in the movies. And I've seen as much of Sheri Starr the porn queen as there is to see, but that don't mean I know her. Or the pope either."

"She had a husband."

"I heard."

The ringing again. It wasn't the chains. The sound came from outside. The bell he'd heard when he first entered the interrogation room corridor. Boyle frowned.

Phelan was watching him, a bemused smile on his face. "That there's the coffee-break cart, captain. Comes around every morning and afternoon."

"It's new."

"Started about a month ago. When they closed the cafeteria."

Boyle nodded, looked down at his blank notebook. He didn't know they'd closed the cafeteria. He said, "They'd talked about getting divorced. Anna and her husband."

"What's his name?" Phelan asked. "The husband? He that gray-haired guy sitting in the back of the courtroom?"

"He's a gray-haired, yes. His name's Bob."

The victim's husband was known to everyone as Robert. Boyle hoped that Phelan would somehow stumble over the name difference and give something away.

"So you're thinking he hired me to kill her."

"Did he?"

Phelan grunted. "Nope."

The cloth felt good on my wrists. . . .

Robert Devereaux had seemed to the interrogating detectives to be the model of a grieving husband. He'd passed a voluntary lie detector test, and it didn't seem very likely that he'd had his wife murdered for a fifty thousand dollar insurance policy.

Anna Devereaux. Thirty-six. Well liked in the town. Wife and mother.

A woman losing the battle to quit smoking.

I took that pretty blue scarf in my hands and killed her with it. And there's nothing else I have to say.

An old scar on her neck—from a cut when she was seventeen; she often wore scarves to conceal it. The day she'd been killed last September, the scarf she'd worn had been a silk Christian Dior, and the shade of blue was described in the police report as aquamarine.

"She was a goodlooking woman, wasn't she?" Boyle asked.

"I don't remember."

The most recent photos of Anna Devereaux that these two men had seen had been in the courtroom. Her eyes were open, frosted with death, and her long-nailed hand was held outward in a plea for mercy. Even in those pictures you could see how beautiful she was.

"I didn't fool around with her, if that's what you're getting at. Or even want to."

The profiling came back negative for lust-driven killing. Phelan had had normal heterosexual responses to the Rorschach and free association tests.

"I'm just thinking out loud, James. You were walking through the forest?"

"That day I killed her? I got bored with the fair and just started walking. I ended up in the forest."

"And there she was, just sitting there, smoking."

"Uh-huh," Phelan responded patiently.

"What did she say to you?"

"I said, 'Hey.' And she said something I couldn't hear. You read that."

"What else happened?"

"Nothing. That was it."

"Maybe you were mad 'cause you didn't like her muttering at you."

"I didn't care. Why'd I care about that?"

"I've heard you say a couple of times the thing you hate most is being bored."

Phelan looked at the cinder block. He seemed to be counting. "Yeah. I don't like to be bored."

"How much?" Boyle asked, "do you hate it?" He gave a laugh. "On a scale of one to—"

"Hell, people don't kill 'causa hate. Oh, they *think* about killing who they hate, they *talk* about it. But they only kill one kinda person—folks they're scared of." Phelan chuckled softly. "Whatta *you* hate, detective? Ponder it for a minute. Lotta things, I'll bet. But you wouldn't kill anyone 'causa that. Would you?"

"She had some jewelry on her."

"That's a question?"

"Did you rob her? And kill her when she wouldn't give you her wedding and engagement rings?"

"If she was getting divorced, why wouldn't she give me her rings?"

Homicide had discounted robbery as a motive immediately. Anna Devereaux's purse, eight feet from her body, had contained eleven credit cards and a hundred eighty dollars in cash.

Boyle picked up the manila folder, read some more, dropped it on the tabletop.

Why . . .

It seemed appropriate that the operative word when it came to James Kit Phelan's life would be a question. Why had he killed Anna Devereaux? Why had he committed the other crimes he'd been arrested for? Many of them gratuitous. Never murder, but dozens of assaults. Drunk-and-disorderlies. A kidnapping that got knocked down to an aggravated assault. And who exactly *was* James Kit Phelan? He'd never talked about his past. Even the *Current Affair* story had managed to track down only a few former cellmates of Phelan's for on-camera interviews. No relatives, no friends, no exwives, no high school teachers or bosses.

Boyle asked, "James, what I hear you saying is, you yourself don't have the faintest idea why you killed her."

Phelan pressed his wrists together and swung the chain so that it rang against the table again. "Maybe it's something in my mind," he said after some reflection.

They'd given him the standard battery of tests and found nothing particularly illuminating, and the department shrink concluded that "the prisoner presents with a fairly strong tendency to act out what are classic antisocial proclivities"—a diagnosis Boyle had responded to by saying, "Thanks, doc, his rap sheet says the same thing. Only in English."

"You know," Phelan continued slowly, "I sometimes feel something gets outta control in me." His pale lids closed over the blue eyes, and Boyle imagined for a moment that the crescents of flesh were translucent and that the eyes continued to peer out into the small room.

"How do you mean, James?" The captain felt his heart-rate increase. Wondered: are we really closing in on the key to the county's perp of the decade?

"Some of it might have to do with my family. There was a lotta crap when I was growing up."

"How bad?"

"Really bad. My papa did time. Theft, domestics, drunk-and-disorderlies. Things like that. He'd beat me a lot. Him and my mother were supposedly this great couple at first. Really in love. That's what I heard, but that's not what it looked like to me. You married, captain?" Phelan glanced at his left hand. There was no band. He never wore one; as a rule Boyle tried to keep his personal life separate from the office.

"I am, yes."

"How long?"

"Twenty years."

"Man," Phelan laughed. "Long time."

"I met Judith when I was in the academy."

"See, after my mother was gone, Papa never had any-body in his life for more'n a year. Part of it was he couldn't never keep a job. We moved all the time. I mean, we lived in twenty states, easy. You don't transfer round much in your line of work, bet."

"Lived three miles from here, in Marymount, going on twenty-one years."

"I've been through there. Pretty place. I lived in plenty of small towns. It was tough. School was the worst. New kid in class. I always got the crap beat out of me. Hey, that'd be one advantage, having a old man who's a cop. Nobody'd pick on you."

Boyle said, "That may be true, but there's another problem. I've got my share of enemies, you can imagine. So we keep moving the kids from one school to another. Try to keep 'em out of public schools."

"You send 'em to private?"

"We're Catholic. They're in a parochial school."

"That one in Granville? That place looks like a college campus. Must set you back some. Man."

"No, they're up in Edgemont. It's smaller, but it still costs a bundle. You ever have kids?"

Phelan put on a tough facade. They were getting close to something. Boyle could sense it.

"In a way."

Encourage him. Gentle, gentle.

"How's that, James?"

"My mother died when I was ten."

"I'm sorry."

"I had two little sisters. Twins. They were four years younger'n me. I pretty much had to take care of them. Papa, he ran around a lot, like I was saying. I sorta learned what it was like to be a father by the time I was twelve."

Boyle nodded. He'd been thirty-six when Jon was born. He still wasn't sure he knew what it was like to be a father. When he told Phelan this, the prisoner laughed. "How old're your kids?"

"Jonathan, he's ten. Alice is nine."

Phelan suddenly grew somber. The chains clinked.

"See, the twins, they were always *wanting* something from me. Toys, my time, my attention, help 'em read this, what does this mean? . . . Jesus."

Boyle noted the anger on the face. Keep going, he urged silently. He didn't write any notes, afraid he might break the man's concentration.

"Man, it damn near drove me nuts. And I had to do it all by myself," Phelan spat out. "Papa was always on a date—well, he called 'em dates—or was passed out drunk." He looked up quickly. "Hell, you don't know what I'm talking about, do you?"

Boyle was stung by the sudden coldness in the prisoner's voice.

"I sure do," the captain said sincerely. "Judith works. A lotta times I end up with the kids. I love them and everything—just like you loved your sisters, I'm sure—but, man, it takes a lot out of you."

Phelan drifted away for a moment. Eyes as glazed as Anna Devereaux's. "Your wife works, does she? My mother wanted to work, too. Papa wouldn't let her."

He calls his father "papa" but his mother by the more formal name. What do I make of that?

"They fought about it all the time. Once he broke her jaw when he found her looking through the want ads."

And when she passed me, I hit her hard in the neck, and she fell down.

"What's your wife do?" Phelan asked.

"She's a nurse. At St. Mary's."

"That's a good job," Phelan said. "My mother liked people, liked to help them. She'da been a good nurse." His face grew dark again. "I think about all those times Papa hit her . . . That's what started her taking pills and stuff. And she never stopped taking 'em. Until she died."

He leaned forward and whispered, "But you know the worst thing?"

"What, James? Tell me."

"See, sometimes I get this feeling . . . I sorta blame it all on my mother. If she hadn't whined so much about getting a job, if she'd just been happy staying home . . . stayed home with me and the girls, then Papa wouldn't've had to hit her."

Then I sat on her and grabbed this scarf she was wearing and pulled it real tight and I squeezed until she stopped moving, then I still kept squeezing.

"And she wouldn't've started drinking and taking those pills and she'd still be here." He choked. "I sometimes feel good thinking about him hitting her."

The cloth felt good on my wrists.

He blew a long stream of air from his lungs. "Ain't a pretty thing to say, is it?"

"Life ain't pretty sometimes, James."

Phelan looked up at the ceiling and seemed to be counting acoustical tiles. "Hell, I don't even know why I'm bringing all this up. It just kinda . . . was there. What was going through my mind." He began to say something else but fell silent. Boyle didn't dare interrupt. When the prisoner spoke again, he was more cheerful. "You do things with your family, captain? That's something I think was the hardest of all. We never did a single damn thing together. Never took a vacation, never went to a ball game.''

"If I wasn't talking to you here right now, I'd be with them on a picnic.''

"Yeah?''

Boyle worried for a moment that Phelan would be jealous of his family life. But the prisoner's eyes lit up. "That's nice, captain. I always pictured us—my mother and Papa, when he wasn't drinking, and the twins. We'd be out, doing just what you're talking about. Having a picnic in some town square, a park, sitting in front of the bandshell, you know.''

I kept hearing this music when I cut back the throttle. And I followed it to this park in the middle of town.

"That what you and your family were going to do?''

"Well, we're unsocial types,'' Boyle admitted, laughing. "We stay away from crowds. My parents've got a place upstate.''

"A family house?'' Phelan asked slowly, maybe picturing it. "What's it like?''

"A little shack really. On Taconic Lake. We share it with my brother and his wife. And Mom and Dad, of course.''

The prisoner fell silent for some moments, then finally said, "You know, captain, I've got this weird idea.'' His eyes counted cinder blocks. "We have all this knowledge in our heads. Everything people ever knew. Or'll know in the future. Like how to kill a mastodon or how to make an atom-powered spaceship or how to talk in a different language. It's all there in everybody's mind. Only they have to find it.''

What's he saying? Boyle wondered. That I know why he killed Anna Devereaux?

"And how you find all this stuff is you sit real quiet and then the thought comes into your head. Just bang, there it is. Does that ever happen to you?''

Boyle didn't know what to say. But Phelan didn't seem to expect an answer.

Outside, in the corridor, footsteps approached, then receded.

Anyway, what it is, I killed her. I took that pretty blue scarf in my hands . . .

Phelan sighed. "It's not that I was trying to keep anything from you all. I just can't really give you the kinda answer you want."

Boyle closed the notebook. "That's all right, James. You've told me plenty. I appreciate it."

I took that pretty blue scarf in my hands and killed her with it. And there's nothing else I have to say.

"GOT IT," BOYLE ANNOUNCED INTO THE PHONE. He stood in the dim corridor between the lockup and the interrogation rooms.

"All right!" the district attorney said from the other end of the line. Most of the senior prosecutors had known that Boyle was going to conduct the final interrogation of James Phelan and were waiting anxiously to find out why he'd killed Anna Devereaux. It had become *the* question in the prosecutor's department. Boyle had even heard rumors that some guys were running a macabre pool, laying serious money on the answer.

"It's complicated," Boyle continued. "I think what happened was we didn't do enough psychological testing. It's got to do with his mother's death."

"Phelan's mother?"

"Yeah. He's got a thing about families. He's mad because his mother abandoned him by dying when he was ten and he had to raise his sisters."

"What?"

"I know, it sounds like psychobabble. But it all fits. Call Dr. Hirschorn. Have him—"

"Boyle, Phelan's parents are still alive. Both of 'em." Silence.

"Boyle? You there?"

After a moment: "Keep going."

"And he was an only child. He didn't have any sisters."

Boyle absently pressed his thumb on the chrome number plate of the phone, leaving a fat swirl of fingerprint on the cold metal.

"Boyle?"

Why would Phelan lie? Was this all just a big joke? He replayed the events in his mind. I ask a dozen times to see him. He refuses until just before he's sentenced. He finally agrees. But why?

Why? . . .

Boyle bolted upright, his solid shoulder slamming into the side of the phone kiosk. Then in despair lifted his left hand to his face and closed his eyes. He realized he'd just given Phelan the name of every member of his family. Where Judith worked, where the kids went to school.

Hell, he'd told them where they were right now. Alone, on their way to Taconic Lake.

Wait, calm down. He's locked up. He can't do anything to anybody. He's not getting out—

Oh no . . .

Boyle's gut ran cold.

Phelan's friend. The biker. Boyle had wondered why Phelan had mentioned him. It seemed like a stupid slip at the time, but he realized now that the reference was calculated. He wanted to get the message to Boyle that Phelan knew someone capable of hurting people for money.

"Hey, Boyle, what the hell's going on?"

The captain stared at his distorted reflection in the chrome number pad, realizing at last the enormity of what had happened. It was all a setup. *My mother . . . Papa.* Phelan's emotional confession about his family. Why, Phelan'd been planning it for months. It was why he'd held out saying anything about the motive, to draw Boyle in close, to get the information out of him and to deliver the message that his family was in danger.

The sound of chains at night . . .

You like horror stories, captain?

The answer to why James Phelan killed Anna Devereaux

meant nothing. The question itself was the murderer's last weapon.

He shouted into the phone, "What're Phelan's phone privileges?"

"What?"

"Tell me!" the captain roared.

"Jesus, Boyle. He's got an absolute right to talk to his lawyer. He—"

"Can we stop him?"

"No way. That'd be a due process issue. The appeal'll be pending for months. Years, if the judge okays the injection."

Hell, Phelan could say he was calling the lawyer and make a one minute call to his biker friend, waiting at a pay phone someplace at a prearranged time. He could—

A jingle nearby.

Boyle glanced around, expecting to see the coffee-break cart wheeling toward the guards' locker room. He saw instead James Phelan, flanked by two guards, hanging up a phone in a kiosk across the hall. The ringing was from his wrist chains as they clinked together. The guards led him back toward the lockup.

Boyle slammed the phone down and, when he got a dial tone, punched in a number. The phone at the lake house began to ring. Five times, six. No one answered.

Boyle watched James Phelan walk into the lockup area as behind him the glass door swung shut with a loud click. Suddenly the prisoner stopped and turned. He looked right at Boyle and mouthed something. The captain couldn't hear through the bulletproof glass, but he knew without a doubt that the man had just uttered the word, "Checkmate."

Boyle lowered his head to the receiver and, as if he were praying, whispered, "Answer, please answer," while, far away, the phone rang again and again and again.

STAR PUPIL

〰

Doug Allyn

"PASSION," I SAID QUIETLY, "IS THE SOURCE OF TRUE literary power. Your own feelings, honestly described, can transform the simplest story into prose with tremendous emotional impact. It can give your writing—" I hesitated. Someone was sobbing at the back of the classroom. An oversized Chicano kid, twentyish, clad in faded dungarees like the rest of them, tears streaming down his stubbled cheeks. A new student this term. Martinez? Something like that.

"It can give your work value," I continued, "even before your writing skills develop. If you can express your emotions clearly, you can—" Some of the students in the front row were getting edgy, shifting around to see what the fuss was about. I decided to press on, to give the guy a chance to pull himself together rather than embarrass him by halting the class.

"Passion," I began again—It wasn't going to work. Martinez was blubbering openly now, and the other students were grinning and nudging each other, most of them eyeing me in open speculation as to how I'd handle the situation. Jailhouse games. The clock above the door showed twenty minutes left in the period, and since all penal-institution classes must begin and end exactly on time I couldn't even dismiss early. Terrific.

I glanced a wordless plea at Indio Zamora, top dog of the Gusanos, the largest Chicano gang here at WaCoCo, the Wayne County Correctional Facility. Indio met my gaze for a moment, his dark eyes unreadable, then nodded a barely perceptible acknowledgment and glanced at Segundo, his second in command. A look, nothing more. Segundo, a slope-shouldered Neanderthal with his hair tied back in a ratty ponytail, slid out of his seat and shambled to the rear of the room. He bent down, murmured something in Martinez's ear. And the kid stopped crying. Instantly.

Segundo eased down beside him at the rear table and rested a blunt-fingered paw on Martinez's shoulder—for comfort or as a threat, I couldn't tell. But Martinez stayed stone-silent through the rest of my lecture.

In the six-odd months I'd been teaching creative writing at the prison, I'd seen this kind of thing before—a whisper here, a look there as effective as the crack of a whip. Detroit's street gangs are active in WaCoCo, and a boss con like Indio Zamora can have the power of life and death over other inmates. Still, as a writer, I've often wondered exactly what the men *say* at such times. Is the force in the message? Or the messenger?

The discussion period at the end of class was the usual stew of abysmal ignorance and surprisingly sharp insights. When I took this job, I frankly expected to be teaching illiterate semi-morons, but though most of the cons are language-deficient and ill-educated, I'd guess the I.Q. levels in my prison class aren't much lower than the Detroit City College classes I teach the rest of the week. And a few of my student convicts, like Indio Zamora, or Ahmad Clark, enforcer for the Black Pharaohs, are intimidatingly bright, with a shrewd, feral intelligence probably superior to the best of my college students.

"Mr. Zamora," I said as the cons filed out to return to their respective cellblocks under the unblinking eyes of the corridor surveillance cameras, "can you spare a minute?"

"Sure," Indio said, "or ten years." Segundo hesitated as well, but, at Indio's nod, went out with the others. I wondered if the two men ever spoke at all, or if they simply communicated by some sort of wolf-pack ESP. Zamora sat on the edge of the front table, dark, hawk-faced, slender as a leather riding crop, his prison denims neatly pressed and tailored, a perfect fit.

"Thanks for helping out with Martinez," I said.

"No charge, Mr. Devlin," Indio shrugged. "He's one of my people and he shouldn't be cryin' in public. Bad for my image."

"Still, I appreciate it. Pity you can't help maintain order in my college classes."

"Maybe I will," he said, straightening, "sometime in the next century. That it?"

"No, that's not it," I said, annoyed. "Aren't you even curious about what my agent thought of your novel?"

"I figure if he said anything interesting, you'd let me know."

"He liked it as much as I do. In fact, he's already submitted it to a major publisher."

"And that's good?"

"Good? It's terrific. I wish he was half as enthusiastic about my work. He said to tell you your book has more commercial potential than anything he's handled in years."

"Sounds krush." Indio straightened. "So. How long will it take for anything to happen?"

"I can't be sure, but, as fired up as Rudolph was, possibly a month or so."

"Or longer?"

"Maybe longer," I admitted. "But the point is, Rudolph Herzel likes your work and he's not an easy man to impress. Damn it, Indio, you just don't realize what this means. For me to say you're talented is one thing, but for Rudolph to say so, and to give your book a special push, is quite another. It means that you can really write, that you can make a life for yourself after you get out of here."

"Or it might mean you two dudes have similar taste and the book does nothing. Look, Mr. Devlin, I know you mean well, but hope's a risky idea to buy into in the joint. You walk around with your head in the clouds, you can do a brodie down a sewer. So if your agent likes my book, that's cool, but maybe I'll wait till the check clears to start the fiesta, you know?"

"The book will sell," I said. "I may not be the world's greatest authority, but I know talent when I see it, and you have it. All you've got to worry about is what to write next."

"Wrong," Indio said evenly. "I've got a few other things to worry about, Teach, like stayin' alive and on top of the dungheap until tomorrow, and then the day after that. Be a shame if my book's a bestseller and I'm suckin' dirt in Forest Lawn, no?"

"I suppose so," I said. "Still, maybe late some night, after lights out and lockdown, you might want to think about what your life could be like as a writer. Because you're going to make it, whether you believe it or not."

"Okay, Mr. Devlin," Indio nodded, with a faint grin— the first one I'd ever seen. "Maybe I'll try thinkin' about it. Just a little, some night after lockdown. I'll see you next Thursday, And, ah, thanks. I won't forget this."

"No charge," I said. "You've earned it."

"Maybe," he said, "*pero*—" He swallowed, then turned and stalked out without a backward glance. But I was almost certain I'd caught a flicker of something in his dark eyes. Hope? I couldn't be sure. But if it was, it made all the headaches of teaching in this hellhole worth it.

I THOUGHT ABOUT INDIO OFTEN DURING THE NEXT WEEK, especially while reading the earnestly muddleheaded offerings of my junior college students. A few of them have potential, I suppose, the talent and the command of language necessary to become good writers, but they lack character. They simply haven't seen or done enough to develop original viewpoints. Their tales of puppy love and parental betrayal are as homogeneous as the pop/pap music they listen to. Not totally their fault. A generation ago a few literate role models still walked the earth. Who do these kids have?

And yet Indio Zamora, a young self-educated gangbanger from East Detroit, had, with minimal instruction from me, assembled a savagely honest first novel, a book so good I paid it the ultimate writer's compliment of wishing I'd written it myself.

I didn't really expect to hear more from my agent immediately—the process of selling a book can take months, or even years. Still, the following Thursday afternoon, I called Rudolph's office.

"Dev, good to hear from you," Herzel's honey-thick Georgian accent rumbled over the line. "Great minds must run in the same rut. I wrote to you today."

"Wrote to me?"

"About that student of yours, Zamora? Dee Grossman at Burke Edwards called me this morning, said she'd read the book at a single sitting, couldn't put it down. She's submitting it to the board on Wednesday, we should receive an offer by the end of the month."

"It's as good as sold and you didn't let me know?"

"I said I just dropped you a note—"

"Couldn't you have called?"

There was a silence on the line. "Yes," Rudolph said, "I suppose I could have, though it's not my usual practice—especially when there's nothing definite."

"It's just that—I think it's more important to Zamora than it would be to someone who's free."

"I see. Well, I'm sorry, Dev, but publishing is a business, and patience is one of its protocols. And if Mr. Zamora hasn't acquired that trait in his present circumstances, I doubt he ever will. How's *your* new book coming?"

"It, ah, it's coming. Slowly, and not as steadily as I'd like."

"You know I never press, Dev, but it's been a while.

Are you sure you're not overextending yourself? With extra teaching, perhaps?"

"I'm all right," I snapped. "I'll work through it."

DESPITE THE GUFF I'D GIVEN RUDOLPH, I DIDN'T TELL INdio the news before class that night. Instead, I glanced at him from time to time as I lectured, hoping to see some hint of anticipation or curiosity. Nothing. If anything, he was even less animated than usual, present in body only. I couldn't understand it. When my first novel was under consideration I hovered around my mailbox like an expectant father, and it irritated me that Indio seemed so disinterested. I was tempted not to tell him at all, to simply wait until he asked, but if we were having a war of nerves, I surrendered, and asked him to stay a moment after class.

"I talked to my agent today," I said. "He expects you're going to get an offer on it soon."

He stared at me blankly. "How soon?"

"I'm not sure—possibly by the end of the month. The point is—"

"It doesn't matter. I won't be here."

"Why not? Where are you going?"

"To hell, probably," he said evenly. "Unless writin' a book balances out the cutting I'm doin' time for."

"What are you talking about?"

"About hope, and how it can mess up your head in the joint. Remember what you said last week about doing some thinking after lights out? About how selling the book could maybe make a difference in my life? Well, I did think about it, and I decided you were right. And I took a shot at changing things." He hesitated, glancing uneasily at the open door, walked over, checked the corridor, then closed the door and leaned back against it. "Look at me," he said. "How much do you figure I weigh?"

"Weigh? I don't see what—"

"I weigh one seventy soakin' wet," he said. "You know what that means? It means I'm not big enough to survive in here on my own. If I'm not ganged up, I'm fresh meat for the first psycho with the hots for me.''

"I still don't—"

"I'm alive because I'm a Gusano,'' he continued, raising his fist, showing me the worm tattoo that writhed up his right forearm from wrist to bicep. "And I'm not just some gangbanger—I'm a top dog, a boss. Not because I'm tough. Plenty of guys under me could break me in half. Segundo for one. But I'm smarter than they are, and they know it. So they follow me. And they trust me. And I hear things. Not just Gusano business, all kinds of things. I could write a book,'' he said drily. "Anyway, I figured that maybe I could do just that to buy my way out. You remember a couple of months back two Feds from the Organized Crime Task Force hauled me outa class for a talk?''

I nodded. "I remember. A short conversation, as I recall.''

"Had to be. Bein' around those guys is dangerous. People wonder if you're rollin' over for 'em. Thing is, they offered me a deal—give 'em enough information about the gangs and I could walk. They'd get my sentence reduced to time served if I cooperated.''

"And you didn't take it?''

"No," he said. "I couldn't see givin' 'em anybody when we'd all be back on the same streets eventually. My life wouldn't be worth spit. Better to just stand up and do my time, you know? Only now I got a chance for somethin' better than bein' just another chump. So I dropped a dime to the Feds, see if the offer was still open.''

"And is it?''

"Sure. The deal is, I talk, they'll fake some scam to take me outa the general population and park me in isolation while they follow up what I give 'em. If it checks out, I can be on the street in a couple of months.''

"But there's a catch?''

"Sort of. There's this guard, Magruder. You know him?''

"I've seen him. Tall? Brushcut?''

"And crooked enough to screw into the ground. He wants a payoff. Five grand. Or he puts the word out about what's goin' down. And I'm a dead man."

"Can't you ask for protection?"

"No way. Even if the Feds believe me, they can't keep me alive. I'd get torched in my cell or maybe poisoned. The gangbangers'd get to me somehow. Which brings me to you."

"I thought it might," I said cautiously. "Only I didn't just get off the boat, Indio, I've been working here a while and I've seen a few jailhouse games."

"You don't believe me?"

"It doesn't matter whether I do or not. Between my child support and car payments, I'm—"

"You didn't answer my question. Do you believe me or not?"

"I honestly don't know," I said, "but if I had any extra money do you think I'd be teaching in this place?"

Indio stared at me, frankly reading me, then shrugged. "Look at these," he said, tossing a pair of photographs on my desk.

I picked up the photos and felt a knot harden in the pit of my stomach. They were snapshots of my ex-wife and seven-year-old daughter, taken at the playground of my daughter's school. "You son of a bitch," I said softly.

"You don't understand. Look at them. When were they taken?"

I examined the photos more carefully. From the light and the clothes they were wearing—"Last fall, I suppose. September sometime. So?"

"September fourteenth," he said, "a few days after you started teaching this class. Do you know how big the Gusanos are, how many men? Maybe three hundred, maybe more. And I'm El Hombre, the main man in here. I have power. Real power. And I didn't get it by missing bets. I started looking for a handle on you the first day we met. I've had these pictures for months. I could've used 'em to pressure you anytime. But I didn't."

"Until now."

"I'm not using them now. I'm giving them to you. And putting my life in your hands. If Segundo or the others find out I'm dealing with the Feds, I won't live a week. Help me, Mr. Devlin."

"Even if I wanted to help, I don't have five—"

"Jesus, I'm not askin' you for money, Teach, I've got the damn cash! But I need to get it to Magruder, and he won't take his payoff from anybody but me. No corroborating witnesses that way. I can't use my own people to bring it in without making them wonder why I need it. You're my only chance."

"But even if I helped, you're searched before you go back to your cellblock, aren't you?"

"Yeah, but I go to work first, in the library. I can stash it there until I hook up with Magruder. Just bring it to me, is that too much to ask?"

"It wouldn't be if I believed you."

"You've read my book, Mr. Devlin, you've seen *mi corazon*—my heart. If you don't know me now, there's nothing more I can say. No hard feelin's. Maybe I'll see you around."

"Indio," I called after him. He paused in the doorway. "Look—" I swallowed hard. "What would I have to do?"

THE WAYNE COUNTY LEGAL AID COOPERATIVE OFFICE was nowhere near as grand as its name. A one-story storefront with raw, graffiti-streaked plywood panels for windows on the wrong side of Montcalm Avenue, downhill Motown. The waiting room was jammed, its mismatched vinyl sofas filled with black and Hispanic street people, the air thick with the aroma of damp clothing, cigarette smoke, despair. I told the black matron at the front desk I had an appointment with Lia Alvarez and she thumbed me toward an office at the rear. I wandered down the narrow corridor, feeling pinpricks of resentment between my shoulderblades. Whitey gets waved on through. And what else is new?

Lia Alvarez glanced up at me over the rims of her half-

framed reading glasses with eyes that were strikingly dark
and intelligent. She was small, a pert raven in a conserva-
tive business suit. Olive skin, tightly curled, gleaming
hair—not conventional cover-girl material, I suppose, and
yet I found her oddly magnetic, almost familiar, though I
was sure we'd never met.

"Can I help you?" she asked. Even her voice seemed
familiar—husky, velvet, like Bacall's in *Key Largo*.

"I hope so," I said. "One of your clients asked me to
see you. Indio Zamora?"

The room temperature chilled at least ten degrees. "Mr.
Zamora is not my client," she said. "What is it you want?"

"I'm not sure," I said. "He asked me to see you—"

"You're Devlin, aren't you?" she frowned. "Thomas
Devlin? The writer? *Poets and Promises*?"

"That's right," I said, surprised she recognized me.

"Indio told me he was taking a writing course from you
at WaCoCo," she said. "And now you're running errands
for him?"

"I'm not an errand boy, exactly," I said. "He's one of
my students. I'm trying to help, that's all."

"I see." She eyed me thoughtfully. "Well, far be it from
me to impede the educational process, Mr. Devlin. His *or*
yours." She took a small envelope from the top desk
drawer and pushed it toward me.

"What is this?"

"A key. To a locker at Metro Airport."

"The airport?"

"You seem surprised."

"Well, I guess I thought I'd just see you and—"

"Mr. Devlin, Indio Zamora is my stepbrother. He was
my sole support through law school, and since I'm partly
to blame for his incarceration I try to—"

And suddenly I realized why she seemed so familiar.
There was a slight family resemblance, of course, but it
was far more than that. "You're Rena, aren't you?" I said.

"I beg your pardon?"

"In Indio's book, the hero has a sister who is—assaulted.

He's sent to prison for avenging her. He describes you very accurately—perfectly, in fact.''

"I see," she said, meeting my gaze. "Well, I suppose I should be flattered. Or something."

"It seems very odd to meet you like this. It's as though you stepped out of a story. Or a dream."

"If that's a compliment, I'll take it," she said brusquely, "but I assure you I'm quite real. And if you're wondering, the rest of it is true as well."

"I'm sorry," I said, "I didn't mean to—"

"It's all right," she said. "I've adjusted to what happened, more or less. What Indio did because of it, well, that's much harder. Because he shouldn't be in jail at all. It was a matter for the police, or maybe the Gusanos. Only Indio felt he had to handle it personally. And publicly. For the sake of my honor. Or his. I was never quite clear on that point. He's really written a book? He said he had, but with Indio—" She shrugged.

"He's not only written it, it'll probably be published within a year. Your brother has tremendous potential as a writer, Ms. Alvarez. He's the best student I've ever had."

"Indio has a great many talents—" she nodded coolly ''—any one of which might have landed him where he is even if I hadn't been hurt. He also has admirable qualities, Mr. Devlin, but he's a complicated man. If I were you, I'd be a bit wary where Indio's concerned."

"And yet you're trying to help him, too," I said, picking up the envelope.

"He's my brother," she said, "he's not yours. And giving you that envelope is the extent of my involvement. Have a nice day, Mr. Devlin." She returned her attention to the papers on her desk, end of interview. I shrugged and turned away.

"Mr. Devlin?" she said as I opened the office door. "I enjoyed *Poets and Promises* very much. It's a wonderful book. When will we see your next?"

"It shouldn't be too much longer," I said. "I've been, ah, having a little trouble, but it should be finished soon."

"I hope so," she said. "I look forward to reading it."

"Thank you," I said. "So do I."

AIRPORT SECURITY AT DETROIT METROPOLITAN IS EX-
tremely tight, metal detectors, guards, the works, which is
probably why Indio chose it for a money drop. It's one of
the few places in Motown you can carry cash without con-
stantly looking over your shoulder.

The key Lia gave me opened a luggage locker just off
the main concourse. It contained a leatherette briefcase with
the K-Mart price stickers still on it. I glanced around, but
no one was near, so I popped the latches on the case. A
moneybelt was folded neatly inside, a cheap, pliable plastic,
one-size-fits-all affair about four inches wide, with a velcro
hookup and a narrow nylon zipper along half its length. I
opened it and rifled through the cash to make sure it was
all there, five thousand in old bills. For a moment I wondered where the money'd come from, whether Lia had
dropped it off or someone else. A gang member? And it
occurred to me that if I had the brains God gave a goose
I'd leave the case where it was and walk away.

But somehow I couldn't. And it wasn't just my promise
to a student, or that Lia Alvarez was a very interesting lady.
It was pride, I suppose, pure and simple. My writing wasn't
going well, and if I backed off now, would it be out of
caution or because I was jealous of Indio's talent? I honestly wasn't sure. I closed the briefcase and took it with
me.

GETTING INTO THE WAYNE COUNTY CORRECTIONS FACIL-
ity is almost as difficult as breaking out. There are three
separate checkpoints at the employees' entrance to the
prison, the first with a metal detector, then two more electronic gates monitored by television cameras. Cofer, the
guard at the first checkpoint, seemed to sense immediately
that something was wrong. He's a large man, fortyish, grey
streaks in his Afro and moustache, and a pillow-sized
paunch bulging at his blue uniform belt. We usually talk

sports as he checks the contents of my briefcase, but he
didn't respond when I asked how the Pistons were doing
and he seemed to search my case with unusual thoroughness. He passed me through without comment, but by now
I was sweating, and if the first electronic gate hadn't opened
as I approached it I might've turned and sprinted for home.
The second gate wasn't as easy. I stood facing the camera
for roughly a year and a half before the damned relay
clicked and the steel door slid open.

It was a lively class—good-natured banter from the students and a short story from a double-lifer that showed real
promise. Still, by the end of the second hour the moneybelt
around my waist weighed a hundred pounds. Or more.

After class, Indio closed the door behind Segundo, the
last of the students to file out. "Mr. Devlin, you look awful." Indio grinned wryly, shaking his head. "You've got
no aptitude for crime at all."

"Thanks, I think," I said, stripping the belt from under
my shirt and passing it to him. "When you get your first
publisher's advance, you owe me a steak dinner."

"I owe you a lot more than that," he said, unzipping the
belt and setting the packets of bills out on my desk, "but
this'll do for a down payment." He hitched up his blue-
denim workshirt and slid the belt around his waist, leaving
the money on the desk.

"What are you doing?" I said.

"Cash on delivery, Mr. Devlin, one belt, five grand. And
one of my people deposited another five in your savings
account today. Ten K for one night's work—not bad, no?
You'll get another ten thousand next week, and ten more
the week after that. Two more belts, that's all I ask, and
then you're off the hook."

"What the hell are you talking about?"

"About power, Mr. Devlin, about how a guy my size
stays alive in a place like this. With the cocaine that's
sealed in the lining of this belt, I'll be richer than Hank the
Deuce. It's worth more than diamonds inside. More than
life."

240 · *Doug Allyn*

I lunged at him, but he pivoted like a matador, seized my wrist in his left hand and whipped it up between my shoulderblades. He flicked his left wrist and a seven-inch sliver of steel appeared in his palm like magic, an inch from my eyes. "Cool out, Teach—you make a scene and you're the one who'll take the fall, not me. They'll know you brought the junk in. And that you got paid. Cops hate it when straight people go bad, they'll love to bust you. Now you back off slow and sit down, you dig?"

"I don't understand," I said, backing to the edge of the desk. "You could get out of here, you have talent—"

"Be a writer, you mean? Somebody like you? Holdin' two jobs tryna make ends meet? Waitin' like a whipped dog for word from some friggin' editor?"

"Maybe it's not a great life," I conceded bitterly, "but at least I'm not in jail."

"Not yet, anyway—" Indio smiled "—and you better hope you never are. I don't think you got what it takes to make it in the joint. You should have read my book better. 'I am the Invictus Worm, buried by the world, yet I strengthen, feeding, thriving in the pit.' Or maybe you should reread Milton—better to rule in hell than to serve in heaven."

"The man who said that stayed in hell."

"But I won't," Indio said, stuffing his shirttails back in his trousers. "I'll cut a deal to get out, *after* I get some serious cash together, and this setup will do it for me. And you, too, if you think straight. Two more belts, thirty grand in the bank, that's not so bad. More than you got for your last book, right?"

"I won't do it," I said, straightening, trying to pull myself together.

"Yes, you will," he said, sliding the shiv back into his sleeve and opening the door. "I didn't use a plastic belt because it was cheap. I used it because it takes fingerprints real well, and yours are all over this one. If you figure you can explain that away, be my guest, but I hope you don't try. You're an intelligent guy, Mr. Devlin, too smart to risk ending up in here. With guys like me. You'll get the next key in the mail with another five grand on account. I'll see you next week. And don't do anything stupid, okay?''

He ducked out into the corridor and stalked away. And I was so furious at the betrayal that I almost shouted for a guard and to hell with the consequences.

But I didn't. Indio had read me well. Either I was too bright, or more likely too cowardly to risk going to prison. So I didn't call out, God help me. I couldn't.

HE'D TOLD ME THE TRUTH. IT WAS ALL THERE IN HIS BOOK. Later that night I brewed a pot of coffee, sat down at the kitchen table of my tiny apartment, and reread the original draft of his manuscript from beginning to end, seeing it clear-eyed, minus the glow of discovery. Indio hadn't concealed what he was. He described his life in the gangs on the Cass Corridor without glamorizing it or making excuses for himself. There was no Sociology 101 "victim of a racist society" drivel that most cons rattle off like a mantra. He was a street-smart ghetto delinquent who'd become a successful criminal by dint of his own labor—a dark mirror image of the American Dream. The stark honesty of his account gave it strength and impact. My mistake had been in assuming that his unflinching examination of his life implied a rejection of it, that his intelligence and his talent had transformed him. I'd been conned. By an expert. And by my own need to validate my teaching by discovering a star pupil. And the hell of it was that even after what had happened, I found it difficult to believe I'd been so wrong about him.

I sat at the table for hours after I'd finished the book, sipping black coffee and chain-smoking, though I'd quit years before, trying to think the situation through. Nothing came. I was too drained emotionally, running on empty. Still, I hadn't wasted my time. Rereading his book had convinced me of two things—one, that Indio was an even better writer than I'd first thought, and two, that I was in deep, deep trouble. The man revealed in that book was perfectly capable of destroying me without a qualm.

I thrashed around in my empty bed like a beached trout for what remained of the night, nightmaring, doing hard time in WaCoCo. I gave it up around 5:00 A.M., slipped on my bathrobe, put on the coffee, and paced restlessly around the apartment, looking for an out. I could tell my sorry little tale to the authorities, but even if they believed me I'd probably wind up in jail. Working at WaCoCo had erased my illusions about the criminal-justice system. It's an arcane game for professionals, and Indio knew the moves and the players far better than I did. He could cut a deal to testify against me and hit the street while I was still trying to explain my stupidity to a lawyer.

At some point in my wandering, I brushed the curtains aside and glanced out my living-room window at the empty street. Only it wasn't quite empty. A car was cruising slowly past, a teenager's car, black with yellow pinstriping, lowered, fender-skirted, its glass pack mufflers rumbling hollowly in the early-morning stillness.

I stared after it as it disappeared around the corner, trying to remember if I'd seen it before. But somehow I wasn't surprised when ten minutes or so later it crawled past again. And suddenly I was galvanized, enraged. I'd tried to do a decent thing and I'd been betrayed. And maybe there was no way out for me, but, by God, the game wasn't over. Not yet.

FIRST THINGS FIRST. INDIO HADN'T EXACTLY THREATENED my family, but he obviously knew where they were. I wanted them out of harm's way while I worked things out. I mulled that over for a few minutes, then called my ex-wife, told her I'd won a non-refundable two-week Hawaiian vacation, and suggested she take our daughter and go, that I'd pick up the tab for everything. It was the first time since our divorce we settled anything without bickering. I thought about going with them, and continuing on to Tahiti or Australia or wherever, but dismissed it. Indio had a belt with cocaine residue in it and my prints on it. He could trade me for a reduced sentence even if I ran.

Still, the idea had its appeal. It was either run or take the payoff and deliver the belts. And who'd be hurt if I did? It wasn't as though he was selling the stuff to school kids, his only customers would be convicts. And he was right about the money. Thirty thousand *was* more than I'd received for my last book.

Books. I kept coming back to that. You've seen my heart, he said. And it was true. But had I seen anything else in his book? Any weakness? Just maybe. After all, Indio wasn't in prison because he was a gangster—he was there because he valued his honor. And because he loved his sister.

I CRUISED THROUGH MY MORNING CLASSES ON AUTOPILOT, my mind like a gerbil in a jogging drum, ideas tumbling endlessly over each other. And always coming up the same way, with the same image. Lia Alvarez. If there was a way out for me, Indio's feelings for her were the key to it. By noon I'd assembled a crude plan. I didn't like it much, but at least it gave me something to do, and an excuse to see Indio's sister again. Or try to.

"Wayne County Legal Aid, Alvarez." Her voice on the phone was curt, all business, and for a moment my heart sank. Suppose she said no?

"Hi, this is Tom Devlin, the writer from Friday afternoon—remember me?"

"Of course, Mr. Devlin," she said coolly, "Indio's teacher and friend. Do you need a lawyer already?"

"Possibly," I admitted, "but that's not why I'm calling. I'm calling about food. Dinner, specifically, at someplace with candles and a view of the city. Does the Sky Room on top of the Renaissance Center sound at all interesting?"

"The Sky Room," she echoed. "My, my, my. Very posh. And very expensive. And what would we talk about? My brother, perhaps?"

"We can talk about anything you like, cats and kings,

whatever. Or we can just enjoy the meal and the view. No strings attached.''

''Sometimes I think I see Detroit all too clearly from my desk.''

''Which proves my point. You need a change in perspective. About sixty stories' worth. What do you say?''

''Are you in trouble?'' she asked suddenly.

''No,'' I lied, ''why do you ask?''

''If you don't know already, then maybe I'd better enlighten you,'' she said brusquely, ''and the Sky Room's as good a place as any. Is tonight at eight convenient for you?''

''Tonight?'' I said, surprised. ''Why, yes, tonight will be fine.''

''Somehow I thought it might be,'' she sighed. ''I'll meet you there, eightish. Have a nice day.''

She rang off without waiting for a reply. I suppose I should have been offended, but instead my spirits lifted a bit. I was still in a jam, but at least I could look forward to a dinner high above the city with an interesting date. And if things didn't work out, I could always take a header off the roof after dessert.

I canceled my last class, drove over to the Cass Corridor, and prowled through a half dozen pawnshops before I found what I wanted—a duplicate of the plastic moneybelt I'd carried into WaCoCo. Then I stopped by the Renaissance Center, the five-tower, sixty-story complex of shops, restaurants, and offices that rises like a stack of poker chips beside the Detroit River, a half-billion-dollar gamble that the heart of Motown can be revived. A winning bet? It's too early in the game to be sure.

I took an express elevator from the mezzanine to the top floor, made reservations at the Sky Room for a table with a view of the river, and arranged for a special service the restaurant offers on request. A photographer.

BY EVENING MY UPBEAT MOOD HAD FADED A BIT, PARTLY because if my little charade flopped I'd be out of options and partly because the more I thought about my idea the less I liked it. I wore my best suit and arrived well before eight to claim our table. I made sure the photographer understood her instructions, then took a seat at the bar while I waited for my date. Or my fate. Or both.

The Sky Room has a sensual, sophisticated ambience, embroidered linens, candleglow dancing on silver carafes, the lights of Detroit and the Canadian side of the river stretching away to the horizon as though the Milky Way had whispered down like snow. The waiters were white tux-ed and black tied, but not snobbish. They joked with the diners and each other, typically Motown, where the only class line that counts is the balance in your bank statement.

And then Lia walked in, and the room seemed to brighten. She was wearing a twin of the dress I'd seen a few days before, a plain dun business frock adorned only with a scarlet wisp of a scarf, and yet I felt my breathing catch. She looked absolutely stunning, underdressed for the room perhaps, but, if anything, more attractive for it. She spoke to the maitre d', who escorted her to the table I'd reserved. I wandered over, carrying the small parcel I'd brought with me and wishing to God I was meeting her under other circumstances.

"Hi," I said, parking the package beside my chair as I sat, "I'm glad you could make it."

"So am I," she said. "You look very natty. I thought writers were supposed to be rumpled."

"Ordinarily I am, but this is a special occasion."

"Yes," she mused, scanning the room, "so it would seem. And yet—"

"And yet?"

"Look, Mr. Devlin—"

"Tom," I interjected.

"No, at this point it's still Mr. Devlin and Ms. Alvarez. And that may be as far as it gets. I'll be blunt, Mr. Devlin. The only times I've ever been here were on business. If this is a business dinner, fine, but can we deal with the agenda first? It might save you an expensive evening."

"I have no particular agenda other than getting to know you better."

"And that's all? There's nothing in particular you'd like to ask me? About my stepbrother, for instance?"

"I do have one question," I said. "Do you think working on the Corridor's made you just a teensy bit paranoid? Or were you always this way?"

"In this town, paranoia's just another name for reality."

"Maybe so," I admitted, "but everybody needs a break from reality now and again. So let's take one. Now, shall I ask for the wine list?"

"Just one last question," she said. "Why the Sky Room? For a first—date? If that's what this is."

"I think that's the term, yes."

"All right, then—why here?"

"Simple," I said. "I wanted to make sure you'd say yes."

"I see," she said slowly. "Well, true or not, that was the right thing to say. Tom. All right, let's ask for the wine list. Bearing in mind that I'm already impressed, so don't overdo it by choosing something terribly expensive, okay?"

"Ms. Alvarez," I said, "I think this could be the beginning of a beautiful friendship."

BUT IT SEEMED MORE LIKE RENEWING A FRIENDSHIP THAN a beginning. She really was familiar, in a way. I had Indio's description of her as background, but it was no more than a sketch, really. He saw her as a sort of streetwise madonna, and she was, but she was also bright and tenacious and compassionate, and funny. And as the evening flew past, I became almost certain that she wasn't involved in Indio's life, except as his sister and his friend. Which made me dislike my scheme even more. Still, I had no choice. And it was almost time.

"Oops, almost forgot," I said, picking up the parcel from the foot of my chair. I placed the moneybelt on the table, then lifted out the small gift-wrapped box and handed it to Lia.

She opened it. "A corsage?" she smiled. "You really take first dates seriously, don't you?"

"Only this one," I said. "Shall I help you put it on?"

"No, I think I'd like to save it, if you wouldn't mind. It's too pretty to wear. And a—moneybelt? Is this some sort of a bribe?"

"It's just something I picked up for a class," I said. "I forgot it was in the bag."

She knew I was lying. Whether it was her training as a lawyer or because we were simpatico, somehow she sensed it. But she would have let it pass, I think, except that the photographer chose that moment to take her shot. Lia glanced up, startled by the flash, then read my eyes and my soul like a cheap novel.

"Just part of the service," I said lamely. "A picture to—"

"Is it?" she said, cutting me off, her gaze still locked on mine. I looked away.

"What's going on here?" she asked.

"Nothing. Why do you ask?"

"Never mind," she said, rising. "Whatever it is, I wish you'd told me. It's been a lovely evening—Mr. Devlin. Thank you. This should cover my half of it." She fished two twenties out of her purse, tossed them on the table, then walked away, moving hastily through the crowd.

"Lia, wait a minute—"

"Here's your photograph, sir," the camera girl said, blocking my path. "It came out perfectly."

"Right, I'll be right back," I said, trying to brush past her as Lia disappeared into the corridor.

"Sir," the girl said, grasping my elbow gently, "didn't you say something about a tip? Fifty, wasn't it?"

It was too late, anyway. Lia was already gone. "Yes," I sighed, taking out my wallet. "Fifty, exactly." The girl handed me the Polaroid snap. She was right, it had turned out very well. And maybe I was off the hook. Instead of delivering the drugs, all I had to do was show Indio the picture of Lia with the moneybelt, tell him that her prints were on it, and that he couldn't burn me without destroying her as well. And he'd never do that. Stalemate. I was free of him.

I should have felt relieved, liberated. But I didn't. Maybe it was the damned snapshot, the glow in Lia's eyes as she held the orchid just as the flashbulb fired.

I CALLED LIA'S OFFICE THE NEXT MORNING, GOT PUT ON hold by her receptionist, and, as I waited, realized I had no idea of what to say, anyway. The truth? More lies? I wasn't sure which would be worse, so I hung up before she came on the line. I thought of her often over the next few days and found myself taking out the photograph at odd moments and staring at it as though it held a message for me. And perhaps it did.

On Tuesday morning, after my ten o'clock class, there was an envelope waiting on the desk in my office. No postage, no return address, just my name on it. I asked the office girl if she'd seen who dropped it off, but she hadn't noticed anyone, and I wasn't surprised.

I closed the office door, sat down at my battered desk, and opened the envelope. Five thousand in cash and an airport locker key. I placed the envelope and Lia's photograph side by side. Did they balance out? Almost certainly. The photograph would neutralize Indio's hold on me. There was only one flaw in my little scheme. I couldn't do it. I just couldn't. I took a last, wistful look at the photograph, then tore it up and dropped the pieces in the wastebasket. Indio was right. I had no talent for this kind of thing. I was back to my original options—take my chances with the authorities, which almost certainly meant going to jail, or make another delivery. I was still staring at Indio's envelope when the warning bell sounded for the next class period. I slipped the envelope into my briefcase and walked out of my office. And into The Dream.

Every teacher has a personal version of The Dream—a

vivid, recurring nightmare that shows up when you're under pressure. You're wandering through a strange school, knowing you're late for class, but can't find your room; or you're lecturing and suddenly realize you're only wearing underwear. Or less.

In my version of the dream, I was addressing a class later that afternoon when I noticed the students seemed to be eyeing me strangely. And I realized I had no idea what I'd been talking about, or even which class this was. Western Civ? American Lit 202? My memory was a blank. Erased. And for a moment the spell of The Dream was so strong that I half expected to wake up in bed. But I didn't. Instead I stood there like an idiot for a century or so, trying to remember where I was, and then just said, "Class dismissed," picked up my case, and walked out.

I drifted down the empty corridor like my own ghost, ducked into the first empty classroom I came to, and collapsed into a desk at the rear. Sanctuary, a quiet place to think. *Think.*

I ran the situation over and over again in my mind, staring blindly up at the empty chalkboard, waiting for an answer to materialize. But nothing came. And after a while, Charlie Volk waddled in, a balding, three-hundred-pound Magoo in a stained white lab coat. He began assembling some sort of apparatus on his desk, humming contentedly to himself, then stopped as he noticed me at the back of the room.

"Hello, Devlin, what are you doing in here?"

"Nothing, Charlie. Just needed a place to hide. I'll get out of your way."

"No rush, my next class isn't for twenty minutes. I came in early to set up an experiment. How's the scribbling going? Still working on the great American novel?"

"When I find time," I said.

"Well, anytime you need a chemistry teacher for a hero, you know who to ask. It'd be nice to have somebody besides Disney write about us."

"Disney?"

"Walt Disney. Or whoever it was that made up that non-sense for the movies. You know, *The Absent-Minded Pro-fessor, Son of Flubber*, all that drivel."

"Oh, that Disney. Sorry, I didn't make the connection."

"You know, you look a little like an absent-minded professor yourself, Dev. Something on your mind?"

"A small problem. Nothing I can't work out," I said, rising stiffly from the desk.

"With one of your stories, you mean?"

"A story?" I echoed. "Yes, I suppose it is in a way."

"Well? Solving problems is what we teach in here, maybe I can help. What is it?"

I stared at him blankly for a moment, then took a deep, ragged breath. I needed to talk to somebody badly. "It's just a plot I'm working out," I said. "About a teacher who gets himself in a jam."

THE NEXT NIGHT AFTER CLASS, I DELIVERED THE SECOND belt to Indio. he seemed almost disappointed. I think he was looking forward to a confrontation, but I had nothing to say to him. He slipped the belt on under his shirt, eyeing me warily.

"You want to talk about this?" he asked.

"About what?"

"This situation we're into here. I know this can't be easy for you."

"I'm touched by your concern."

"Believe it or not, I do care about you, Devlin. You tried to help me and I haven't forgotten it. Plus I want to make sure you don't do anything stupid now and burn us both. Try thinkin' of this as an educational experience. You've taught me some things, now I'm returning the favor and you're gonna come out ahead of the game, wiser and richer both. Might even make you a better writer to know how the other half lives. So enjoy your walk on the wild side, Mr. Devlin. And be cool. You're doin' the smart thing."

"I hope so," I said.

"You are," he said. "Trust me."

"You've got to be kidding."

"Just a figure of speech," he grinned. "I'll see you next week."

BUT HE DIDN'T. INDIO WAS ABSENT THE FOLLOWING WEEK. I asked Segundo where his boss was and he said he was in isolation block. There'd been a fire in the library. The guards knew it was arson, but couldn't nail anybody for it, so they punished all six of the cons who worked there— ten days in solitary each.

"Sorry to hear it," I said.

"You got any message you want to get to him?" Segundo asked.

"I thought you said he was in isolation."

"He is. But he's still El Hombre."

"Yes, I suppose he is," I said. "No. No message."

"YOU HAVE A SLIGHT EDGE OVER WRITERS ON THE OUT-side," I said, facing the following Thursday-night class of thugs and felons. "You've seen and done things that most people haven't or you wouldn't be in here. It makes your viewpoint unique, and you can make that work for you." I continued on this tack for a bit, talking about former convicts who'd become respected authors—Eldridge Cleaver, James Ellroy, and others. Inspiration by example, I hoped. The class was edgy, unresponsive. I felt I was living The Dream again, lecturing to a Diego Rivera mural. Indio Zamora was back, sitting at a desk in the rear, silent as a stone idol, Segundo, as usual, at his right hand.

I managed to get through the session, made assignments for the following week, and dismissed them. Segundo ushered the others out into the corridor and took up a station in the hallway just outside the door. Indio unfolded from his seat and sauntered toward me. He looked like a man just out of solitary, hollow-cheeked, his dark eyes sunken, opaque.

"Maybe you think you're off the hook," he said quietly, stopping a foot or so away.

"Almost," I said. "I guessed you'd probably hide the belts in the same place, so they went up in smoke together. As for your money, it's in my bank in a savings account. In your name. You can pick it up when you get out. If you ever do."

"And if I told you I still have the first belt?"

"I wouldn't believe you. The guards knew the fire was arson and they turned the library upside down. If the belt was there, they'd have found it. They didn't. It burned. It must have."

"When you're right, you're right," Indio shrugged. "Both belts burned. An expensive fire. How did you do it? Some kind of chemical, right?"

"White phosphorus, and consulfuric acid. The acid ate through the lining, the phosphorus burns as soon as it's exposed to air."

"You're a chemist, too? I'm impressed."

"I'm not a chemist, just did a little basic research."

"And the coke that was in the belt?"

"I flushed it down the toilet where it belongs. By the way, Mr. Herzel called me while you were—away. Your book will be published—the advance will be ten thousand."

"Good, I can use the money. I'm about to change careers. I'm getting out of here, going into the witness-protection program."

"Is there an echo in here? I think I've heard this before."

"Maybe so—" he smiled narrowly "—only this time it's true. I took deposits to deliver merchandise, and then my stash gets torched. And now people figure I was runnin' a scam and burned the library to cover myself. They have no faith in humanity, you know? If I stay here, either some strung-out junkie'll waste me or there'll be a gang war and a lot of my people will get hurt. So I'm cutting a deal to get out, tryin' to trade the Feds enough to earn a walk without betraying any Gusanos. And then maybe I'll take my shot at the straight life."

"You'll do all right if you work at it. You're a bright

guy, Indio, probably the best student I've ever had.''

"No hard feelings, then?"

"Wrong," I said. "All kinds of hard feelings."

"Whatever," he shrugged. "But for what it's worth, I've worked a lot of hustles in my time, Devlin, but I never had a new blood beat me in a deal before. I guess that makes you my star pupil, no?"

"What it makes us is quits, Indio, dead-even. I don't want to see you again, in here or anywhere else."

"Like the song says, Teach, you can't always get what you want. If I'm really as good a writer as you say, maybe you'll see me around, like it or not."

"I doubt it. I think you're at home in prison, Indio. Afraid of the outside. I think you'll die in this place. Or one like it."

"Perhaps," he said softly, moving closer to me, his eyes only inches from mine, "but sometime, Devlin, maybe late some night, after lights out and lockdown, you'll think back on this and admit you learned as much from me as I did from you."

"I doubt that very much."

"No, I think you *will*. And you know what else you'll remember? What a rush it is to walk on the wild side. And you'll miss it. Maybe you'll even miss me."

"No," I said, "not a chance in hell."

"Maybe not," he shrugged, turning toward the door. "*Adios*, Teach. Thanks for everything. It's been interesting."

"That it has," I said. "Good luck," I added, surprising myself.

He didn't reply. Segundo opened the door for him, then shambled after him down the corridor. I began erasing my notes from the chalkboard, but paused in mid-swipe, thinking about what Indio said about missing the wild side. And I knew he was wrong. If I'd learned anything from him, it was that some people need the adrenalin highs of that life but I wasn't one of them. Nor is there any chance I'll miss him. He's an amoral sociopath with no more conscience than that worm tattooed on his wrist. WaCoCo, or some other prison, is exactly where he belongs.

Still, wherever he ends up, I hope they give him a typewriter. Because if not, I'll send him one myself. A teacher only gets one star pupil in a lifetime, and inside the walls or out Indio Zamora's going to be a fine writer. And in spite of everything, I can't wait to read his next book.

ON DEATH ROW

※

Steven Peters

RAZA VALKUNIN WILL DIE AT PRECISELY 12:30 A.M. tomorrow. I am able to specify the exact time because the State will electrocute him then and promptness is characteristic of the State when executing convicted murderers. In other matters, such as paying its employees, the State frequently procrastinates. I know because I am employed by the State Prison as a psychologist.

My primary responsibility is prisoner rehabilitation but the State recognizes the impossibility of rehabilitating a corpse and so does not require me to have contact with murderers. However, I am interested in investigating the psychological factors which drive men to murder, and for some time now I have conducted a research project of my own along these lines, which is how I met Raza Valkunin.

Since the day Raza was condemned to die, he has not been permitted to leave his cell on Death Row. Instead of the usual comfortable consultation in my office with the patient delivered to me, I had trudged down endless corridors to Raza's cell. Out of sheer deprivation of human contact——only the warden and the chaplain were allowed to visit him——he had agreed to talk to me.

"Did you know, Doc," he said to me during our first

session, "I always wanted to be a cop? I even took the exams to get on the force."

No murderer had ever told me that before and it heightened my interest in Raza. While he spoke, I studied him carefully. He was twenty-eight years old, about five feet ten inches tall, and in excellent physical condition. He wore prison garb—a blue denim shirt, open at the throat, and formless pants without cuffs. The only departures from standard issue were the paper sandals on his feet and the absence of a belt. His hair was already cut quite short, as if in anticipation of his impending execution.

"Yeah," Raza went on, "I crammed hard for three months for those exams to get in. I was ready to drop by the time they rolled around. I couldn't sleep at night or nothing. Boy, was I jittery—all that coffee I drank to stay awake and study."

"You really pushed yourself," I commented, encouraging him to continue.

"You know it, Doc," he replied. "I kept telling myself I hadn't studied near hard enough. You jerk, I kept saying, you want to flunk that exam? You want to be a cop, don't you? Then get going on those books. At the end of three months I knew that stuff cold, but I was still jumpy about the exam."

"What happened when you took it?" I asked.

"Just what I was afraid of, Doc. I goofed. Hell, I knew the stuff, but my mind went blank on the exam. I like, froze up, you know what I mean?"

"I know," I replied.

"Now why the hell would I tighten up like that?" Raza asked.

"A lot of people panic when they are tested on what they know. Not many of us like to be put on the spot," I explained.

"The exam was nothing like the way I tightened up on the range that afternoon," Raza replied. "I picked up the gun and it felt so heavy I had to use my other hand to hold my wrist up. I aimed at the dummy and got the shakes so bad my teeth damn near jumped out of my head. I felt cold and sick, like I was going to lose my lunch right there in front of all those guys. All I wanted was to get the hell out of there. I dropped the gun and ran and I never went back.''

"You were really upset," I said, "so much so that I am curious as to why you wanted to become a policeman in the first place?"

"I don't know," Raza replied. "Ever since I was a kid I wanted to be a cop." He paused a moment and stared at the naked bulb suspended out of reach from the ceiling of his cell. "Funny, I've always felt like I wanted to be sure I was on the right side of the law, you know what I mean?"

"Yes," I said, "as a policeman you felt people would identify you with law and order."

"Yeah," Raza agreed, "I wanted people to—I don't know how to put it—I always felt like people would look at me and—well, like think I was the kind of guy that—uh, you know, would do violent things."

It was difficult for him to express this thought. He appeared embarrassed by this insight into himself. His comment, however, provided me with an opening to probe about the murder, and I forged ahead.

"You mean people expected that you might kill?" I asked. I noticed that a small muscle on the side of his jaw convulsed as I asked the question. Other than that he betrayed no sign that the question disturbed him.

"You think they were right, don't you?" he asked quietly. Then with more concern for my feelings than I had evidenced for his, he continued without awaiting my answer. "I felt lousy after I flunked the exam. For a couple of weeks I didn't do anything or go any place, just sat in my room. I didn't want to eat or sleep. Then one day I got this idea that I wasn't good enough to be a cop."

"What made you feel you did not deserve to be a policeman?" I asked.

"I don't know. Like I said, I wasn't good enough. It just made sense to me. It was right and I felt better, kind of excited, like now I knew something I should've known all along." He stopped and chuckled. "Sounds backwards, doesn't it, Doc? I mean thinking bad about myself like that made me feel good inside."

"It does seem strange," I said.

"Anyway, after that, I started going out, doing things, you know. That's when I met her, my girl friend. I loved her, Doc, more than anything, even after I found out she was two-timing me."

"Are you saying that you didn't kill her?" I asked.

"No," he replied. "I'm not saying that. I oughta die."

Raza then proceeded to tell me about the girl, with all the standard clichés of a man in love. Since we had already been talking for well over an hour and a half, I decided to terminate the session on this positive note.

"Come back and see me when you can, Doc," Raza said as I left. "I'll still be here for a while yet."

It was three days before my work eased enough to allow me to schedule another talk with Raza. I found him in good spirits even though the date of his execution was less than a week away.

"What do you want to know about me today, Doc?" he asked.

"I thought you might tell me something about your childhood," I said.

"Sure," he agreed, and for the next hour, starting with the present, he worked back through his life. Shortly before our time was up I remarked, "You haven't told me anything about your parents."

There was a pause and then he said, "There's not much to tell. My old lady died about eight years ago, from a stroke. I hurt her enough. I'm glad she didn't live to know about—about this."

"How did you hurt her?" I asked.

"I don't want to talk about it," he said, becoming agitated.

"Perhaps you can tell me about your father," I suggested.

Raza suddenly stood up and strode to the door of his

cell. He grabbed the bars and stood with his back to me.

"I never knew him too well," he said slowly. "He died when I was six." He turned to face me and I saw tears streaming down his face. He took a menacing step toward me. "I don't want to talk about him."

"I'm sorry," I said. "I asked you to remember some things that were not very pleasant. Maybe you'll feel more like talking about it another day."

"Maybe, Doc, maybe. There isn't much time left, you know."

"I know," I said, and called for the guard to let me out.

I was perplexed about Raza. He was different from other murderers I had known. Most of them—except for the professional killer—saw themselves as temperate people, until that moment when their one violent act shattered forever their self-delusion. But Raza thought of himself as a man capable of doing violent things.

He had even attempted to discipline that violent side of himself by becoming a police officer, but it refused to be constrained. It had paralyzed his mind on the examination and his failure had thrown him into a depression. Raza also impressed me as a man driven by guilt—not guilt over his crime as many murderers feel, but guilt over some violence in his past. My curiosity about Raza prompted me to review more thoroughly the account of his crime and trial in his prison record.

Raza's girl friend had been found shot to death in her apartment. Her relationship with Raza was common knowledge among the tenants of the building. The police readily obtained this information and routinely brought Raza in for questioning. He appeared stunned when informed of her death, but then collapsed and admitted his guilt. He steadfastly refused to discuss the details of the murder, but the police easily established motive and opportunity. There was no direct physical evidence, since the murder gun was never found.

The actual trial was quite short. The State relied on the usual motive in such cases, jealousy. The girl had been seeing another man behind Raza's back, and he was duly produced as a star witness. He supported the prosecution's case for first-degree murder. The defense argued it was a crime of passion, unpremeditated, and hence, second-degree murder. Raza's counsel complained of his client's failure to cooperate fully in assisting him to prepare a defense, a complaint given credence by Raza's indifferent attitude toward the entire proceedings.

The jury returned a verdict of guilty in the first degree after a scant thirty minutes of deliberation. They did not recommend mercy. The judge, as required by law, pronounced the death sentence by electrocution. Justice had been done and only vengeance remained to be satisfied.

In the remaining few days before the execution I made repeated requests to see Raza, but he refused them all. Then, unexpectedly, the day before he was to die, he asked to see me. Seated opposite him on a bench in his cell, I was impressed by his calmness, as if he were finally at peace with himself. I would not have been so calm if I knew I was going to die the next day.

"Hello, Doc," he said. "Thanks for coming. I've been hashing stuff over a lot since your last visit. I don't have much to do besides talk to myself, you know?" He paused as if gathering energy for what was to come. "You're like him, Doc, so I want to tell you something."

"About your father?" I asked.

"How'd you know?" Raza replied. "Yeah, it's about my old man. I told you he died when I was just a kid and I didn't know him well, but that's not true. I really loved the guy. He was good to me—hard, you know, but soft in his own way." Then he said in a voice so low I could barely hear him. "I'm sorry I killed him."

I straightened up in surprise. "You killed him?" I said. Raza nodded. "Tell me what happened," I urged.

"My father was a nut about hunting. He loved guns and wanted me to love them too. One day, when I was six, he was getting ready to go deer hunting. He took me into the kitchen and put his rifle in my hands. He got down beside me on one knee and showed me how to sight it and how to pull the trigger.''

He paused and stared at the corner of his cell, recapturing that day from a distant childhood. I was silent, and in a moment he resumed speaking.

"It was great, him doing that like I was grown up. The more I think about it, it's just like yesterday. I wanted to go with him so bad, and I told him so, too. He got a kick out of it, messed up my hair, and said I was still a kid and had to stay home with the old lady. Then he left me with the rifle and went to get the rest of his hunting junk.

"I was mad about not going. I wanted to show him I was a man. I saw the box of shells on the table and shoved one in the gun, like he showed me. When he came back into the room, I poked the gun at him, jerked the trigger, and yelled Boom!

"The bullet hit him in the heart; he died right there. The noise shook the hell outa me. I let go of that gun like it was red-hot. I called to him but he wouldn't answer me. I was still yelling my guts out when the old lady ran into the room.''

Raza told me all this in a flat tone of voice, scarcely changing his inflection. When he finished he said simply, "All my life I've been bugged by that. Any guy that killed his old man shouldn't oughta live, right, Doc? I'm sorry I did it. I'm sorry.'' He dropped his head into his hands to hide his tears.

When I tried to console him he refused to respond. He displayed no further interest in what he had revealed, or in me. He would only say, in a monotone, "That's it. I don't want to talk no more. Now that I told you, get out.''

Finally I gave up and left. I returned to my office, cancelled my patients for the rest of the day, and went home. Raza's story had depressed me. At supper I pushed away my meal, half eaten. I started reading a novel and then flung it aside after ten minutes.

Finally I grabbed my coat and left my dismal apartment for the neighborhood theater. I slouched in my seat through most of a miserable double feature, but all I saw on the screen was a little boy with a rifle standing over the dead body of his father. I left and shuffled home again. All evening some repressed thought had been gnawing at a corner of my mind, trying to eat its way into consciousness. I felt uneasy, on edge, as if there were something I should know but didn't.

I went into my den, closed the door, and slumped into an armchair. I stared at the abstract painting on the opposite wall until I thought my eyes would drown in the colors. Suddenly it was no longer an abstraction, but a concrete image of a gun, a child, and a murdered father frozen in time immediately after the shooting. Then the figure of the child startled into movement, dropped the gun as if it were hot and—and—and threw up on the corpse of his father.

My feet crashed to the floor as I leaped from my chair. Now what had led to a ridiculous association like that? Or was it ridiculous? There was something Raza had said— let's see—wait—yes, "I felt cold and sick, like I was going to lose my lunch right there in front of all those guys."

He was on the shooting range—the gun was heavy, leaden—he had to support his gun arm—cold—body shaking—teeth chattering—and he felt nauseated—panic—he dropped the gun and ran!

He had been describing an acute anxiety attack, of course. Suddenly I realized why. He had been afraid to fire the gun at that dummy target of a man. He was morbidly afraid of guns and *could not fire one!*

The full impact of this knowledge staggered me. Raza was innocent! He might have stabbed, beaten, or strangled his girl friend to death, but he was psychologically incapable of shooting her. Raza wanted to die in atonement for killing his father.

Raza Valkunin was to die at 12:30 this morning. I lunged for the phone on my desk and in my haste knocked over the clock beside it. The upturned dial read: 12:35.